THE YOUTH DRUG

F.W. WATT

 **FriesenPress**

Suite 300 – 990 Fort Street
Victoria, BC, Canada V8W 3K2
www.friesenpress.com

ISBN
978-1-4602-4436-4 (Paperback)
978-1-4602-4437-1 (eBook)

1. Fiction, Science Fiction, General

Distributed to the trade by The Ingram Book Company

John Hornby and Norman Shearer were both thirty-five years of age, and they had not yet changed the course of history.

Every day while Dr. Shearer mostly saw patients and collected data on cancer cases in the Carter-Trudeau Memorial Hospital, Dr. Hornby mostly worked in their laboratory on the seventh floor of the adjoining Cancer Research Institute. (Every day including for him, since he was a bachelor, many Saturdays and Sundays.) Every day they hoped their team would make a great advance in understanding what causes cancerous cells to act as they do, and how to stop them from doing it.

Along with many thousands of doctors and scientists around the world, they went home at the end of their day's work disappointed. Or rather, since they were too realistic for that -- a little less optimistic and a little older.

They were friends from medical school days and now research colleagues. They met every afternoon on weekdays for a brief conference. Norman Shearer came in to see John Hornby at the laboratory, before leaving for his home and family out on Lakeshore East. Sometimes, like this first Thursday of January, the meeting was so brief that Dr. Shearer didn't bother to take off his overcoat and snow boots, which he put on before leaving the adjacent Hospital to avoid having to carry them. Dr. Hornby lived in a nearby climate-controlled apartment complex, so that he hardly even knew what season of the year it was.

When Dr. Shearer came in as usual and sat on the edge of the table beside Dr. Hornby's sight microscope and note cards, Hornby only waved vaguely, distractedly. As if too tired to bother entering a discussion. Something in his friend's bearing, however – Hornby was a short, fair-haired man, whose white coat was buttoned unevenly over a prematurely middle-aged paunch – made Dr. Shearer look down thoughtfully from his lean six-foot-four-inch height, and pause before interrupting.

"Going to stay here all night, my friend?" Shearer ventured, after several minutes passed without a word.

"I just might, Norman, I just might."

John Hornby slumped back on his stool and at last looked up at his colleague. Now, face to face, it was clear that Hornby was not tired, but slightly euphoric, which made his usually calm expression seem angelic.

"What have you got there, John?" Shearer asked, leaning over to look into the microscope. He didn't want to get too interested, too hopeful, but the blood stirred a little.

"It's a biopsy from one of our D elevens," Hornby replied, naming the group of rodents from which the slide had been prepared.

Shearer was making some adjustments to the focus. He clucked his tongue twice until he had it set the way he wanted it. "D eleven," he murmured, as he peered intently at the slide. "One of the pregnant stock, that hasn't produced yet?"

"Right. And here's E eleven, their control group."

Hornby replaced the slide which had aroused his feelings so strongly with one from the other group. In a moment Shearer whistled in disgust. "Advanced case?"

"E elevens are all dying or dead," Hornby said crisply. And then in a lower tone, almost a whisper. "But as you can see, this one from a D eleven looks like normal, healthy tissue, at this level of magnification. That's with twenty days of the serum."

The two friends stared at each other, both digesting the implications, and afraid to put them into words.

For three years the Hornby-Shearer team had been making comparative studies of healthy and cancerous cells, human and rodent, while conducting experiments on mice with varieties of serums developed through a sophisticated technique of gene-splicing. The institution for which they worked required, as a matter of policy, this teaming of medical and pure research staff, under the terms of its foundation. So far nothing directly useful was discovered about cancer, except that the laboratory could produce it more and more easily in mice, without being able to control it or cure it any the better. There had been false alarms and will o' the wisps before, but nothing quite as close to a breakthrough as this.

Dr. Shearer immediately displayed his occupational bias. He was the official representative of applied medicine on the team.

"Clinical indications? What are our D elevens doing? Any signs of changes in behaviour or function?"

"Come and see for yourself," Hornby said, leading the way out into the corridor and down the hall, his friend towering behind him and almost treading on his heels with his long athletic stride.

It was feeding time in the room containing the glass cages. A young white-coated laboratory assistant was releasing the feed mechanically, with the technique designed to avoid risk of contamination or infection. In a moment he nodded to his seniors and left the room.

The cage marked D eleven was a scene of energetic activity, the whitish hairless pink-nosed creatures jostling and pushing and climbing over each other in a mass to reach the feed. In the E eleven cage, housing the control group, the atmosphere was very different. The population was obviously diminished, there were several bloated, supine specimens off by themselves, and barely nosing at their feed. In a separate cage, also marked E eleven, several mice had managed to produce litters, sickly as the mothers and families looked.

"No offspring from D eleven yet? Odd, isn't it?" Norman observed.

A shadow crossed Hornby's face as he returned Shearer's look. Then he shrugged philosophically and smiled. "The treatment seems to have retarded the course of pregnancy. We'll have to wait and see what develops."

"Meantime carry on with the present high dosage treatment?"

"Meantime carry on."

All traces of euphoria were gone now from John Hornby's face. It returned to its usual appearance of comfortable round ruddiness, resembling that of a German beer-hall waiter or a successful bank manager. He had always known that even if they were blessed or lucky enough to come upon the elusive cancer cure, it would hardly be simple. Nothing in the world of science ever was. More than likely there would be side-effects worse than the disease itself. And yet . . . .

"Look at them," he said with real delight as he held the door open for Shearer to go out ahead of him.

The two men stood in the doorway, Norman Shearer in unzipped snow boots, coat over his arm, John Hornby in his white rumpled smock, brushing his fair hair back from his forehead. They watched the greedily cavorting and gambling animals of D eleven, who were evidently benefitting so much from the daily serum injections.

"Not very matronly behavior," Shearer said.

"A bunch of silly school girls," Hornby replied, as he was closing the door quietly behind him. "Well, we may not have cured them of cancer, but we've certainly made life a lot more fun for them."

Every six months the Hornby-Shearer project had to come before the powerful Environmental Hazards Committee of the International Science Research Council of North America. To have its status reviewed. The requirement was of course automatic for any experimental work which involved gene-splicing – a procedure well-accepted and familiar in the scientific world, but still a mysterious and rather alarming game to the general public, a suspect tinkering with the origins of life to some. The Committee, established only recently, when a series of calamities and near-calamities made it clear just how dangerous uncontrolled scientific experimentation could be, had the power to stop any project in its tracks.

"Dog license day, have you forgotten?" Norman Shearer said to John Hornby, as he surprised his friend by stepping briskly into the laboratory, dressed in his best one-piece dark suit, early on a Tuesday morning in March.

"Oh my God," Hornby grimaced, putting down his pencil on the pile of notes in front of him. "Poor you."

"I don't know. I'm getting rather to enjoy these sessions. I think I'm going to go into Educational TV."

Shearer reached a long arm to Hornby's neat sheaf of notes, plucked up a handful at random, and proceeded to mime an eloquent, charming lecture from them for the benefit of imaginary TV cameras.

"Bravo," said Hornby, applauding over his white-coated paunch without quite allowing his hands to meet. "May I assume you'll impress the Committee that you're enough of a scientific genius to get our permit renewed?"

Shearer abruptly got serious. He dropped his friend's papers back on the table and pulled a chair to sit beside Hornby. "We've got to decide how much to say to these guys this time," he began, pulling a small, minutely penned note card from his inside breast pocket. "This is what I had in mind. Tell me what you think."

An hour later, his consultation with John Hornby completed, Dr. Norman Shearer strode quickly to the elevator on his way to the Senior Conference Room of the Carter-Trudeau Memorial Cancer Research Institute, where the Committee was already in session. He was a little late, in fact, but he had no doubt that the sessions would be running behind time. They always did. And especially so today when they involved a prominent new U.S. government representative, a sort of international celebrity, serving for the first time on the Committee.

The Conference Room was on the main floor of the Institute. Its luxurious waiting room was decorated with numerous large photographs of the two public leaders after whom the building was named. They were pictures taken in a variety of places and poses, formal dress and shirt sleeves, at work and play, individual and together, meeting workers and corporate executives, Quebeckers and Mexicans, in those happier days of international harmony and personal happiness – before their public images and wide popularity had begun fade from the new generations. As eventually it does, even for the best of political leaders.

The waiting room was empty. Norman Shearer paced its length once or twice, drawing near and then walking away from the double doors, behind which one or other of his Institute colleagues was now being grilled.

It was a sign of the Institute's stature in medical research that the Environmental Hazards Committee – or to be more exact, the active travelling sub-Committee of that larger group – was prepared to come to them for their semi-annual reviews, instead of obliging them to go down to the New York headquarters. There were only half a dozen other centers in North America which they visited in this way.

Norman Shearer began to rehearse in his mind once again the outlines of his presentation. Despite himself, he felt a tightening of his throat and a slight pounding at the temples. These meetings could be awkward, at least unpredictable, involving as they did not only scientists and doctors but laymen, representatives of the public interest, watchdogs as they often thought of themselves. In fact, nothing was more difficult than having to explain complex scientific and medical matters in front of your colleagues and other experts, but in simple terms for the benefit of laymen present. All the more so, if the laymen were stupid or wary, or both, which had been known to be the case.

However, as he said to John Hornby on his way out of the laboratory, it was always an interesting challenge.

The double doors abruptly swung open. Shearer found himself standing in the middle of the waiting room as a grey-haired wiry little man in a rumpled old-fashioned tweed jacket and slacks stepped out, followed by the Institute's chief officer, Dr. Wayland Finger. Dr. Finger remained in the doorway, ready to usher in Shearer. The grey-haired man leaving was familiar enough to Shearer. He gave a wry look and a jerk of his head back towards the Conference Room he had just left, as if to prepare Shearer for an ordeal. In fact, Norman Shearer was a little disconcerted to see the elderly Dr. G. K. Shields emerging from a meeting with the Committee in that frame of mind. Dr. Shields was in charge of the Hospital's radiation treatments, hardly in the forefront of experimentation. It should have been smooth sailing for him.

But of course, Shearer remembered, there had been a bit of play recently in the international media about the effects of radiation on hospital staff, and genetically on patients who had undergone prolonged treatment. Well, no doubt Dr. Shields survived his grilling with nothing more to show than a little increase in his exasperation quotient.

"Come in, Norman," Wayland Finger said, putting out his hand in an avuncular greeting -- an urbane man whose main aim at these sessions was to keep the Institute and Hospital out of controversy, to protect their base of public grants. "The members are all ready for you."

Around the oak table within, five men and two women were standing to stretch their legs, as Dr. Finger made the introductions. "This is Dr. Shearer, ladies and gentlemen, appearing on behalf of Dr. John Hornby and himself, for the Institute's project classified as number L 15, 189. You'll find the technical description and latest digest report in full on . . . . " Here Dr. Finger paused until he could consult his files assembled at one end of the table.

"On pages thirty-eight to forty-one."

Shearer took his stand at the only empty chair on his side of the table, and awaited the gaze of each member of the Committee in turn.

"You've met our Chairman, Dr. Milanova Rudi, on previous occasions. . . ."

"Indeed," Shearer said, smiling at the calm attentive woman in her late forties or early fifties, dressed as severely as himself, in a grey one-piece suit complete with collar and tie. Dr. Rudi nodded and sat down.

"I believe you've also met Dr. Murphy of Johns Hopkins, and Dr. Subreen, delegate of the International Cancer Research Council."

They also sat down, Dr. Murphy picking up his unlit filtered 'pure air' pipe, and going to work on it industriously with tamper and small silver screwdriver, Dr. Subreen plunging into his file and reading in it intently through a pocket magnifier.

Dr. Finger turned with a flourish to the remaining male member, a man in his middle or later fifties, taller even than Norman Shearer, graying hair at the temples but deeply tanned and strikingly handsome in a soft, roll-collar, expensive overall suit that didn't look at all too young on his athletic frame. The bronzed face was familiar enough to Shearer, from TV and the newspapers and magazines. But the sense of live personal presence was much stronger than he had anticipated. "And the newest member of the Committee . . . ."

"Yeah, I'm the freshman," the tall, energetic man broke in, reaching his long arm across the table to join hands with Shearer. "Chad Hamilton. Nice to meet you, Doctor."

Shearer returned the warm grip. Before sitting down, he waited a moment longer for the last introduction.

"And of course, this is the Committee's chief executive secretary, Alice Devers."

"Without whose help," Chad Hamilton called across in a booming voice, "I for one couldn't make head nor tail of these proceedings."

He beamed down the table at the green-eyed dark brunette, who looked to be barely out of her twenties, but who was ordering with calm efficiency all the files and recorders which occupied the end of the table opposite to Dr. Finger. She acknowledged both Hamilton and Norman Shearer with a tolerant smile. Her immaculately tailored chalk stripe jacket, trousers and vest suggested a physique that would have been equally at home, though in completely different garb, on Norman Shearer's favorite TV network, the Blue.

As they settled into their chairs, Shearer found himself looking not at Dr. Rudi, who was directly opposite him, not at Alice Devers, engaging as she was, setting the dials of her recorders, but at the much publicized Chad Hamilton. Multimillionaire, media tycoon, owner of the largest world newspaper, the New York and London Times, director of international corporations, sportsman, socialite, the man with the golden way of life built on deep foundations of power and authority.

It was odd and rather piquant, Norman thought, that an obscure medical researcher like himself should hold the attention, for however short a time, of a man of this public magnitude. Usually the only time a doctor and a man this rich held each other's attention was in the sick-room. However, 'I consider it the duty of responsible men in the financial and business community to help to preserve our environment for our children and our children's children,' Hamilton had said to reporters, when the President of the United States made the official announcement of his appointment to the Environmental Hazards Committee. Evidently he did not consider the job to be merely honorific. In fact, there was some evidence from his public pronouncements thereafter that he really saw it as an opportunity to straighten out modern experimental science, and put it on the right track for generations to come.

Dr. Rudi had been speaking so quietly for a moment or two, in a grave contralto voice, her heavy-lidded eyes on the papers in front of her, that Shearer almost missed her opening comments. In a moment he gathered that she was reminding the assembled members that the Carter-Trudeau Memorial Cancer Research Institute project they were reviewing had begun six years earlier, before the licensing requirements were enacted, with Dr. Philip Gonz in charge. That three years ago Dr. Gonz had turned over his work entirely to his two younger colleagues, Dr. Hornby and Dr. Shearer, and that the bi-annual renewal of license had been granted to these two researchers ever since. She was going on to offer some details about the nature of the research, before asking Dr. Shearer to speak about its present status, when Chad Hamilton interrupted.

"Tell me, Madame Chairman, if I may ask for an initial clarification . . . ." He turned to smile broadly at Norman. "Out of supreme ignorance, I assure you. I'm trying to learn the basics as fast as I can – why did this project have to have a license in the first place?"

Shearer could understand the impatience of his predecessor in this chair. Evidently Chad Hamilton did not intend to sit back and be intimidated by the mysteries of science and medicine. He made a mental note to try to leave nothing unexplained when it came to his own turn to speak.

Dr. Rudi was meticulously outlining for Hamilton the two categories of the regulations enforced by the Hazards Committee into which the Hornby-Shearer project fitted. First, there was the aspect of genetic experimentation involved in developing a new serum with the potential to affect cancer cell production. Second, there was the aspect of clinical application of serums developed in this way, the use of potentially hazardous man-created organisms, in the treatment of human cancer patients.

Chad Hamilton listened carefully to the explanation, nodding his head from time to time and making notes with a gold pen on the pad in front of him. Then he sat back and watched attentively, as Dr. Rudi invited Dr. Shearer to offer a brief account of the current stage of research. The crucial moment had now arrived. Norman's nervousness was beyond his own expectations, despite the genial and encouraging gaze of Dr. Wayland Finger, designed to show that the audience was basically sympathetic and that the Hospital was behind him.

The problem was, that Dr. Norman Shearer wanted to tell the Committee less than he knew, and he wasn't very practiced at deception.

At the end of his brief exposition, both Dr. Subreen, tapping his lips with his pocket magnifier and peering at Shearer short-sightedly, and Dr. Murphy, still adjusting the air vents in the bowl of his 'pure air' pipe, asked some technical questions of an incidental sort. About the particular bacterium they were using, and the precautions being taken to control it, precautions which were pretty well standard by now. These were mere formalities. Norman had the feeling that they understood very well the kinds of reservations he might be guilty of, and were sympathetic to a researcher's dilemma in not wanting to get ahead of hard scientific evidence. As professional colleagues, they were willing to go a long way in trusting a fellow scientist. But Chad Hamilton inevitably proved to be the one to stir up the trouble.

"If I could just ask a couple of questions – out of complete ignorance again, I'm afraid . . . . " Once more the broad grin, the open-palmed gesture of apology. "So you've been making some new kind of virus in that lab of yours, and feeding it to mice for five years or so -- and nothing useful's come out of it yet? Surely you've got something to show for your trouble, or you would have quit by now and gone on to something else."

Norman returned his smile. He had to admit to himself that Chad Hamilton had got to the heart of the matter in his blunt, simple-minded, business-like manner.

"While it would be more accurate to say we've had some promising progress, we've modified the active virus in our serum in several significant respects over that period of time – and are still modifying it – basically you're right. Our gene-splicing experiments have all been in the same direction. And you're right also in surmising that our work has not been entirely without positive indications."

The three professional members of the Committee all looked at Dr. Shearer more attentively, he was well aware, as he continued to speak. He knew that he already was going a little beyond the formal, written presentation he and Hornby had made. Beyond what it was wise to say this early. But Chad Hamilton's open challenge piqued him a little. He felt confident enough to venture a hint or two about what he and Hornby had agreed not to discuss in public as yet.

"But you've never tried the stuff on people, have you? And you've been killing mice right and left."

Chad Hamilton emphasized his two points with two smacks on the table and a rise of an octave in his booming voice. Out of the corner of his eye, Shearer could see Alice Devers smiling with mild amusement. And why not? Obviously Chad Hamilton's presence transformed these meetings into something more than dry formalities. Moreover, Hamilton's lively glances down the table made it clear he was the kind of man who flourished on a receptive audience, especially a female audience.

"No, Mr. Hamilton, we haven't yet attempted any clinical use of the serum we're developing. As our reports to this Committee indicate over the past few years, the laboratory experiments have produced interesting but rather ambiguous results. We've continued to make systematic comparative studies of human and animal cancer cells at varying stages of growth. We're amassing the kind of information that will be extremely useful when we take the leap to clinical application, as we certainly hope to do, sooner or later."

Hamilton's voice emerged with a quieter, more comical tone as he commented over bronzed hands clasped on the table in front of him. Perhaps he felt he had been a little too belligerent earlier. "That sounds a bit ominous. 'Leap' makes me think of Niagara Falls or the Empire State Building."

Everyone joined in his chuckle, not entirely at Shearer's expense. Shearer felt a small surge of aggression himself, a push of pride, even ambition. He enjoyed, he was prepared to admit, a desire to impress Chad Hamilton and not be diminished in his eyes.

"It's always a leap to go from lab to clinic, and especially in the field of genetic experimentation," Shearer said, sitting up to his full height and looking directly at Hamilton, who returned his gaze candidly. "But when you're dealing with a disease like cancer, you sometimes feel that a little urge towards precipitation is understandable."

"True," Hamilton replied, nodding his handsome head slowly, "I agree with you. I do."

Encouraged a little, Shearer went further. "And that is why we have included in our presentation this half-year a request to be permitted clinical applications of our serum, or modifications thereof, under Restricted Surgical and Medicinal Procedures, Regulation B3."

"Remind me! What in hell is that?" Hamilton called out instantly.

At this point Dr. Wayland Finger saw fit to take part from his end of the table.

"B 3 is a highly limited category, Mr. Hamilton, as your colleagues on the Committee are aware. It's the one that offers the option to a medical practitioner, with the agreement of a hospital chief and another consulting physician, of giving experimental treatments (within limits specified in the regulation) to . . . ." Here Dr. Finger paused a moment as if to be sure Chad Hamilton was ready to receive the main point, "to terminally ill cancer patients who haven't responded to other forms of therapy."

"Ah," Hamilton said, leaning back in his chair, evidently quite satisfied, if not a little abashed. But in a moment, barely touching the back of his chair, he bounced forward and boomed another question at Shearer over the table.

"What is it that makes you think this new virus of yours will do any good?" After a split second's hesitation, Norman Shearer decided he would lay at least one card on the table.

"As I said before, the laboratory results to date are inconclusive. But recently, very recently, there have been some indications that we would describe as encouraging. Within six months – before I have the privilege of addressing this Committee again – we hope to have data sufficiently reliable to justify consideration of clinical trials on a limited basis."

There was a distinct stillness in the bearing of the three professionals listening. It was almost as if they could scent the suggestive facts that Dr. Shearer and Dr. Hornby considered it premature to divulge, certainly not yet in the form of scientific publication. If they did, they respected his situation too deeply to show any overt signs. But not so, Chad Hamilton.

"What do you mean, Dr. Shearer? Are some of your guinea pigs managing to survive?"

Dr. Shearer pursued his lips in a small smile. He was getting a dangerous pleasure out of Hamilton's interest.

"There are some promising indications."

"Yeah, but what kind of promising indications?"

At this point Dr. Rudi, whether out of sympathy for a badgered Shearer, or simply a desire to see some end to the interview, spoke up in her chairperson's authoritative voice.

"We have the bi-annual progress report on the project in front of us, Mr. Hamilton. We assume it's reasonably up-to-date. But we can hardly expect a definitive account of research that is still under way up to the time we hold our hearings. Any further comment from Dr. Shearer might be misleading, or cause improper expectations. I daresay he may feel that way."

Chad Hamilton turned in his chair to face Dr. Rudi, directly. He raised both his hands and grinned.

"Oh, come on Milanova, honey, you know these hearings are in camera, strictly confidential. Anyway, I'm not going to rush out yelling about a cancer cure around the country, and I'm sure no one else here is. I just think . . . " And here he turned back to look a little appealingly at Dr. Shearer, "the doctor should be able to tell us a bit more where he's got to. How else can this committee deal with his application for renewal in an intelligent way? Don't you agree, Dr. Shearer?"

Norman sat for moment, smiling, looking around the table. It was really more of a problem for them, would continue to be as long as Chad Hamilton stayed on the Committee, than it was for him. Nevertheless, he decided to plunge in.

"Of course. At the present moment, Dr. John Hornby reports that massive daily injections of the experimental serum we've been developing, in its latest form, appears to be having a pronounced effect in retarding cancer activity in a certain group of white mice. That's exactly where we've got to, as of today."

There was silence around the table.

"Well," Chad Hamilton said at last. "That sounds like something worth writing home about."

"We think so." Shearer's voice was quietly confident. "However, the limitations of the trial are extremely narrow, and there are ambiguous elements in the results which we've hardly begun to understand. We may be a long way from any publishable conclusions. But we're very encouraged."

"So you damn well should be," Hamilton exclaimed, with rising enthusiasm and respect in his voice.

"Would you want to say anything for the record about the limitations?" Dr. Rudi asked.

Shearer recognized that she was inviting him to join forces in cooling Chad Hamilton's rashness. He tacitly agreed with her that it was very necessary.

"First of all, the dosage seems to have its most pronounced effect on pregnant specimens. We think the explanation may lie in the hormonal balance within these animals. Second, the side-effects of the serum include at least one which is particularly significant: a process of uterine re-absorption seems to take place in pregnant animals subjected to levels of treatment sufficient to retard cancerous activity."

"What does that mean, Doctor, uterine . . . . What was that again?" Hamilton asked, running a thumb behind one ear in a bemused fashion.

"It means," Dr. Wayland Finger interjected, perhaps in the hope of hastening the conclusion of this disconcertingly unorthodox session, "that the womb of the pregnant female reabsorbs the fetus. The female without aborting appears to be no longer pregnant."

Chad Hamilton shook his graying head in astonishment.

"By God, Dr. Shearer, I don't know what it has to do with cancer – but it looks like you may be on your way to putting the abortion clinics out of business!"

Shearer found himself getting carried away a little by Hamilton's flippancy and unprofessional exuberance. He couldn't help responding in kind.

"Actually, what we find happening," he said, almost boyishly wanting to please the older man, "is that these mice seem to get younger – altogether younger in their behaviour and appearance. But unfortunately at the high level of dosage we're using, so far their vital organs undergo certain disruptive effects. They tend in the end to deteriorate, from one malfunction or another. Of course there are a number of options, modifying the serum, adjusting the dosage levels and so on. We've still got a long way to go, as you can see."

Dr. Subreen, who had been hiding his face behind his pocket magnifier as though embarrassed by the unconventional tenor of the discussion, abruptly dropped his shield on the table and spoke up. It was almost as if he had decided to capitalize on the breach of professional decorum, and satisfy his own curiosity.

"We all recognize that the results of genetic code re-direction are difficult to predict. For the data you've gathered so far, have you any hypothesis to account for the uterine re-absorption effect?"

"Yeah," Chad Hamilton chimed in, lowering his voice in a stage aside to Dr. Rudi, "how does the damned stuff work on them?"

By now, Shearer's last diplomatic inhibitions were leaving him. He had a final moment's uneasiness as he reflected on how he would ever explain to John Hornby why the meeting had gone so differently from what they had anticipated and agreed upon.

"We're really not too sure how close the facts are to our working hypothesis. What we've been trying to do, of course, is to produce, through gene-splicing, a serum that operates to some extent in the way of a normal enzyme-signaling. That is," he went on, struggling for the words that would make Hamilton understand and not get lost in the technicalities of molecular biology, "a serum containing enzymes that enter the cells with the same freedom as normal enzymes do. To direct and develop the cell growth. All healthy cells are programmed to develop according to genetic blueprints. They use messenger enzymes to help carry out the blueprint. Unhealthy or cancerous cells are ones that have got off the track, and are responding to a programme of division and multiplication that harms the organism as a whole. By using what we know now about the genetic code, we've tried to create new information enzymes to signal a simple retarding or reversal of cell division. We're attempting to focus and control the effects of our new invading enzymes much in the way that radiation is aimed at malignant growth in conventional radiation therapy."

Shearer stopped abruptly and took a deep breath.

"I'm afraid I may have lost you, Mr. Hamilton. It's a hard matter to explain."

He felt a deep frustration at the effort to put such a vital and delicate and complicated argument in words understandable to someone whose life was not dedicated to the probing of the most mysterious of the life sciences. Then with a single gesture Chad Hamilton made it all right.

"OK, OK, enough. Thank you, Dr. Shearer. You're very kind to . . . very patient with an ignorant old non-scientist like myself. I'm grateful to you. Madame Chairman, I have no further questions. I just want to say to Dr. Shearer, that I wish him the best of luck, and I look forward to hearing his progress report six months from now."

Dr. Rudi did not dispute this abrupt way of bringing the interview to an end, or guard her chairperson's prerogative. The members of the Committee all stood as Dr. Shearer turned to walk out. Chad Hamilton came around the table to follow Wayland Finger and Shearer to the door.

"If you're ever in my town, Los Angeles, Doctor, give me a ring, won't you? Do you play golf?"

Shearer stood in the doorway for a moment, enjoying the weight of the great man's hand on his shoulder. "A little," he said with a smile. "Not at your level, though, I'm afraid."

He knew from the magazines and newspapers that at his best Hamilton could play with the professionals. Hamilton looked him up and down for a moment, assessing his tall, lean athletic build and offering his estimate. "No worse than the low eighties, I'd say."

"You flatter me," Shearer said. "High eighties, on a great day."

Hamilton gave his shoulder a shake and let it go to reach into his pocket.

"I'll spot you five strokes, not a single one more. Here, please take this. Come and see how you like my home course."

Hamilton slipped a small card into Shearer's suit pocket with his left hand, and reached to shake hands with him with his right. Shearer fingered the card in his pocket as he walked past a couple of his Institute colleagues, seated in the waiting room ready for their turns before the Committee. Ticket to a far paradise he would never use. Then he rushed off along the corridor, caught the elevator just as its doors were closing, and stepped out a few moment later through the seventh floor glass doors marked 'Authorized Personnel Only'.

He was rapidly turning over in his mind how he would defend himself when John Hornby discovered he had been so indiscreet about the project, the work which both their lives revolved around, but John's even more than his. Maybe it would be better not to go into any details with John until the weekend, when Hornby was due to pay the Shearer home one of his rare visits. For now he would fob him off by saying simply that everything went very well.

On the spur of the moment, restless with nervous energy, Shearer decided to see if he couldn't manage to take the afternoon off, or at least leave the Hospital to go home early to his wife and daughter.

It took Norman Shearer an hour by what members of his little Lakeshore East community liked to call 'personal transport' – as opposed to public transport – to get from the Hospital to his old-fashioned brick house. It would have been only fifteen minutes by the Overhead. Norman didn't mind the trip his way. He went along the lakeshore highway with its glimpses of the waterfront at a comfortable forty miles an hour in his electric runabout, licensed for entry into the city limits. Anyway, a generation before, when there were simply no restrictions on the use of city roads, his father had taken almost as long on the same route in a big eight-cylinder gas guzzler, bumper to bumper with thousands of others, every morning and every evening. It was mind-boggling to remember.

Somewhere during the trip, at about the half way mark, Norman's thoughts usually began to shift from what he was leaving, the Hospital, the Institute, John Hornby, his patients, to what he was approaching. To his house in the bourgeois comfort of Lakeshore East, which was trying so hard, in face of the relentless march of urbanism and computerism, to preserve its mid-twentieth century neighbourhood character. To his sixteen-year-old daughter, who was bored with all that and didn't know what to do with her life, like most young people these days. To his wife . . . well, she was bored with all that too, but was realistic enough to know that there might not be anywhere else that was any better, or could offer her anything she might really want to do. Sometimes it seemed that pure boredom was the greatest curse of civilization, unless you were one of the lucky ones like Norman, born or brought up that way, with work he could put his heart and soul into.

By the time Norman turned off the highway and eased his way past the electronic safety blocks that lowered speeds in the community to fifteen miles an hour, he had already rehearsed three or four scenarios for his arrival today. At one extreme was the nostalgic and romantic -- wife at the door in cuddly pullover and slacks, welcoming arms following hard on surprised look.

"Sweetheart, you're early. And you remembered the groceries. Put that box down and come here right now."

In the background, a voice from upstairs.

"Dad, hi, I'm sure glad you're home. When that other woman lets you go, please come up here and help me with my math. I'm in a terrible mess and I need my very own daddy genius to get me out."

Then of course there was the melodramatic. No answer at the door. Curtains drawn. Silence within, despite soft and then louder calls. Creeping up the stairs, full of dreadful premonitions to find . . . . Take your pick of several versions. One, the bathroom door open, and in the bathtub, limbs floating in bloody water . . . . Two, hair spread over the pillows of their double bed, mattress slashed and soaked. Three, bedroom door closed, sounds of murmuring, laughing, panting voices, rising to ecstasy. Four . . . . Without realizing it, Norman found himself drifting into the plots of the last month's Blue Television Friday night horror stories. He shook them off. Life was never as exciting as that. The mind struggled futilely against the weight of conformity, urbanization, computerism, mechanization, trying to fly – but soon dropped down to middle aged ordinariness again.

A block and a half from his house, he pulled in at the neighborhood grocery store. Some local families treated the store as merely a symbolic gesture, a token resistance to the inhumanity of computer shopping and the mechanized supermarket, but the Shearers and many others patronized it fully, despite the higher costs and, frankly speaking, the damned inconvenience of it.

"Hello, Mrs. Catroni, did Mrs. Shearer phone this morning?"

"Good day, good day, Doctor. Oh yes, I have everything ready, all ready for you."

A genuine Italian grocer's wife of two hundred pounds weight and a perpetually cheerful nature, Mrs. Catroni bent down behind the wooden counter and fished out a large cardboard box full of groceries. She half opened the wrappings on one parcel at the top.

"You see, beautiful bird, from farm, capon, sweet white meat. You'll like it, I promise."

"I'm sure I will," Norman said, taking hold of the box and preparing to move quickly to avoid a long neighbourly conversation.

"How is Mrs. Shearer? Last time she came in she looked a little pale, just a little. Sick every morning she tells me. I tell her, she should get out more, it's good for the little one, make him grow big and strong."

Mrs. Catroni mimed the way the muscles of a pregnant woman's stomach would tug an embryonic athlete to her, and smiled encouragingly. Her own belly clearly was of the capacity suitable for quintuplets.

"That's just what I tell her too," Norman said over his shoulder, with an irony he knew she would miss, and a little sly miming in his own movements, the box clutched to his stomach as he waddled out to the car.

"Good bye, Doctor, take care. My best to Mrs. Shearer."

"Thank you, thank you."

Well, you wouldn't get the friendliness, the family interest, or the farm capon, from the computerized shopping deliveries. But Norman could understand the mixture of fondness and exasperation with which his wife Ella viewed the whole futile neighbourly mystique of their district. It was clearly a losing battle.

"Let's move then," he would say.

"What, into some dismal, push-button high-rise like the one your friend John Hornby lives in? Indistinguishable from a thousand like it? Is that any place to raise a teen-age girl? Do you think I want to have a baby somewhere where we'll never get any real air or sun, and you're surrounded day and night by computers and domestic robots?"

Then of course the tears. Always the tears. Norman was thinking of them as he pulled into the driveway and touched the signal on the dashboard to alert the automatic garage door. Sometimes it seemed to Norman that Ella had been crying ever since he got her pregnant fifteen or sixteen years ago, when they were both still in school. But he had to admit that the first years trying to complete an education, despite the troubles of a young couple with a baby, were full of laughter. Or was it because of their troubles? Their having certain things they had to do, whether they liked it or not, if they were going to survive. Both of them remembered that. Which was probably the main reason why Ella decided to get pregnant again. To do something that got you involved, that demanded things of you. Something deliberate this time, decisive, creative. She'd tried just about everything else to restore some happiness and purpose. This was a kind of last resort. However, two months into it she was already showing signs of changing her mind.

Norman picked up the box of groceries and carried it to the front door. Before he could shift it onto one hip to free a hand, the door swung open and Donna Shearer, his teen-age daughter, dressed in a high-collared long coat and knee boots, stepped out.

"Dad, what are you doing home at this time of day? Can I borrow the runabout? I was just going down to the lakeshore highway to see if I could hitch a ride. I promise not to dint the sides like the last time."

Norman stood looking down at her over the box of groceries until she was finished. He grinned at her wryly.

"Hello Donna, sweetheart, thanks for the welcome."

She tossed her auburn hair, richer and longer than her mother's, off her shoulders impatiently.

"Oh, Dad, I hope you aren't in one of your moods."

Norman walked into the hallway and placed the box on the chair just inside. "One of what moods?" he asked, slowly taking off his overcoat.

Standing in the doorway his daughter grew more impatient. "You know what I mean. Dad, I have to go. Can I borrow the runabout?" She started precipitously towards the steps as if to leave, whether with or without the transportation he could provide.

"Where are you off to at this time of day, anyway?" he called to her, raising his voice and obliging her to stop to avoid having him raise it still farther, embarrassing her in front of the neighbours.

"Mom said I could go. It's an exhibition in Sunnyside Park. The weather's just right and it's due to start at sunset."

Norman stood on one leg to take off a snow boot. He felt an obscure need to keep her talking, even though he knew it would only anger her.

"An exhibition. What kind of an exhibition? Maybe I'll come with you."

She laughed sarcastically. "Hardly your kind of thing, Father. There won't be paint or a piece of marble or metal or plastic in it anywhere."

"One of those obscene theatricals by your downtown liberation friends?'

"They're not obscene. And this has nothing to do with my friends. It's a visiting aeronautical artists' club from Florida. They're doing an evening of cloud sculpture."

"Cloud sculpture," Norman scoffed, dropping his second boot beside the door. "The silliest of all the silly fads. Sky doodling, that's all it is."

Donna Shearer's pose, hands on hips, was sublimely contemptuous. "What do you know about it? You've never even seen cloud sculpture." Then her voice quavered a little, as the injustice of the older generation's attitudes came home to her. "It's beautiful, really beautiful. You just couldn't appreciate anything that beautiful. Anything new and different. You're too old and stuffy."

She stamped down the steps towards the street. Norman followed her onto the porch, his heart tugging at the sight of her graceful female shape leaving him. Maybe for a few youthful years she could fly free of the traps of ordinary adult life, but it seemed unlikely. He reached into his pocket to pull out the runabout's keys.

"Here, honey, catch. And if there's so much as a scratch on that new paint job I'll smack your bottom."

She stooped to pick the keys from the snow, where they had slipped through her fingers, deliberately turning to him that shapely part of her anatomy he was threatening.

"If I scratch the paint," she said straightening up, "I won't come back. I'll just keep driving till the battery runs down."

Then, as she turned to activate the garage doors, she grinned up at him, forgiving all. "Thanks a lot, Dad. See you tomorrow."

It was too late for him to question what time she would be coming back, if she didn't think she'd see him again tonight, a thought which hadn't crossed his mind. Shaking his head, he closed the door and walked into the living room, where he could hear the sound of the TV set.

The curtains were half drawn. In the shadows he could barely make out the shape of his wife in her typical pose, stretched out on the chesterfield, gazing at the bright images on the wall screen. She was wearing a caftan, and holding a tall drink in both hands in front of her. She reached an arm in his direction without taking her eyes off the screen.

"You're going to wear out that video," he said, taking her hand in his and settling onto the sofa by her head.

He recognized the film as a favourite of hers, one she played again and again, from their collection of early greats. *The Magnificent Ambersons,* a romance going back to the pre-technological days of the horseless carriage. She took a sip of her drink, and tried to silence him with a squeeze of her hand. He should have poured himself a drink and joined her to watch the film out. Drift with her in her adolescent dreaming. What harm was there in a little nostalgia. Impatience prevented him.

"You're spoiling that girl, letting her run around town whenever she wants to. She should be studying for her entrance exams. She hardly even tunes in for lectures anymore."

"She doesn't want a college degree. You can't force her. Besides, you're the one who spoils her by letting her have the car."

She settled down to watch again, one hand back under her long auburn hair.

"It's better than letting her go down to the highway and get picked up by God knows who," Norman protested.

Ella took her eyes off the screen for a moment to look at him and laugh sarcastically.

"It's a bit late in the day to play the heavy father with her, isn't it? Besides, whether she gets picked up, or whether she picks up someone herself, what difference does it make? They'll spend their time together, these kids, and do what they want to do, whatever you think about it. That's the way their generation is. That's the way the young are."

The movie was coming to its end. The music was bringing it to its poignant close. There were tears in Ella's eyes, whether from the movie or from what they were talking about, Norman wasn't sure.

"OK, so that's the way the young are," he echoed her. "And you're just sorry you can't still be one of them."

He said it as a matter of fact, rather than as a challenge or a taunt. She took it that way. She offered him a sip from her drink, and said to him softly as he drank, "Oh yes, I'm sorry all right. But there's no point in that. I know that once you've lived through a phase of life you can't ever go back. The question is, what's ahead? What else is there?"

He could almost cry with her. He shared her sense of youth passing, of age creeping in, of the loss of freedom and spontaneity and fun – and more than anything else, perhaps, beauty. It was terrible to contemplate, to observe, growing old and tired and ugly. In their different ways, both he and his wife were drawn towards images of beauty.

"Well, there's this," he murmured, slipping down on the floor beside the chesterfield and resting his head on her belly, which was not yet showing the extent of her womb's commitment to the future.

She pressed his head against her body. "I don't want to have a baby now," she moaned. "It's all so futile. Who would want to bring a baby into this world?" she went on sounding a familiar cry that had resounded around the globe for a generation without significantly reducing the earth's population.

Norman refused to take up that cry, refused to accept it or to argue the inarguable. He was silent, letting his long arms roam over her quietly sobbing body. Almost despite himself, he found his feelings quickening.

"Well then," he murmured, a hand resting on the softness and warmth between her legs, "there's this."

"Oh that," she whispered, not stirring as he eased up her caftan, and passively accepting his hand's familiar exploration, "you're a man who can hardly stay interested 'till a woman's thirty-five."

Before she could say anything more ruthlessly true, before she could spoil the evening by following up a hundred distracting and discouraging associations, he raised himself to lie beside her and show her the extent of his immediate interest.

And then, for quite a long while, it was very good. Much more specifically enjoyable than anything Norman had in mind when he decided to come home early, but very good, all the better for not having been planned.

Of course the mood couldn't last. As they each went their ways to wash and change and prepare their everyday faces for the dinner table, the temperature dropped to ordinary. Ella became even cooler, to the point of being sardonic, during the course of dinner.

"Don't sour it," Norman begged.

He poured her another glass of hock, hoping that if his plea failed, the wine would succeed in making her stop trying to suggest that his ardor was the result of some new drug he had discovered, or last night's Blue Television show, or a visit to some beautiful young nurse or woman doctor in the city. To stave her off still more, Norman did what he usually avoided, talked shop.

"I spent the morning before the Environmental Hazards Committee. They gave me quite a time of it."

"I thought all that was just a formality," she said, picking uninterestedly at her food. "Or are you really becoming a hazard nowadays, you and that fanatical friend of yours, John Hornby."

"John isn't fanatical. He just loves his work, difficult as that may be for you to understand. You've never forgiven him, have you, for refusing your invitation to Christmas dinner when he and I first teamed up six years ago."

F. W. WATT

The subject was not an awkward one between them. Norman used to make the same mistake as Ella, in thinking that because John Hornby was a bachelor he must be lonely and in need of kind attentions from luckier people during the festive seasons. They were both a little put out to discover that John on the whole preferred to be by himself on such occasions, though he did enjoy and contribute very successfully to dinners and parties from time to time during the rest of the year. For Norman, it was really a case of the shoe being on the other foot. He had come to admire his friend's calm, ageless and evenly independent way of life, though he still couldn't quite understand it.

Ella drank deeply from her glass and accepted more. "I forgive John Hornby everything," she said, "now that I know what a fanatic he is."

Norman decided not to pursue a quarrel with her terms. He liked to think about John, about John's differences from himself as well as what they had in common. They were a good team, Norman with his more impatient, moody and at the same time practical attitudes and approaches, John with his serene, reflective and detached cast of mind and his bent towards the theoretical. Friendship was in some ways the most mysterious kind of relationship. It wasn't sharing the research project that made them friends. It was being friends that had led them to pool their efforts as professional colleagues. Why they were friends wasn't exactly clear.

"Yes," Norman said, turning his wine glass around in his hand by the stem, "work means a great deal more to John than it does to me. He really believes in it. Not just in the particular job we're trying to do, but in the whole idea of scientific advancement."

"He's very naive, very young," Ella said, indulgently. "He's never grown up."

She liked John as much as anyone Norman had introduced her to among his colleagues.

"Not really. He knows all the limitations of science, its perversions and dangers and so on. But he just has this conception – it's a fine conception in fact – that what's essential about man is his ability to know. His desire to know, his need to know. Whatever the consequences. John's motto is, man is mortal, science immortal. He wants that on his tombstone."

Ella dipped a finger into her wine glass and began to dabble the back of Norman's hand.

"Like I said – he's a fanatic. He's the one who should have gone before the Committee this morning. Why is it always you?"

"Because he hates that kind of thing. He'd rather stay in the lab. Besides, I'm the one with the gift of the gab, haven't you noticed?"

Norman softened his boast by taking hold of Ella's moist finger and sucking the wine drops from it. He then began to tell her at length about his appearance before the Committee, and tried to amuse her with his account of the illustrious Chadwick Hamilton's part in the occasion. In fact, he was still enjoying a sense of heightened interest in the life of power and money, having for the first time met one of the select few in the flesh. He was well aware that even at second-hand the effect on Ella would be seductive.

How bored she was, how frustrated at the way they lived. It made her more vivacious and lively to hear talk of someone from a sphere so different. Abruptly Norman felt the urge to bring her back to reality. It was inexplicable to him why these reactions came to him. He couldn't seem to resist.

"He's getting old of course, our friend Chadwick Hamilton. Well preserved, immensely charming, handsome. But age will have its day soon enough."

"Why did you have to say that?" Ella withdrew her hand from his and sat back in her chair. "You've got a destructive streak in you, haven't you?" she said, with a touch of bitter, renewed recognition of this trait in him.

He was tired of it all too. He pushed his chair back from the table and stood up.

"And you," he said from his great height over the candles, "you've never grown up yourself. You're a person who's been ruined by the youth generation. The first generation in which the entire world began to systematically despise and undercut the elders and everything the elders stand for, and hand society over to the young. That's the generation that shaped your character. Now that you're getting old too, you don't know what the hell to do with yourself."

He strode out one door to the downstairs den while she, fighting back her tears on the way out the other, began to clatter dishes into the dishwasher and tidy away the kitchen chaos. The evening was going to end as so many had done in the past months and years, with her playing old movies on the upstairs TV, while he sat in the gloom of the den and watched the Blue Television network until he was satiated.

At one o'clock Norman was ready to join Ella in their bedroom, but Donna hadn't come home yet. He turned off the TV and went upstairs to mix a drink in the kitchen, determined to wait her out. Fifteen or twenty minutes later he heard the garage doors slide up and down. In a moment Donna was passing the kitchen door on the way upstairs to bed. Her voice was tired.

"Hi Dad. No scratches, no dints."

She reached in the doorway to toss the keys on the kitchen counter. Her auburn hair was tousled. Something in her weary, relaxed manner particularly annoyed Norman.

"You realize it's after one o'clock?"

"One twenty-two to be exact," she answered with a cheerful smile, having glanced up at the wall clock to check. She started on her way again.

Norman's annoyance flared up. "This is the third night this week you've been out till after twelve o'clock. And you're supposed to be studying for your entrance exams. Besides that, since when have you had free run of this city without telling your mother or me where you're going and who you're with?"

Donna stepped back into the kitchen and leaned wearily against the counter. She spoke in her most reasonable tones. "Father, I'm seventeen years old. I've been driving for a year and a half, and never had an accident – except for a few scrapes and scratches – and I did tell you where I was going. To the Sunnybrook Park cloud sculpture exhibition."

Norman hated himself for continuing. He knew where it was bound to end. But his anger wouldn't let him stop. "Sunnybrook Park? Until one o'clock in the morning? Who are you trying to kid? I wasn't born yesterday."

Donna found herself having to get into detail she clearly didn't care to discuss. "I drove Sandy Cairns home. He lives in Westview."

"And why, might I ask, didn't Sandy Cairns drive himself home? That's forty miles, for God sake."

"Father, you don't have to swear at me. Sandy's father isn't a *doctor*. He isn't lucky enough to have a car or license to drive in the city. Anyway, he's my best friend."

References to his privileges always had a chastening effect on Norman. They made him feel apologetic. "Alright," he said grudgingly, "but what does 'best friend' mean to you these days?"

Donna pretended to be shocked at this invasion of her privacy. "I don't think you have any right to ask about my private relationships."

He didn't really think he had any right either. But he floundered on despite himself.

"I have a right if you get yourself in too deep. I'm the one who'll be asked to take care of everything if you get pregnant."

Donna's face was a picture of pitying exasperation. She shook her head slowly, looking at him in disbelief."Really, Father, you're so out of date. I said I'm almost eighteen years old. Mother's given me my annual pill for the last three years."

Her sense of truth, or perhaps a fear of consequent questions, made her be more exact. "Well, the last two years anyway."

Norman's anger began to shift from his daughter to his wife. What could you expect from the girl, encouraged in that way by her own mother. On the other hand, Donna herself would probably never have been conceived, sixteen years ago, if Ella's mother had been sensible about birth control, and taught her daughter to take care of herself. Arguing with the young, with Donna, was always a frustrating experience. Norman grew very tired suddenly.

"Just because you're on the pill doesn't mean you can play around with everybody you meet."

Donna could see that the battle was over. She was mild with the loser. "I don't play around with everybody I meet, as you put it, Father. I'm very choosy."

She stepped into the kitchen and gave Norman a quick kiss on the cheek, before darting out to the hall and up the stairs.

"Did you remember to plug in the car?" he called after her, but it was too late. Her bedroom door was already shut. Wearily he trudged into the garage himself to make sure the runabout's battery was on charge, and ready for the trip to the city in the morning.

Dr. Shearer liked to arrive at the Hospital early on Wednesday mornings, because on those days his friend John Hornby now accompanied him on the regular rounds. For several years the patients Dr. Shearer visited were primarily statistics and case records and biopsies to Dr. Hornby. But since the Hornby-Shearer serum was at last being used to treat advanced cases which had responded to none of the more established kinds of therapy, the time had come for Dr. Hornby to join in the clinical observations.

On the whole it was not an enjoyable experience. Of the half dozen cases treated to date, just one offered any encouraging signs. This kind of immediate result was to be expected. Only hopeless cases, to be blunt about it, were normally available for such experimental applications at this stage of research and verification. Usually these patients were in such extremity that it was unclear as to what effect a particular treatment was actually having.

The first case, a one-time leading relief pitcher in the National League, might have been responding in his fight against leukemia, but he died after a couple of weeks from kidney malfunction and pneumonia. A sixty-year-old asbestos worker with one lung removed, and on the way to losing the other, seemed to have stabilized, though at an unacceptable level of survival dependent on the hospital support systems.

In some ways the most interesting case was that of an octogenarian retired physics professor and former Nobel Prize winner in the 1950s. He had an advanced rectal malignancy for which he refused to accept surgery – hardly a worthwhile ordeal for him in any case. He cross-examined the doctors extensively about their research, and agreed willingly in the end to be a guinea pig for them. His cardiovascular system gave out in three weeks, before evidence about the impact of massive serum dosage on his malignant cell growth was conclusive. But not before he responded to treatment, or perhaps just to the interest and excitement he felt about the treatment, by becoming a positively sprightly old satyr. To the amusement and occasional alarm of the nursing staff.

The first turning point in these early days came with one of the most delightful of many interesting and prominent people to enter the Carter-Trudeau Memorial Cancer Hospital. John Hornby and Norman Shearer had no conception to begin with of how important this case was going to be for them.

John Hornby was seated at his microscope in one of his significantly distracted moods, when Norman Shearer came by on a Thursday evening. At last, having watched and waited until he exhausted his patience and courtesy, Norman tapped his friend on his mop of fair hair.

"Get your nose out of that and talk to me. What's so interesting?"

With a sigh, Hornby slumped back from the table, pushed both hands into his pockets, and looked up. "It's the notorious Faye Delisle," he said with a grin, a jab of his thumb directing attention to the slide.

"Faye Delisle is attracting a lot of interest at the Hospital these days," Shearer said. Without taking off his coat he quickly leaned past Hornby and peered into the microscope.

"I don't doubt it," Hornby replied, reaching for another slide from the holder on his table. "You can hardly expect to keep the most ravishing body on the whole Blue Television Network to yourself. That's her right breast there. This is her left."

Miss Delisle was originally slated for routine mastectomy. But the malignancy was so advanced, despite first impressions, not only in the breast but in the uterus and even more widely, that surgery no longer seemed to be justified. After it was explained to her, she eagerly accepted the outside chance offered by the Hornby-Shearer experimental therapy.

Hornby slipped out the slide Shearer was inspecting, and replaced it with the one in his hand. His friend made several small adjustments in the setting without saying a word. Then, after studying it for a minute or two, he turned from the instrument and sat on the table again, looking down at Hornby. "It looks pretty certain, then? The carcinoma in the right breast is checked?"

Returning Shearer's stare, Hornby answered quietly. "I would say there's no longer any doubt about the right breast."

"But the left is even more interesting," Norman suggested, tapping his own chest at the appropriate place, his overcoat now open. "Once again, normal, healthy tissue seems to be undergoing a reaction too. What do you make of it?"

Hornby was seated again at the sight microscope, and he answered while peering into it steadily. "Not too much at this level of magnification. You'd have to say healthy looking cell activity, extraordinary tone. Unusual stimulation, if anything."

"What about the cervical biopsy?" Norman asked.

"Same thing. Retarding of the activity of carcinomatous cells. Some kind of rejuvenation of normal tissue."

Norman Shearer spread his arms and grinned in the special crooked way reserved for gallows humour and the usual medical joking. "Millions of lovers of Miss Delisle's skin will be grateful," he cried. Then abruptly he grew serious again. "You're sending the biopsies on to Microscopy in the usual way? Same instructions?"

Hornby nodded as he begun to tidy up his table. "I think so. For now. We'll wait and see what they make of them before putting any more ideas into their heads."

"OK, but you'll come with me tomorrow morning and have another look at Faye before the general staff conference – I want you to stay for that."

Hornby made a face and shrugged his shoulders. He much preferred to remain in the lab, but of course he agreed with the principle of their partnership. He would go and see the patient in the flesh. Since the results were proving to be so interesting and, despite ambiguities, so promising, he would make a special trip, having already gone the rounds with Dr. Shearer for that week. Even more important, he would take part in the Hospital staff conference which, practically speaking, determined the pecking order for the introduction and extension of experimental therapy at the Hospital.

The next morning the two doctors met on the fourth floor of the private patient's pavilion, passing together without hindrance through the glass doors and electronic surveillance of the restricted area.

Faye Delisle was half asleep. She barely stirred while they inspected her chart and Dr. Shearer examined her. Despite her pallor and lethargy, which negated any impression of the beauty queen about her, the visit supported the evidence of the biopsies. The patient had been in a distinctly lower mental and physical state when they took her on. They were about to leave when Miss Delisle's low, husky voice caught them at the door.

"Tell me, won't you? What do you think? Am I getting any better?"

Dr. Shearer came back to the bedside, looking down at the young woman from his great height. Dr. Hornby remained by the door.

"It's too early to tell very much." Dr. Shearer mouthed the easy, familiar phrase while wondering whether to say anything more. "We'll have to continue the treatment for weeks, probably months, before the results have any significance."

"I understand. I understand all that, Doctor," she said, raising her voice a little.

Surely she must, too, having been subjected to a variety of unsuccessful treatments, almost every kind, except for surgery, for the past year. She had even contemplated the most drastic operations on her magnificent body, her pride and her principal asset, until the surgeons had to withdraw assurances. She had faced the extremes of helplessness and hopelessness.

"Isn't there anything you can tell yet? I feel a little different. Aren't there any signs?"

Dr. Shearer stood for a moment longer, weighing the possible answers, from easy to true. The easiest was not really all that easy. It might even be better to try the hard. Finally he settled his tall frame onto the chair beside her for a moment, and took one of her hands in his long fingers. It gave him a curious sensation, not in the slightest erotic in that set of surroundings, but faintly and pleasantly reminiscent of sexuality. Even in sickness her personality was very strong. And after all, he was one of her most dedicated television fans. He decided to offer her one of his speeches.

"Miss Delisle, cancer has been with the human race for many centuries, probably from the beginning of human life. For several decades medical science has been getting closer and closer to a genuine understanding of the disease. But too many false hopes have been destroyed by cures that didn't work or didn't last. Or were worse than the disease. Today, well, anyone who claims to have found a cure for cancer without having thorough proofs, thorough clinical evidence, will only add more to human misery. All I can say to you for the present time is . . . . "

Dr. Shearer paused a last time to glance over at Dr. Hornby, still standing by the door, listening in a posture as still as a statue. Dr. Shearer met his eyes and Hornby gave an almost imperceptible nod. "All I can say is, there's some degree of encouragement in the way your body is responding to the serum."

Faye Delisle said nothing, but she squeezed the doctor's hand hard as tears moistened her eyes.

"Some encouragement," he repeated, returning the pressure. "So we must just continue from day to day in the same spirit. . . . I'll see you again tomorrow."

As he rose to join Dr. Hornby, he could hear her faint thank you following them out.

"That's what I pay you for, Norman," John Hornby said, holding the other's elbow as they marched side by side towards the elevator. His face showed the extent of his distaste for this kind of ordeal, and his admiration for his colleague's way of coping with it. "I would have made a terrible mess of that."

"The hell you would. Come on," Shearer said, pulling his friend into the elevator and grinning down at him. "If we do half as well with our colleagues at the staff conference we're in business."

In the Hospital's weekly staff conference, there was inevitably a certain amount of subtle vying among the assembled doctors and support staff, most of whom had their own projects which they had faith in and wanted to see expanded. Today was an important occasion for the two friends. They were making their strongest pitch yet – moving them from a comfortable low profile into a vulnerable prominence.

Although it wouldn't be true to say that the Hornby-Shearer experimental project swept the board in the lively half-hour that followed, it gained enough ground, from Dr. Shearer's review of existing case histories and Dr. Hornby's few comments on the laboratory research background, to gain support for the use of the serum in limited additional cases. They were moving in the right direction. Some of these were very likely going to be not quite as advanced as those they had been offered to date. In light of the premature stage of their research and the element of hazard involved in the application of any genetic experimentation, the two doctors could expect nothing more. They were highly pleased.

As had happened before with trials of this kind, within a few weeks the skepticism and wariness of the Hospital staff, and of Dr. Wayland Finger as its chief executive officer, began to weaken. And despite habitual conservatism and determined efforts of policy to keep the lid on, in the corridors and coffee-shops and cafeterias of the Carter-Trudeau complex, talk was turning more and more curiously to the signs of change in patients undergoing the Shearer-Hornby course of injections.

It was something of a dilemma for the two doctors. They wanted Hospital support, in fact they needed it to make any rapid progress, but the last thing they wanted was public attention at this stage. Having Faye Delisle under treatment inevitably stimulated interest. It was on no account the young woman's fault, however -- she was discretion itself. She accepted without question the firm requests of Drs. Shearer and Hornby to keep her own hopes within bounds, and to maintain silence as far as statements in public were concerned. And she did remain their most encouraging case.

Dr. Shearer was delivering a research paper to a medical society in New York on the day it had been agreed upon that (if the patient's condition permitted it) Faye Delisle could leave the Hospital for a week at home – under strict quarantine conditions. Dr. Hornby found himself obliged to visit her all by himself to complete the formalities for her release.

She was much more vital than on any earlier visit. Her cheeks were flushed with excitement. Dr. Hornby felt it necessary to remind her about the need for care and for avoiding any public discussion of her case.

"I'll keep my promise," she said fervently. "But I do feel good, really good. Better than I have for years. I feel . . . well, it's the only way I can put it – like a girl again."

She laughed at the signs of embarrassment on Dr. Shearer's face at her outburst. It was almost as if his male conservatism provoked her. Abruptly, as if he had never before had the privilege of seeing her body, she pulled up her nighty from under the sheets and tugged it over her head and arms in one movement.

"There," she cried, beaming at him, holding her naked body upright as if for the closing credits of Blue Television sequence, "see for yourself! Don't I even *look* so much better?"

Dr. Hornby could hardly not accept the invitation, a strawberry flush slowly spreading from his neck to his forehead and into his fair-haired scalp. His eyes ran over her body. The famous breasts were indeed striking, unmarred by lumps or swellings, unscathed by surgeon's scalpels, presenting themselves richly but without a hint of grossness, carrying their dark-haloed nipples with a touch of buoyant uplift that could even be called youthful. Dr. Hornby scratched his jaw judiciously before announcing a conclusion.

"Miss Delisle, I believe you're right," he said, with a touch of a shy smile. "You do look a lot, ah, happier, than when you arrived."

As she watched his reaction across the room, where he stood awkwardly in a posture that would have been boyish if it weren't for his portly middle, Faye Delisle relented. She wanted to please, not embarrass. Now she thought she recognized him for what he was.

"You're not married, are you, Dr. Hornby?"

F. W. WATT

Hornby's reply came out as a slightly choked laugh. "Ah, no, no, ah, not at all."

"And I'll bet you've never watched my TV programme."

"I'm afraid I haven't, Miss Delisle. It's kind of late at night for a person of my habits," he went on to explain apologetically.

"Be honest, Dr. Hornby," she pursued him, with a teasing smile, "you disapprove. You're a moralist."

The word 'moralist' seemed suddenly to put Dr. Hornby at his ease. It allowed him to settle onto an intellectual ground on which he felt at home. After all, it wasn't really that he was afraid for himself, afraid to be made a fool of, but that he was afraid of hurting, of saying the wrong thing or taking the wrong stance to someone else's discomfiture.

"Not so, Miss Delisle. I'm not a moralist. I'm a scientist."

Faye Delisle laughed as if he had made a joke, before she quite grasped what he had said. Then her face changed to look a little more serious as she digested his answer.

"I would have thought . . . . Can't you be both? Scientist and moralist?"

For a moment Dr. Hornby mentally summoned up the presence of his friend Norman Shearer. What delight Norman would have derived from the spectacle of scientist and porn film actress engaging in a Socratic dialogue.

"Lots of people would agree with you, Miss Delisle. But not me. I think a man can be both scientist and moralist, but not at the same time. The scientist's job is one thing only – to know everything that can be known. Give him any other job and it will interfere with his essential function. He'll want to be doing things, changing things, as well as knowing. And before you realize it, there'll be certain things he won't want to know any longer, won't dare to know, or won't be able to know."

Miss Delisle was looking at him with blue eyes wide open.

"You know, Dr. Hornby, you've been here at least a dozen times since I came. And in all that while I've never heard you say so many words one right after another."

He flushed again, and stood for a moment longer, hands fidgeting in the pockets of his white smock, a tight smile on his lips. "Maybe I feel I have to make up for Dr. Shearer's absence."

A few moments later, he was turning away with a half bow in her direction, closing the door behind him. Taking with him the memory of her laughing face, the little wave of her hand, and her final words.

"And what was it she said?" Norman Shearer demanded, when John was telling the story, word for word, while they walked together along the lakeshore boardwalk the next Saturday.

John Hornby sat down on a bench for a moment to shake sand out of his shoes. He deliberately kept Norman waiting a little for his answer. Then he gave it with a mildly triumphant air. "She said, 'I don't know about making up for Dr. Shearer's absence. But I certainly loved talking with you.'"

"You're making that up," Norman objected.

John shrugged his shoulders as if it were a matter of indifference to him whether Norman believed him or not. "And then she said, 'Please, why don't you watch one of my programmes. I'd like you to see me as I was at my best.'"

Norman looked down at his friend in amazement. "I don't believe you! She didn't say that, did she?"

John Hornby got up and continued the walk, letting his friend follow. His serene expression made it clear that as far as he was concerned the subject was finished. Unsatisfying as it might be this time to Norman, it was easy to change subjects quickly on these walks.

There was a touch of excitement for both of them in meeting outside their usual places, the Institute and the Hospital. Hornby came out to Lakeshore East only every few months at the most, a visit for each season, perhaps, though not that systematically. They always toured the lake front, whatever the weather. Today was a brisk, clear, bright spring day. The lake looked deceptively clean and fresh, but it was just as badly polluted as all the other Great Lakes. Off to the west the skyscrapers and the covering climate-control domes of the city were diminished by distance. To the east the regional water-purifying plant, opening its sluice-gates at the lake's edge, loomed like a medieval grey stone castle, except for its high smokeless stacks.

Knowing he would get nothing more from his friend about Faye Delisle, at least for now, Norman picked up his ordinary stride, and soon it was John who was puffing along half a step behind him again.

"Smell that air," Norman insisted, drawing in deep breaths and exhaling noisily.

"It smells like dead fish," Hornby gasped, his face a bright strawberry colour as a result of the unusual exertion.

"You're corrupted from living all your days and nights with air-conditioning and purifiers and perfume dispensers," Shearer scoffed. "You don't deserve the privilege of natural air."

"Dead fish," Hornby muttered defiantly, tugging at Shearer's sleeve to hold him up.

Undeniably there was an actual dead fish where the water lapped the sands on the lake side of the board walk. Its eye looked up at them balefully as its body swayed a little, half-submerged, its head resting on the grey sands.

"It's that damned purification plant," said Shearer, ruefully scratching his head as he stared down at the fish.

Hornby glanced up in disbelief, wondering if Norman was still mocking him. "Don't be absurd, Norman. Chlorine and fluoride have been used for half a century without a trace of environmental damage. It's been a long time since anyone claimed his gold fish were being killed."

Shearer in answer pointed along the lakeshore to the massive grey buildings of the plant, with its outlet and intake streams marked by whitecaps at the lake's edge.

"Last month they had a spill. Not fluoride or chlorine or oil or anything like that -- just plain warm water. You know, amongst other things they do there, they re-circulate the water from the nuclear power plant next door. They use it to heat greenhouses back there inland. The temperature was, I think, ten or twelve degrees higher than it should have been. Amazing how delicate the environment is sometimes. It was enough of a shock to kill hundreds of fish along the edges of their spillage. Hundreds, gasping out their last."

"Just as I said, dead fish." Hornby raised both arms to the sky.

Shearer turned away from him in disgust. "Nonsense. They cleaned most of the mess up weeks ago. Anyway, you can't really smell the odd dead fish on a beautiful fresh day like this." Without another glance at the offending corpse, he strode off down the board walk, inhaling and exhaling again enthusiastically, leaving Hornby to jog along behind as best he could.

Three quarters of a mile farther they came to a promontory on which stood an empty lifesavers' platform, its electronic scanner not yet in place for the summer.

"My favourite spot," Shearer said, as he always did at this point in the walk. He immediately stepped forward to climb the iron ladder.

Hornby watched the long athletic figure of his friend snaking upwards higher and higher. Fifteen feet above the ground, Shearer looked down from the platform, ready to offer assistance. Hornby sighed wearily and began his laborious ascent. He knew he was not built for this kind of activity. Gasping for breath, he allowed himself to be pulled onto the square platform. Off to the west the city was more clearly visible now. They sat side by side for a few moments contemplating it, gods on their little Olympus.

"Sometimes I think I'd like never to go back to that place," Shearer said thoughtfully, turning away sideways to look over the lake instead. "It's a trap, a big, dreary, fatal trap."

Hornby sympathized with these moods of Shearer, though he never really felt the same way. For him, things were what they were. "Where would you go?"

Norman was silent for a while, not particularly thinking of any likely possibility. It was an idle exercise. Where else was there, for a medical researcher, than a big centre of money and technology and knowledge? Then a thought popped into his mind.

"I'd take up Chadwick Hamilton's invitation. I'd go down to California."

A week earlier Drs. Hornby and Shearer had each received identical letters, form letters really, despite their handsome letter-head, from the officers in charge of the newly established Hamilton Medical Research Centre in a place called Notlimah, California, which they'd never heard of. It announced the founding of the Centre, and gave a description of the range of activities it was going to undertake. And it invited parties interested in joining the staff to get in touch with the authorities there.

Neither Hornby nor Shearer took the letter seriously, although it was signed by Hamilton himself. It was not their idea of pleasure or profit to join a new medical institution, in which inevitably administration and politics tended to take precedence over research.

"Chad Hamilton's got everything he wants," Norman had said to his wife Ella, the day it arrived, thinking the letter might amuse her, "so he's decided to buy himself a hospital. It will be a lovely toy."

California, California. Norman murmured the name as he let John Hornby sit a little longer on the life saving platform and catch his breath, and he himself mentally transformed the lake view in front of him into a climate purer and milder and more luxurious, peopled with golden skinned beauties. By natural association, no doubt, a more tangible, attainable idea came into his mind.

"You know what, John," Norman said, clapping his friend on the shoulder, "you're going to stay with us overnight tonight. We'll have a bottle or two of my best, and we'll watch the Saturday night double bill on the Blue. It's always a blockbuster. Remember, you promised Faye Delisle you'd have a look, and tonight's the night."

On their way back to the house, despite Hornby's repeated attempts to fend off the invitation, Norman grew more insistent, until he finally swept all resistance away. And after all, Dr. Hornby could claim to be carrying further his research into the case history of a most interesting and important patient. It would be combining business and pleasure. John knew that when his friend was in one of his bouncy, facetious moods, there was no use arguing with him. He allowed the evening to drift on as Norman wanted it to.

When the programme ended after three in the morning, Norman staggered off to join Ella, who had been in bed for hours, and John Hornby stumbled down the hallway to the guestroom. Both were very drunk in an owlish, solemn way, and very satisfied with themselves and the evening. It had been a wonderful escape into a dream world inhabited by images of beauty, sexuality, and perpetual youth. While the spell was on them, neither of them wanted to associate what they saw on the screen with the living woman who was one of their handful of human guinea pigs.

In the following week Miss Faye Delisle was returned by her attendant nurses a few days earlier than expected, to her room on the fourth floor of the private patients' pavilion. Whether from earlier therapy, from the impact of the carcinoma growths themselves, or from the massive injections of the Hornby-Shearer serum, she was experiencing heart palpitations which the medical staff believed should be monitored in the Hospital.

Nevertheless, when they visited her on their rounds, the next day being Wednesday and Hornby's day, the two doctors found her in excellent spirits.

Dr. Hornby stayed even farther in the background than usual. It was a little less easy to divorce the patient being visited from the porn actress, now that he had watched one – no, a double bill – of her sensational performances. Which made it amply clear why she had such a name for herself among North American males. And also, now that she seemed to be so full of energy and feminine radiance, like someone just back from a holiday in the Caribbean.

"Except for those little flutters in my chest," she said, as Dr. Shearer put his stethoscope against her at the point where her new nighty swooped down from her neck, "I feel good. Really good."

"You look . . . 'really good'," Dr. Shearer murmured, with his usual touch of genial teasing, as he moved the stethoscope about.

"My producer flew in from the West Coast to see me. Sticking to all the rules, of course, just the way the nurses said. The first thing he said to me was, 'Faye, I wish I'd brought the camera crew, I've never seen you looking more beautiful.' He wasn't just being nice, either. He's full of ideas about a new series when the one that's on now runs out. You know, we've only got a dozen more shows in the can, and then . . . ."

Dr. Shearer stood back a few steps from the bed and let Miss Delisle's excited chatter run down. She quieted in a moment, but her eyes remained bright and her smile cheerful.

"I know what you're thinking, Doctor. But you needn't worry. I'm not being silly about it. I'm only living one day at a time, as we agreed. It's just that it's so wonderful to be feeling this way that I let myself dream a little. The fact is," she went on, turning her eyes to bring Dr. Hornby into her orbit, "you two should patent this medicine of yours – it has to be the nicest tonic there ever was. It's like I was a girl again. I swear my body's got ten years younger in the past few months."

Dr. Shearer glanced around at Dr. Hornby, hearing these words. They exchanged looks for a moment. Then Dr. Hornby took a step forward. "Miss Delisle, may I ask you, why do you say 'younger'. Can you be any more precise than that?"

She laughed a little uncertainly, wondering if he was making a joke or teasing her in his straight-faced way. "It's not just me," she said defensively. "My producer – we're very good friends, you know – he says my body looks to him like it did ten years ago, when I did my first audition."

Almost as if she were unconsciously re-enacting one of her roles, she ran her hands in a serious, exploratory way from her hips up her sides and under her breasts, cupping herself a little and gazing down.

"I'm more slender now, more . . . . Well, not quite so full, whereas I used to be, you could say, a little bit . . . . "

She raised her eyes slowly to gaze from under her blond hair at the two fascinated men. She was appealing to them to help her with the words.

"More . . . voluptuous, perhaps?" Dr. Shearer ventured, with a broad smile, memories of the advertisements for dozens of episodes on Blue TV flooding through his mind, and arousing his appreciation of the accuracy of the cliché.

"Thank you, Doctor, I knew you could put it the right way."

"But are there other things you've noticed, too?" Dr. Hornby persisted.

"Well, it's more in my head than anything, I suppose. I have these crazy, flighty ideas of what I want to do, just the way I was when I was in my teens and early twenties. Even though I know they're all nonsense. It's kind of fun, but it scares me a little too. You can't be thirty-one and twenty-one at the same time, can you?"

She laughed at her own expression, which sounded ridiculous and made her think they would laugh at her too.

Dr. Hornby still stood behind, with one arm across his paunch and the other raised so he could scratch his round cheek meditatively. He was watching Faye closely and brooding deeply, not realizing how uncomfortable he was making her. Finally from where he stood he broke the embarrassing silence.

"It's not surprising that you should have some unusual psychological as well as physical reactions. It doesn't sound too alarming at the moment, however. Please keep us up-to-date on how it is with you. In the meantime we'll continue the treatment along the lines we've been following . . . ."

"Unless," Norman Shearer interjected with a laugh, "you have any objections to the idea of feeling younger every day."

One of the great advantages of working in the Carter-Trudeau Memorial Cancer Research Institute was that it housed all the expensive and sophisticated equipment a medical research scientist might want to use, and the technical staff to operate it. Particularly important to the Hornby-Shearer project was the availability of a large computer complex for helping to unlock the mysteries of the genetic code, and a Microscopy Department with the most highly developed electronic microscopes for examining the minute structure and activity of cells. The precise impact of experimental treatments on the life within cells could be analyzed there to an extent hardly possible anywhere, comparably at only a few centers of research on the continent.

Dr. Hornby and Shearer spent many hours assessing the detailed technical reports that came back to the laboratory on the animal and human specimens they were treating. The most advanced (and still the most successful) case history remained that of Faye Delisle. It was also the most puzzling. Every week that went by added to the excitement and perplexity with which Hornby and Shearer approached their discussions of the case, and paid their visits to the patient.

"The laboratory and the clinical aspects of this case still don't seem to jibe," Hornby said, late in the summer, as Shearer entered in shirt-sleeves, carrying his jacket, and seated himself on the table beside Hornby's sight microscope.

There was nothing new, basically, in what Hornby was saying. But they both found it useful to think out loud and try to push their thoughts further in the process.

"The reports from Microscopy go on suggesting that the serum must be having some destructive effect on healthy tissue. And it's true, there does seem to be a sort of tissue reduction. Most dramatically, of course, with our pregnant mice."

Shearer picked up the thread and carried on. "But if that's so, if the serum really is eroding the healthy cells in some way, as well as retarding the growth of carcinomatous cells, why do some of these organisms seem to be thriving, instead of wasting away?"

"Actually," Hornby corrected his friend, "they seem to be thriving *and* wasting away. How could that be?"

"There's got to be an explanation."

"There's got to be."

Shearer sat swinging his long leg back and forth while Hornby re-read the latest report on a biopsy sent on to the Microscopy Department. The only sound was the tapping of his pencil on the table.

Norman Shearer was the first to break the silence. It was obvious to him that the time had come. His friend was not going to say it, so he would.

"John, you're going to have to spell it out for the Microscopy gang. You've got to tell them what to search for."

Hornby looked up with a disgusted expression on this face.

"How can we do that? They'll think we've gone round the bend. Surely if they keep doing their job, and if what we think is even remotely possible, they'll come up with something on their own. Without our prejudicing them. Or without our making them think we're crazy and giving up on us altogether."

Norman shook his head emphatically. "We can't wait any longer, John. We have to go forward or back, given the situation with our clinical cases. It could be months or years before anything shows up if we go on letting the technical people do their analyses on present assumptions. They're looking for damage, and their finding it. In the theoretical framework you've set up for them, you can't expect anything else. We're got to give them a new lead and take the risks."

Hornby sat tapping his pencil and staring gloomily at the papers in his hands. They had come close to this point many times in the past few weeks, and backed off. Norman continued more urgently, his impatience rising. "John, let's face it, Faye Delisle is our best case, we may not have another like it this year. And with those cardiac symptoms she could go anytime. We've got to make some progress while she's still . . . . "

"Still able to help us," John Hornby concluded the sentence grimly. He threw down the pencil and gave his agreement. "O.K., Norman, we'll do it. If they laugh at us, it's too damn bad."

"Right," Norman followed on, standing up to his full height and raising his voice in mock exuberance. "After all, every great scientific advance was laughed at in the beginning. It's a price you pay for a great leap forward."

That left John a bit more down to earth. "Shall we go and see Faye Delisle before I write out the new guidelines – for the next great leap forward."

Norman grinned at the suggestion, which was the one he was about to make himself.

"I think you enjoy these visits now more than I do, you devil, however much you play the virgin and saint."

"I'll leave the eroticism for you," Hornby answered, as he prepared to close up the laboratory. "Besides, you're the one who goes in for cradle-robbing, aren't you?"

It was a somewhat cryptic jibe, the first that had passed between the two of this kind. It took Shearer a moment to get the link, the connection, between his early marriage and Faye Delisle's present condition. But what was no joke was that Norman Shearer and John Hornby were getting closer to making known, within the Institute and the Hospital, the strange hypothesis they believed might explain and make sense of their experimental results to date.

Miss Faye Delisle was still a long way from belonging in the cradle. But to look at her now, sitting up in bed with a video of the latest Hollywood movie playing on the wall screen, her long blond hair over her half-bare shoulders, her blue eyes turned in their direction as the two doctors entered the room, was to imagine for a moment that you were seeing a precocious teenager.

"Hi, come right in," she called, touching the remote to close down the picture on the screen in mid-sentence. "This is a surprise. I thought you'd already had enough of me for this week."

Dr. Hornby kept his station to the rear while Dr. Shearer came forward grinning appreciatively. He was carrying a small cardboard box. "We've come to wish you happy twenty-first birthday."

He handed her the box. She took it with a delighted cry, though she knew right away how they were teasing her.

"Thirty-five, you mean, let's be honest. How did you remember? What have you brought me? Will it explode?"

Fearlessly, she ripped the cardboard of the box open like a child with a Christmas present. Inside was a small recorder, the kind that adjusts automatically to present voice levels and has a multi-hour capacity.

"What fun," she cried, switching on the machine and speaking into it in her sultriest actress's voice.

"Happy twenty-first birthday to Faye Delisle from her very dear friends, Dr. Shearer and Dr. Hornby, you lovely lovely men, thank you so very much. I'll keep this at my bedside and talk to it every night before I go to sleep."

Instantly she put it on to automatic Replay, and back came the message in lifelike tones. Then with a laugh she switched it off, lay it down on the bedside table, and turned to them in a more subdued mood.

"Now tell me what you two really mean by all this."

Dr. Shearer glanced at Dr. Hornby behind him as if for moral support, before sitting at her bedside to explain. "Faye, you've been receiving therapy for longer now than any other patient on this course of treatment. And we're particularly anxious to know as much about how you're responding as we possibly can. In a physical way, but also in other ways, mental, psychological. You've told us many times about how the treatments seem to make you feel . . . different."

"Younger," Faye broke in emphatically. "It's true. It really is. I've sometimes felt rather silly saying so, but I can't help it."

"Good, we want you to talk freely. We thought you might agree to record your reactions more fully, more on the spur of the moment, when you're actually having them. Not just when Dr. Hornby or I happen to be here. Do you think you'd be willing to do that?"

Faye Delisle picked up the recorder from the bedside table and looked at it dubiously.

"What would you do then? I'm sure it would sound even sillier, hearing me talk about myself for . . . for posterity."

Dr. Shearer reached a long arm forward take the recorder from her hand. He switched it on and spoke into it solemnly.

"I, Dr. Norman Shearer, do hereby swear that these recordings of Faye Delisle's voice are strictly for private medical and scientific purposes, and will never be used for public performance or reproduction."

He handed it behind him to a somewhat startled Dr. Hornby. Dr. Hornby took it, looked down at it, cleared his throat in an embarrassed way, while Faye lay back against the pillows and smiled at him expectantly, cleared his throat a second time, and then said abruptly into the receiving grill:

"I, Dr. John Hornby, do hereby also swear . . . which is something I don't often do."

He quickly handed back the recorder to Shearer, who passed it on to Faye Delisle.

"All right," Faye said, as if her anxieties eased to a degree by their performances, "if you really want me too, I will. But you must promise not to make fun of me when you hear the silly things I have to say."

Dr. Shearer spoke directly and seriously to her. "Anything you say will be heard only by John Hornby and myself. And we'll be grateful to you for helping us to understand the possible psychological effects of this form of therapy. Very grateful."

"Well, then," Faye said, folding her arms, and settling back into her pillows, "we're agreed. Actually, I think this will be fun. I get so gabby these days. Now

I'll have an audience any time I want. Just like when I first started keeping a diary. When I was fifteen."

Faye Delisle suddenly realized that the two men were leaning forward a little and watching her carefully as she chattered on. "You two got awfully interested in my nonsense all of a sudden. What's this really all about?"

She turned her wide blue eyes on them with a mixture of worry and charm, which disconcerted them.

Dr. Shearer and Dr. Hornby had agreed not to say too much to her, for fear of putting suggestions into her head and prejudicing their study of her responses. But Dr. Shearer couldn't resist a further word. "There's nothing particularly mysterious about it, Faye. It's just that you seem to be reacting in a fairly consistent way. We'd like to get a little more detail about your reactions, day to day. You know, when you say you feel younger, what exactly do you mean? That sort of thing."

"I see," she said, with a renewed sense of excitement, "Like when I flush a lot" (giving a good spontaneous illustration of this reaction) "the way I used to when I was in high school. It's really embarrassing how much that kind of thing shows up when you're a blonde. And when I get those funny restless twinges in my arms and legs. Mother used to call them growing pains. And when . . . ." She paused, looking a little doubtful about how to go on. "When I get these tingly feelings here . . . and here."

She put the palm of one hand over her bosom and the palm of the other hand over her upper thighs, with an expression that was almost shy. "As if I were a . . . a virgin school-girl all over again."

Then, as if they needed any reminder that she had, instead, grown up to become the most mature and experienced of porn movie queens, she chuckled throatily and stretched back in the bed, hands high over her head, legs reaching down and spreading luxuriously under the covers. "I really love it. It feels so good. Like being high all day long."

On the way to the elevator, the two doctors discussed the patient's chart, which Hornby had taken the opportunity to study again. "She remains stable enough for the moment, as far as the chief functions go. Nothing too alarming about the palpitations either for weeks. But she's losing weight rapidly still," Hornby said.

The two nurses they happened to be sharing the elevator with were looking discreetly away, listening hard, but in the traditional hospital manner pretending that they didn't exist.

"Well I imagine," Dr. Shearer answered with an ironic smile, "she would have been about ninety or ninety-five pounds as a teenager before she matured?"

The two nurses were about to step out on the floor above the doctors' stop. Dr. Shearer couldn't resist a further comment on the case within their earshot, aware how odd it must sound to their impassive white backs as they left the car. "Then the question is, how big a twelve-year-old was she?"

F. W. WATT

The two doctors rode down the rest of the way in silence, still digesting the implications of the case, and the realities of having to bring their growing understanding to the surface for themselves – and for others who might find it far more incredible than they did. They knew that they were entering a new, even more difficult phase in the history of their research – God knows, perhaps a new phase in the history of the world.

When Dr. Shearer arrived at his home one evening, later that month, he found his Ella in an unusual state of excitement. She was not lying in front of the TV screen. She was obviously waiting anxiously for his return, hovering in the hallway while he put the runabout in the garage and plugged it in, and carried the groceries up the front steps.

"There's a long distance message for you," Ella blurted out as soon as he stepped in the door. "I put the operator's number by the telescreen."

Norman raised his eyebrows in comic astonishment.

"Thanks for the welcome, my dear," he said, pushing the big cardboard box from Catroni's Grocery Store into her arms.

"It's quite urgent," Ella insisted, turning with an indignant flare of her caftan, and carrying the box into the kitchen. "It's from Chadwick Hamilton in Los Angeles, person to person – but when he heard I was your wife, he spoke to me anyway," she called out over her shoulder, almost spitefully, as she went through the doorway.

"Well," Norman muttered to himself.

He stood by the telescreen as he took off his coat. There in Ella's round hand was the name and the operator's number on the pad. Looking at the blank telescreen, Norman tried to imagine Chad Hamilton's handsome face peering out at Ella. It must have been rather surprising and interesting. No wonder she was so keyed up.

"Did he say what he wanted?" he called into the kitchen after her. He didn't have the slightest urge to play it cool, and vex her further. He was every bit as curious as she, and quite prepared to show it. Ella returned from the kitchen a little mollified by his tone.

"No, he didn't tell me. But he insisted – very nicely – that you call him as soon as you get in. He tried you at the Hospital but they said you'd left for the day."

"O.K.." Norman gave her a hug on his way upstairs. "I'll get in the mood."

He spent a few minutes washing his face and changing into slacks to collect his thoughts, before attempting the return call. He had a very good guess as to what Chad Hamilton was going to say. He spent a minute in his study preparing himself as best he could. If his guess was right, he wasn't sure what to answer. Of course, with someone like Hamilton it was probably wise not to take anything for granted. Norman could be far off in his expectations.

What threatened to put Norman in a real quandary was the situation that had developed in the Hospital and Research Institute in the past few weeks.

At the very least, things had taken a turn for the worst for the Hornby-Shearer project. After a couple of disturbing unsympathetic staff conferences, Dr. Wayland Finger had called both John Hornby and himself in to break the bad news. They were being given the 'go slow' signal, though it wasn't put that bluntly. There was no use arguing.

"It was bound to happen sooner or later," John insisted, when Norman tried to assume the blame. "We just weren't getting the clinical results to go ahead on a larger scale. People were bound to start asking more and more difficult questions."

The problem wasn't that patients on the Hornby-Shearer serum persisted in dying. The same thing was happening with most of the other experimental treatments used in the Carter-Trudeau Memorial Cancer Hospital, and indeed with the more established forms of therapy too. The Hospital was often a place of last resort, drawing patients from all over the continent. Poor statistical results were inevitable. The difficulty lay in trying to keep a level of scientific theory and experimental practice which seemed credible to colleagues and officers in the Hospital. Here is where the two doctors got into trouble.

They had had to make a fundamental alteration in the theoretical basis of their research. However conservatively it was veiled in careful technicalities, they couldn't avoid revealing an hypothesis that crossed the border-line, which in any case is often quite narrow, between respectable research and irresponsible adventuring. Their colleagues had supported them when they proposed a method for curing cancer. The support evaporated when it appeared that they were flirting with bizarre ideas about how this method might affect the normal aging process of healthy cells.

Norman had these considerations in the forefront of his mind as he prepared himself to speak to Hamilton. He smoothed back his hair a little nervously, and adjusted the tie he had slipped on especially for telescreen effect, before taking his chair and calling the long distance operator.

The screen lit up with its alert pattern as the connections were made down the continent. Then, somewhat to his surprise, Norman found himself eye to eye, not with Chadwick Hamilton's face, but with the image of an attractive young woman who seemed familiar to him.

"Hello, Dr. Shearer," the woman's quiet, confident tones began, "thank you for returning Mr. Hamilton's call. He's on another line at the moment, but he won't be long. He's most anxious to talk with you. In the meantime, he's asked me to fill in some of the background of his call."

As she spoke, it came to Norman who she was, why she seemed familiar to him. And then a glance at the letter of many months ago, from the Hamilton Medical Research Center, which in anticipation Norman had brought to the telescreen and had spread out in front of him, verified what he hadn't focused on at first. On the letter-head was the name of the Secretary of the Board of Directors – A. L. Devers. He now recalled the young woman vividly enough, sitting at the end of the table when he last met with the Environmental Hazards Committee.

"All right then, thank you, please go ahead," Norman said to her, smiling agreeably at having solved a small puzzle. "It's Alice Devers, isn't it? I didn't recognize you in your new incarnation."

"I wondered, you looked a little doubtful," Alice Devers said, returning his smile. "Let me tell you something about the Hamilton Medical Research Center."

For three minutes without pause, Miss Devers briefed him on the background of the Centre, beginning by identifying it as the Smith Cancer Research Centre of Los Angeles under another name.

Of course. Norman nodded his recognition of one of the most prestigious small research institutes on the West Coast. A steady stream of publication in the medical journals had come from that address for more than a decade, after which it apparently went into decline, possibly attempting to be too far ahead of the times.

Now, as Miss Devers explained, the institution had been taken over by Chadwick Hamilton, and had been given a new financial and moral impetus. Mr. Hamilton was making strenuous efforts to bring together advanced researchers from around the world in the hopes of making the breakthrough in cancer therapy that seemed so long overdue. Though he had cut his term short on the Environmental Hazards Committee, for reasons she didn't go into, the experience had helped him to know where to locate the latest developments on the frontiers of medical science – obviously with the cooperation of Miss Devers, whom he must have stolen from the Committee.

"The new Centre is of course very interested in the current research and clinical experimentation being conducted by you and Dr. John Hornby. Mr. Hamilton has refused to accept your declining the Centre's invitation as a final decision. He wants to talk with you personally about transferring your work to California. He's particularly anxious to discuss the matter in view of your recent publications and the latest monthly progress reports you submitted to the Environmental Hazards Committee."

"I'm flattered by his interest, Miss Devers," Norman said, a little more drily than he intended. "But I'm rather surprised, frankly, to find that he's taken such a positive view of our project. We haven't a great deal to show as yet, and we've had our discouragements."

"I understand your surprise," Miss Devers replied, with such a steady confidence that she almost persuaded Norman that she did. "It will become clearer to you when you've spoken with Mr. Hamilton. There are some things he'll want to talk about himself. If you can hold on a moment, I think he's ready to come on now."

The screen darkened for an instant, and then was filled with the energetic features of Chad Hamilton's aristocratic face. He wasted no time with preliminaries.

"Look, Dr. Shearer, I'd like you and your friend Dr. Hornby to come down here to Los Angeles and become part of our organization. We think we're going to have the finest facilities in the cancer field outside of the big six. And we offer a hell of a lot more freedom and encouragement for young men like yourselves than you'll ever get from the old gang. You've got to come down and see for yourselves. What do you say, are you interested?"

Norman found himself pulled along by the avalanche of energy, and consciously trying to keep his bearings. It wasn't as easy as that, surely, he wanted to protest.

"You'll have to excuse me if I seem a little caught off guard, Mr. Hamilton," he began. "I didn't realize you were so involved in this venture. In fact, I didn't think that you were personally involved at all. I'm wondering . . . ."

"Dr. Shearer," Hamilton broke in, his voice lowering an octave and deepening in gravity, his eyes trying to search out Norman's through the electronic stream that connected the two men across so many of miles of space. "I'm as personally involved as I've ever been in anything in my life. I have to tell you – I'm putting this to you to show how serious I am, but I'll ask you to keep it strictly confidential, as confidential as any information passed between patient and doctor – can you do that?"

"Surely," Shearer said at once, wondering what it was he was committing himself to silence about.

"This business *is* absolutely personal. Because I've got cancer myself."

"Ah," Norman said, as suddenly the whole feverish enterprise began to make sense. "I had no idea."

"I have. Cancer of the bowel. They give me about a year, more maybe if I have that damnable operation. You know the one. No thank you."

Norman felt a sudden surge of dismay. Partly it was the sense of his golden image of Chadwick Hamilton crumbling. Partly it was dread at the thought of having raised false expectation in Hamilton, perhaps in others too.

"Mr. Hamilton," he began, with great earnestness, "Dr. Hornby and I are nowhere near being able to report clinical evidence in support of our serum's effectiveness. I can understand now how you might think . . . ."

"Hold on, Doctor," Chad Hamilton's booming voice interrupted, "I'm not sure you do understand. I'm no babe in the woods. I'm not asking you to come down here because I think you've got some miracle cure. Christ, I could have a thousand people trying to peddle me one crank remedy after another. What I want is to bring together all the legitimate advanced knowledge on the subject and just let things go ahead as fast as they can in the most favorable conditions. Sooner or later you medical people are going to crack the problem. If I can help to make it sooner, and soon enough for me personally, I'm going to make damned good and sure it works out that way. If I can't, then my son and his kids and other people around the world will get the benefit after I'm gone. . . ."

Chad Hamilton's face seemed to crowd the telescreen in the effort to get closer and communicate the message clearly.

"So don't get me wrong. What we're offering you here is a perfectly legitimate kind of research opportunity, you and Dr. Hornby. With the kind of facilities that will allow you to get the job done. And as for money and that kind of thing – well, just write your own contract. I think you'll find I'm a reasonable man. Come on, what do you say?"

There was a pause, the longest in the whole conversation to that point. Norman was thinking hard, and Chad Hamilton obviously knew how to play poker.

"To be quite blunt about it, Mr. Hamilton, I have to say that I didn't give your invitation very serious thought when I first read it. I was quite happy with the way our work was going at the Carter-Trudeau. Now I'm not quite so happy."

"In what way? What can we do here that would make you happier? You name it."

"I liked what you said about freedom and encouragement, Mr. Hamilton. We feel we're a little hemmed in here right now. We're not making as much progress as we think we could with a little more scope on the clinical side."

"That settles it, Dr. Shearer, you're talking our kind of language. You belong down here."

They went on for five minutes more, while Norman insisted that the matter was far from settled. He hadn't even discussed the possibility seriously with John Hornby, they hadn't considered what sort of disruption in their work a major change in location like this would entail, he hadn't contemplated what might be involved in uprooting and moving his family to Los Angeles.

"I forgot you were a family man, Dr. Shearer. Look here, you have to bring your family down for a visit right away. Say for three or four days next week? Could you get away? You and Dr. Hornby can inspect the set-up here, meet the staff we've got working here already, get an idea what we've got and whatever else you might need, your family can see the environment where they'll be living – everybody seems to love it here – and then you can have a real talk with me and Alice Devers and the people we've got running things. I'll send my plane in for you. Let's see – Alice? How does Wednesday the twenty-first look on our side? O.K.? Now, Dr. Shearer, what do you say?"

When a few moments later Norman turned away from the telescreen, having given his answer, he could see that as far as Ella was concerned, it was the right one. She stood a few feet behind him, holding a drink for each of them, her face lit up with fascination. They sat drinking after dinner, well into the night, and in fact without realizing it, by bedtime they found that for the first time in what seemed like years, they had got drunk together.

Early next day, the frenzied discussion with John Hornby rushed the two doctors into an impetuous agreement. We have to take this incredible proposition seriously. We have to get out of our rut, see at firsthand what this guy has to offer. Find out if it sounds too good to be true. At mid-week , moving still (it seemed to Norman) within the powerful magnetic field set up by Chadwick Hamilton in that telescreen conversation, he sat with his wife and daughter, and a fully engaged John Hornby, in a jet helicopter hovering over Hamilton's private landing strip in central California.

It had transpired by this time that Los Angeles for Hamilton was actually his huge estate, Notlimah, almost a country of its own, a hundred and twenty miles inland. It consisted of a large encircling ring of ten or twenty acre properties – called, naturally enough, the Circle – connected via roads to a collecting area on the west side, where the Centre was located, the airstrip, and a link with the rapid transit service of outer Los Angeles. Within the ring of the Circle was a central enclave of several hundred acres shielded by forest areas, which Chad Hamilton had reserved for private purposes. Principally a Lodge, which was his residence, and a Farm – which evidently he did *not* inhabit.

The Hamilton Medical Research Centre had been moved, lock stock and barrel, from central Los Angeles to a site on a hill between the transit depot and the air field. Ten minutes, as the steward of Hamilton's private plane told them, from the middle of Los Angeles by high speed helicopter, three quarter of an hour by the rapid transit Overhead.

"Who says money can't buy everything?" Norman murmured to his wife as they looked in the directions pointed out by the steward and listened to his explanations, while the helicopter did a great circle over Notlimah. They were being treated to a bird's eye view of the ring of fine landscaped estates, the forests, and what seemed to be well cultivated fields and rich pasture lands and meadows, dotted with farm buildings.

"Where is Mr. Hamilton's Lodge?" Ella asked, expecting perhaps a very special monument, a baronial castle, among all those splendid possibilities.

"You can't see much from above," the steward replied with an understanding smile. "Mr. Hamilton likes his privacy. Actually, if you look very carefully at that big hill almost dead centre of the district, you'll see a series of circling driveways and paths. Can you make them out? Well, they lead up to the front entrance of Mr. Hamilton's Lodge. But the house itself is underground. Mostly under water, to be more exact," he corrected himself, laughing at their puzzled expressions, but showing no sign of wanting to clear up the mystery.

Norman peered down at the big hill as they passed over it. In its flattened top was what looked like a large spring-fed quarry lake, its deep-set waters glinting in the sunlight, crystalline with a bluish tint in this light. He began to get the picture, or thought he did, but he assumed that the steward knew enough to leave some surprises for Chad Hamilton to present to his visitors.

There were two electric limousines waiting for them when they landed. A couple of pleasant, tanned, short-haired young men in white shorts and shirt sleeves helped them efficiently out of the plane and into the cars, Norman and John Hornby in one, Ella and Donna in the other. Alice Devers stepped briskly out of the one-storey white stucco airport building when they were ready to drive away. She looked as cool and confident – and just as striking as Norman remembered her -- in her cream-coloured safari suit that showed off her dark hair. After greeting the two doctors cheerfully, and telling them that Mr. Hamilton was expecting them at the Centre, she got in with Ella and Donna.

"We'll go over and look at the housing situation," she said to Ella and her daughter, "and we'll see the men again over lunch. If that's all right with you?"

If it wasn't entirely all right at the beginning for Ella, who didn't like to leave Norman so soon, mainly out of fear that he would make some sort of commitment without her being there, it soon became so. Alice Devers treated Ella like a sister being given a first tour of her new neighborhood, about to move in to join the family. Donna, sitting in the front seat with the agreeably young driver, was so delighted with all the diversions of the trip so far that she was drifting along happily wherever they went.

As they drove into the landscaped and wooded estate area, the Circle, Alice Devers explained the terrain and a little of the philosophy of Notlimah that lay behind the rather curious arrangements they were beginning to explore.

"These estates are all owned by Mr. Hamilton, so he can decide who comes to live in them. They're what he calls his 'moat' – better than a high fence or a stone wall or a thousand Doberman Pinschers. He hands them out on renewable annual leases to people he thinks will enjoy them and will fit into his scheme of things, staff from the Lodge and the Centre and others. Most of them want to stay forever."

The route they took gave them a little glimpse of the different estate buildings, all shapes and sizes from magnificent, to comfortable, to small and tidy, with ground facilities ranging from resort-like tennis courts and swimming pools to wilderness gardens. What they had in common, as Ella and Donna discovered when they inspected three of varying sizes that were currently empty, were completely modern domestic appliances, from kitchen and shopping computers to micro-ovens to telescreens to self-cleaning floors and temperature and humidity controls and garbage disposals.

"Most of the staff of the Centre have their families somewhere in the Circle," Alice explained. "There's also a set of apartments and town houses adjoining the Medical Research Centre itself for those who prefer that style of life. Some of our 'singles' are living there, especially those who seem to like being close to their work."

"The fanatics," Ella said, thinking a little enviously of John Hornby, and how modest would be the problems of moving for him.

"If you like," Alice said agreeably. She obviously could share Ella's perspectives when she wanted.

"Now we'll go and see the Lodge and the Farm," she added, with a suggestion of having saved the best for the last, leading the way back to the waiting car.

The road they took to penetrate inside the Circle led through a buffer of evergreens and was blocked by a white gate, beside which stood a white cottage. At a signal from the car's dashboard the gate slowly rose and let them through. Alice and the driver waved at a couple of young women, in the white shirts and shorts which the visitors now recognized as a kind of uniform, who were cutting the grass. All the staff seemed young and cheerful and energetic.

On the other side of the gate the road began to pass though cultivated fields and orchards and over irrigation canals and small streams and through pastures with cattle and horses grazing. It was almost too idyllic to be real.

"This must be Shangri-la," Donna called to the women in the back seat, remembering another of her mother's favorite old movies, her eyes bright with excitement and her auburn hair flowing in the breeze from the open window.

"You see?" Alice Devers said triumphantly to Ella.

She had just been telling Ella that the Farm was populated with young people, and that young people always took to the place instinctively. It was part of Chad Hamilton's great design that the comfortable upper middle-class life of the Circle should have an escape valve for its young. He was very aware of the fact that it's really the off-spring of the wealthy, far more so than of the working class, who seem to have most difficulty getting along with their parents' life-style and the society of their elders, and who are always running away from home or getting into serious trouble.

Instead of trying to hold onto the young and making them conform to standards which they resist, the Circle was encouraged to be more liberal about it, to let its young run away – to the Farm. Here there was freedom and spontaneity impossible in their family homes, and the chance to behave in ways that would shock – did shock – their elders. But at least there was some sense of where they were and what was happening to them, and some limits to the scope of possible evils.

"Who runs the Farm, then?" Ella asked. "Who's responsible?"

"That's really how the whole thing started," Alice said. "Mr. Hamilton's son, Garth. It all began with Garth, when he was eighteen. As a kind of youth commune, with a difference. Garth went through some difficult psychological stages as an adolescent. Mr. Hamilton knows something from first-hand experience about what it's like dealing with the younger generation."

"I don't think I knew Mr. Hamilton had a son."

"Very few people do. He's lived out of the public eye all his life. By his own choice. It suits him, obviously. You'll certainly meet him though, if you come to live here. Garth Hamilton is the Chief of the Chiefs on the Farm,"

Alice Devers laughed at the odd phrase as she uttered it, so Ella wasn't quite sure how to take it. In any case she was trying to keep a tight rein on her feelings, trying to quell her rising sense of excitement. If she had been seeing all this on one of her videos she might have sat back and enjoyed it without a thought. But to be seriously considering committing yourself to this environment was a different matter. It was necessary to be detached, critical. There had to be some catches. She was no longer adolescent enough to believe it could be that easy.

"Don't worry about it now," Alice Devers said, as if she could read Ella's mind. "Just look around and enjoy yourself. Then when you get home again, you can add everything up and make your decision. . . . Here we are now – the Lodge."

They had been circling and rising from the base of the large hill in the middle of the estate. Their eyes had been turned outwards to take in the growing vistas of farm lands and wooden farm buildings dotted here and there in the midst of trees and shrubbery, and then, beyond, the encircling forest of evergreens on the circumference. But the driveways and lanes had now brought them up onto the plateau of the hill-top, covered in grassy stretches and trees and giant flowering shrubs and secluded patio patches, with benches and footpaths leading to the edge of the strikingly clear sunken lake of the quarry.

Then abruptly the driveway descended through a cleft in the high rock rim that hemmed in the water.

Suddenly they could see that the clean white rock on all sides of the water actually formed the roof of a pillared underground parking space. As the car drove in and they got out to stand on the patio slates under the rock ceiling and look around, they realized that the beautiful clear lake was in fact surrounded by the windows and open patios of a vast habitable complex under the same roof, lapped at by the water of the lake on the inside, and extending back an unknown distance away from the lake and into the stone of the quarry, none of it visible from the roadway or from the sky.

"How lovely," Donna cried, walking to the edge of the parking area and gazing across the sunlit water at the profusion of doors and windows and open lounging areas fronting on the lake, and sheltered by the natural-seeming roof. "It's a kind of treasure cave, a palace underground."

"Under water," Alice Devers said with a smile, repeating a phrase which had puzzled them before. "Come in and I'll show you around. We'll have an hour or so before the others arrive."

Two wide sliding doors opened automatically at the back of the parking area. Alice led them into a carpeted corridor, saying over her shoulder.

"As I told Chad when I first saw this place, it's really terribly gross and vulgar. But it's fun too. Chad's favorite toy."

At the end of the corridor was an upholstered elevator car with comfortable padded walls.

"Up or down?" the mechanical voice chirped at them from the control panel.

"Down, please," said Alice with a descending intonation.

The car silently dropped them to a soft stop, and the doors opened on a corridor like the one they had left, except that it was in white and this one was in blue. A short walk took them to another automatic door. Ella and Donna both caught their breath as Alice Devers stepped aside to let them through.

"It's always fun introducing people to this place," Alice said, enjoying their exclamations and amazement. "It's a showpiece, but it's for living in too. Chad spends most of his time here when he's at home."

The room itself was vast, though divided by furnishings into lounging, drinking, eating and working areas – one central section contained a huge round desk with a telescreen and recorders and the other paraphernalia of a business office – but it was hard to pay attention to what was on the floor and walls . . . because of the ceiling.

Looking up, they saw that they were under water.

The water of the lake was above them, making up the entire ceiling, supported by some glass or plastic so close to being invisible that there seemed to be only water, translucent, limpid, streaking splendidly with the movement of fish and occasional plants and the gentle shimmering of its surface. It made you want to lie on your back and gaze upwards forever. Restful was hardly the word for it. It didn't put you to sleep. It woke you to a conscious sense of perpetual motion, perpetual peace, timelessness.

"It's beautiful," Donna breathed at last, realizing there was no adequate way to express that first impression.

"Yes," Alice Devers said, looking at the girl's eyes, and putting an arm around her shoulders, "it is beautiful, isn't it?"

The mood of that first moment remained so strong for the mother and daughter that it was hardly disturbed by the more energetic and noisy presence of the three men, when they arrived a half hour later.

After giving Norman and John long enough to react to the Lodge's unique architecture and for himself to enjoy their reaction, Chad Hamilton boomed out a general invitation to go for a swim before their meal.

At both ends of the Lake Room were quarters supplied with everything necessary, showers and swimsuits and air driers. When all three men were changed, Hamilton, looking fit and athletic in his white swim shorts, led them into another tiled room with a high open ceiling, a kind of deep shaft, which showed the blue sky above.

"Do you want to float up or blast out, gentlemen?" Hamilton asked with a boyish grin.

"Float for me, I guess," said John Hornby hesitantly, portly and lily white in the bright red swim-suit he had chosen from the cupboards.

"The same," Norman decided, though reluctant not to explore the possibilities.

"Right you are. Then I'll blast out. You two first."

Hamilton lifted his head and spoke sharply up to the sky. "Ready number one, if you please."

Immediately a metal hatch at floor level opened and a large rubber raft was ejected with a plop onto the tile floor at their feet. A moment later clear tepid water began to sluice in at floor level from all sides, with alarming speed.

"Climb aboard if you like," Hamilton suggested, pointing to the raft.

As John settled himself aboard, the water was already beginning to lift the raft.

"You see that window running up the side of the wall to the top? Watch. I'll beat you to the surface by three minutes," Hamilton said, stooping to splash water on himself.

Norman watched the sluicing water rise up to his knees and then his waist. He put a hand on the raft and gave it a gentle push so John could feel it move and bump against the wall. John sat carefully in the middle, not moving. Chad Hamilton stepped into a kind of glass closet which opened into the wall at the base of the vertical window strip.

"I'll be waiting for you," he said with a grin and a wave, as he let the glass doors shut behind him, enclosing him like a torpedo in a tube.

Abruptly, before they knew what had happened, they could see his bronzed shape surge upwards, a flash of brown and white on the other side of the glass, and he was gone.

"It's like diving!" Norman laughed like a boy, holding on to the raft with one hand, bobbing up and down now almost out of his depth, "only instead of down you go up."

A moment later he couldn't feel the floor and was rapidly rising along with the raft. As they approached the surface opening, no longer very high above their heads, Norman let the tremors of childish excitement take over and he cried out playfully to John.

"Help!"

That was a mistake. Suddenly the whole process went into reverse. The sluicing water began to retreat, the level sank with a rush, and in a moment the raft had shot down like an elevator and touched bottom, leaving John still seated in the middle of it, like an overgrown child in a sandbox. Norman stood in awkward embarrassment beside him, dripping water onto the wet tiles. The door of the room swung open, and a pair of athletic-looking short-haired young men stepped forward ready for action.

"I'm very sorry, did I do that?" Norman sputtered.

The two men took in the situation immediately.

"Don't worry," one of them laughed, "it happens all the time. The lock room machinery hasn't learned how to take a joke."

"What can I say?" Norman pleaded comically, seeing that the situation was redeemable. "You saved my life."

"Glad to be of service," the second young man said. "Actually we treat these things as drills to keep us sharp. Living with all this water around you, you never know when there might be an accident."

"Have a good swim," the first man said, and then up to the ceiling, sharply: "Ready number one, if you please."

This time, as the two young men stepped quickly out and closed the door behind them, Norman meekly climbed aboard the raft beside John, and remained there in silence. In a few moments they found themselves on the same level as the surface of the lake, looking across lock gates about to open, at the bobbing heads of the three women and Chad Hamilton, enjoying the slanting of the late afternoon sun on the lake surface.

It was after midnight before Norman and Ella settled down in a big bed in front of open French doors overlooking the moonlit lake. Somewhere around the rim of the lake, John Hornby had another guest room. Donna, if she ever came in to use it, had a bedroom a few doors down the corridor in the other direction.

Donna had asked if she could go off for a walk in the fresh air after dinner. An hour later she had telephoned from a farmhouse a mile away to say she had met some people who wanted to take her to a "farm concert". There were flustered consultations between Ella and Norman, until Chad Hamilton intervened.

"Keep her on the line for a minute. I'll have a word with Garth" he said.

He sat down at a telescreen on his big table, and in a moment his screen filled with the dark bearded face of a youngish man with obvious resemblances to Chad Hamilton, but eyes if anything even more direct.

"Garth, do you know I've got a few guests at the Lodge, and their teenage daughter is down visiting your people?"

"Hold on a moment, please."

The screen went dark. During the pause, Chad turned reassuringly to the Shearers.

"Nothing much goes on down there that my son doesn't know about."

Garth's face reappeared. "She's with Don Planter and his friends. She'll be all right. When would you like her back?"

Before Norman could say anything, Ella broke in.

"Tell him, that as long as he thinks it's all right, and she's enjoying herself, she can come back whenever she wants."

As they lay side by side in bed, Ella justified her words energetically. If they were seriously thinking of moving to Notlimah, they'd better face the realities right away. Many of the young people from the Circle where they would be living naturally gravitated to the Farm. If they didn't want to give their children that kind of freedom, if they were suspicious and protective, they'd better not live here at all. It would only get worse.

"Besides," she concluded, "I'm sure it's much safer than at home, letting her go into the city at night by herself. I think Garth Hamilton looks like the kind of man who would take good care of her. He looks like . . . like a holy man."

Norman snorted his derision at that description. "You're drunk."

Ella insisted. "He does. He looks like a saint. Sort of sad, too, as if he were going to be a martyr. He looks like Christ."

Norman laughed out loud. "You *are* drunk."

"What's so funny about that?"

In a moment Norman was serious enough to explain. "I agree, my dear, he does look a little like . . . like God the Son. Just as Chad Hamilton looks like my idea of God the Father, without a long white beard. But from the odd thing I've heard about him, he's not quite as spiritual as you think. Any more than Chad Hamilton is."

That was as much as Ella could get from him. In a few seconds he was dozing, despite her desire to go on talking and asking questions. It had been a strenuous day. They were soon both sound asleep, whatever Donna might be doing.

Don Planter and his current best friend, Thelma Dean, who was three months pregnant, walked Donna up the hill and made sure she was inside the front doors of the Lodge a few hours later. It was a bright night still, though by then (after four o'clock) the moon was getting too far down to show the lake at its best.

Donna was very happy. Why, she would never be able to tell her father and mother. But she very much hoped – in fact, as she got under the sheet in her bedroom two doors down from theirs, she prayed – that they would decide to move to Notlimah permanently. She believed she had at last found a place and a way of life that mattered to her.

It had been a night like none she had ever known. She hadn't left the Lodge after dinner out of boredom or restlessness at being in the company of her parents and elders for too long, as in another situation she might have. Actually, it was interesting to be with people like Mr. Hamilton, who was wonderfully good-looking for his age, and had done so many interesting things and gone to so many places around the world and who had met just about everybody who was anything. And Alice Devers treated Donna just like a younger sister, making her wish she really had an older sister, at least one as beautiful and confident and talented as Alice.

But when dinner was finished, and the others were settling down for drinks and more talk in the Lake Room, Donna was just too excited in an almost physical way to sit still. She had to do something with her hands and feet. She was only intending to walk around the lake and look at the view, which Alice said she would love.

From the top of the hill it was possible to see as far as the evergreen ring on all sides, and, in between the Lodge and the forest, the whole Farm spread out under her in the fading light of the summer evening. There were small shapes of people moving down there in the distance, across fields, in barnyards, several driving horse-pulled wagons, a few on horseback. On the highest point of the hill, where she came to stand, was a circular wooden hut open on all sides but covered over with a shingle roof. Under it was a telescope on a tripod. Donna amused herself by focusing it, and bringing everything she could see so close she could almost touch it.

One cluster of farm buildings, the largest and most central she could discover, bordered on a winding stream that came out of the forest to the east, bent southwards around the hill, and passed on through the forest to the west. At a long wooden table, as Donna could make out when she adjusted the telescope, a group of young people sat eating or drinking and talking after the evening meal. Under a tree at the stream's edge, a figure lay, evidently strumming a guitar, with another beside him, perhaps singing.

As Donna moved the telescope back and forth, a man with a broad-brimmed hat and a dark beard stood up at the centre of the table, and then leaped up onto the table itself. Everyone seemed to be paying rapt attention. He was either singing or talking, Donna couldn't tell. After a long while he leaped down again and sat among the others for a few minutes. Then he abruptly got up, walked away into the farmhouse nearby – and gradually, as if the magnet that held them together had been turned off, the others began to wander off in different directions.

It was like watching a movie with the sound off. Mysterious, intriguing, tantalizing. The clear blue sky was beginning to colour magnificently as the sun sank. The fields and trees and the river with its ditches and canals leading off on both sides, the flowering shrubs and the white-washed farm buildings – it all drew Donna. Especially the people who seemed so young and easy and relaxed, moving with natural grace through their idyllic world. She wanted to get closer. She abruptly got up and started walking down the pathways, always choosing the turn that took her closer to the bottom of the hill.

In fifteen minutes she had reached the first fields. Soon she was passing through lanes with pastures and orchards and crops on each side, and sometimes cattle and sheep and horses grazing. The first cottages that she passed showed her no signs of life. Then she heard the clop of horses' hooves behind her, and soon stood to one side of the lane to let a young couple pass by, trotting along on two fat grey horses. They eased to a walk as they approached her.

The young man in jeans and T-shirt, half a length behind the young woman in a long blue cotton skirt who was also sitting astride, was the first to speak. Donna didn't know quite what to say, or whether she was trespassing.

"Hi, are you from Heaven?" the young man asked.

The two riders stopped now, and looked down with amusement at Donna's bewildered expression.

"What?" Donna asked, laughing up at them in return, but wondering if this was supposed to be a compliment.

"From up there," the young woman said, pointing to the hill which, as Donna turned to follow her gesture, she realized must be visible from everywhere on the Farm.

"Yes, I guess I am," Donna said, and then quickly, "I mean, I'm just visiting with my parents up there."

She didn't like the sound of that either, so she rushed on. "We're thinking of moving to Notlimah for good. We're just looking things over for a few days."

"Come with us then," the young woman said, reining her horse ahead at the walk. "We live just over there, and we'll show you around the Farm when we've turned the horses out."

A little while later, after a glass of red wine and a snack of cheese and crackers, local cheese, local wine, and local crackers, as Don Planter and Thelma Dean explained, the three strolled down into the heart of the Farm, the cluster of buildings Donna had seen from the hill. People were gathering in the yard of the high roofed old barn, which was to house the concert for the evening.

Donna hadn't told her parents what kind of concert it was, because, when she had asked her two new friends, they simply smiled and shrugged their shoulders, saying, You never know. It would be whatever the Chief of Entertainment had suggested to him and had agreed on. You would find out when you got there.

As they moved through the assembling young people, Don Planter threw out casual introductions, usually variations on the 'visitor from Heaven' theme. They were making their way to the river bank, where a group was gathered around a huge oak tree and a big man in a rich wine-coloured caftan seated on a wooden awning-covered tree-swing. The group lying on the grass around him were laughing at some story he was telling. He looked across at the trio approaching, but continued with his story to its conclusion, which broke up the listeners with shouts and laughing comments. Then he gave Donna Shearer all his attention.

He was deeply tanned, like someone accustomed to spending most of his time out of doors, eyes so penetrating they were almost fierce, and a rich dark beard. He looked slightly familiar to Donna, but she was sure she would never have forgotten if she had met him before. Though now she did identify him with the man she had seen through the telescope on the hill earlier in the evening.

"This is Donna," Planter said, taking the girl by the hand and virtually presenting her, "a visitor from Heaven. Donna, this is our man Garth."

Garth accepted Donna's hand and drew her to the seat beside him. Her feet didn't quite touch the ground, so that when his long legs began to push the swing gently, she drifted back and forth easily and helplessly.

"I've been expecting you," he said puckishly, turning a little sideways to inspect her in a friendly, candid way. "My father tells me he's very anxious that you should enjoy yourself, you and your parents."

"I know now," Donna said. "You're Mr. Hamilton's son."

"And you," Garth answered, pushing the swing a little higher with his sandaled feet, "are the daughter of a famous medical scientist."

"I don't know how famous," Donna answered, not wanting to be there under false pretences, "but I know he's very smart. He keeps telling Mother and me."

Garth pushed the swing higher still, and then began to pump rhythmically, his caftan flowing, thrusting his tanned legs out in front of him, bared to the thigh in the breeze. He held the side-ropes, one of his arms behind Donna's back. Donna tried to pretend she wasn't in the slightest bit surprised or frightened.

"Don't be so modest," Garth said. "Our Chief of Health knows about your father. He was just saying your father writes in the best research journals -- he's into genetic experiments and all that far out stuff."

As the swing rose higher and higher, it began to reach over the stream, as if on its forward motion it would take off from its ropes and fly. Then it went back and down with a giddy sweep and upwards the other way, until it felt as though they would be tipped out and onto the ground far below. Back and forth. Higher and higher, higher and higher.

Suddenly Donna's nerve gave and she screamed. In the same instant Garth stopped pumping and wrapped an arm around her. She buried her face in this chest and hung on, eyes shut tight, feeling his muscular arm firm around her, as the sickening semi-circling hurtle and drop gradually shortened and slowed. The two sat still for a moment in their spontaneous embrace, and then suddenly the dozen or so spectators cheered. Donna jumped free and stood looking about in a confused way, as if she'd forgotten where she was. Garth stood up beside her, to his full height, letting his wine-coloured caftan settle in folds to the ground. He towered over the girl. Smiling to the others over her head at her confusion, he took her by the hand.

"Let's go in. The concert will start now."

Inside the barn, the big wooden benches were filling up. Garth led Donna down the side aisle to the front row, where he put her beside himself with Thelma Dean and Don Planter.

"A Farm specialty," he said to Donna, after offering a slim wooden case of thin brown cigarettes to Planter and Thelma.

He took one and lit it for Donna, before lighting his own. She breathed a sweetish flavor, basically familiar, but not quite like anything she'd tried before.

Others were lighting up all around her. The bare stage in front of them was touched softly now by sidelights, and far at its back they could see a couple, both with hair to their waists, settling down to the controls of some instruments she didn't recognize. Soon some soft wailing and percussive sounds were coming out over the audience, soothing but attention-catching at the same time, enjoyably enough even to Donna, who had thought she hated electronic music. Thin ribbons of smoke were rising up to the high rafters all around from the nearly full audience, everyone sitting in a quiet, relaxed way, waiting with a sense of pleasant and not too strenuous expectation.

The music began to rise in volume and quicken in pace. It rapidly reached ear-hurting proportions, and then abruptly it was over, to a response of sporadic claps and good-natured cheers from the audience.

The lights over the whole building went out, leaving the place in total darkness, except for the glowing and fading of dozens of cigarette ends. The audience sat silently letting the sense of expectation build up again. Thelma Dean reached over and took Donna's hand in hers, guessing that the girl might not be as comfortable in the dark with a strange crowd as the others were.

She had time to give it a squeeze and receive one from Donna in return, when the entire backdrop of the stage was suddenly lit up with a magnificent, overwhelming brilliance of pure white. Donna gasped and covered her eyes for a second at the first impact. In a moment she was staring with fascination, with the crowd, as a dot of the brightest red appeared without visible origin high in the left hand corner of the white expanse.

The small intensely red spot was motionless, perfect and complete in itself, hypnotic in its simplicity and singleness. But like an egg, a seed, a drop of blood, it seemed, the dot surged and spread diagonally across the whole vast sheet of white, a widening gash, a flash, a visual cry growing louder and louder.

The shape turned back on itself and took another direction, pulling in viewers' eyes with it, and went on moving in unpredictable leaps and dives. When the motion and colour traversing the white space began to seem too much, abruptly it stopped, became set, permanent – but a dot of blue appeared on the right hand bottom corner. After another hypnotic pause, it became a vivid spread of the new colour, meeting and avoiding and fusing with the red.

The process repeated itself again and again, for a length of time Donna couldn't even guess. The white background filled and swirled and danced and warred and danced again with shapes and colors of all kinds, until all memory of pure white was gone, until the mind was lost in the complexity and intricacy and endless variety of shape and colour and texture, building and building mysteriously before their eyes, until pure possibility had become complete realization.

The sounds of electronic music had been growing louder. When the room was filled to overflowing with sound and colour, suddenly the music stopped and the massive visual structure, vibrating in front of their eyes, absorbing them into its world, disappeared as if it had never existed, leaving the hall in total darkness and complete silence.

A spotlight sprang on the figure of a young man seated, hunched over a sloped table at the front of the stage, to the extreme right hand side. The audience at once burst into clapping and cries of praise. The young man got off his stool and stood a little disconsolately in the bright light, pulling off the band from his shoulder-length hair with one hand and waving a clutch of painter's brushes at the audience with the other.

"Our artist," Garth murmured to Donna, and then in a booming voice, joining the others: "Bravo, Roberto."

"How does he do it?" Donna whispered to Thelma, a little disappointed that such magnificence had come from the actions of a human being with an ordinary body and a name.

"It's a way Roberto developed himself," Thelma answered under the noises of approval. "He used to do oils and water colors and that kind of thing, but he says he can't stand to do anything permanent and static any more. He's built a kind of projector that instantly takes off the work he creates from a special screen he works on. He says it's the closest thing to direct communication of his artistic vision he's been able to invent so far . . . . Did you like it?"

"It was beautiful," Donna breathed, not caring how naïve she might sound.

The second performer wasn't quite so much to her liking. In fact, fascinating as she found him in all sorts of ways, she didn't really understand what it was all about. This time she was too shy to try to find out if she was the only one who reacted that way.

A young man leaped into the spotlight, dressed only in a leather apron, his body wonderfully bronzed and muscled, his head completely shaved, his skin oiled and polished so it seemed to glow like fine wood, carrying a bow and arrow in his hands and with a hatchet tied to his waist. He did a little athletic dance in complete silence, turning and glaring threateningly in each direction, one after the other, and straight up to the sky. Then he faced the audience and began to speak.

Or at least, it was a kind of speech that came out of his mouth. There were recognizable words and phrases and even sentences. But there were strange and foreign-sounding words too, or noises, that seemed to be all vowels and no consonants. But what was strangest of all was the tonal rise and fall of the voice, and the incredible vibrancy, so rich and subtle that it seemed to send a listener's whole body, bones and guts, vibrating as though touched by a violinist's fingers and bow. It was a few moment before Donna realized that the performer was treating his voice box as if it were a musical instrument, and in some delicate way not visible to the audience, he had amplified his throat. The combination of natural and electronic was eerie, at times haunting, so intimately relating hearer to utterance that it was claustrophobic, overwhelming.

"Our poet," Garth commented as the performer at last ended and stepped forwarded to accept the audience's applause.

"It's one of the Farm's favorite poems," Thelma explained. "Eric has tried to capture some of the aboriginal feeling for earth and sky, mother nature, while projecting it into the atmosphere of the future, you know, the time of machines and so on, modern technology. You really have to hear it several times to appreciate it fully."

Donna was grateful for that remark. Not that she cared whether she understood or not. She was wonderfully relaxed and happy. She didn't want the evening ever to finish. And besides, the next performance was a delight from beginning to end.

"Ah," Garth said, in obvious satisfaction as the sidelights came on to begin illuminating the still shape of a young woman in the centre of the stage. She was clothed in a white dress, full length with voluminous clinging folds, and she was lying on the floor curled up in the fetal position, her long black hair wrapped around her head and neck. As the illumination increased, electronic music began quietly and grew in intensity. The woman remained motionless.

"Our dancer," Garth said into Donna's ear. "You'll like this."

Soon a little movement could be detected in the fetal shape, a kind of quivering of body and limbs, in the woman's form, nothing that could be identified with purposeful actions. Gradually the movement increased until, like a flower growing and unfolding, the figure stirred and stretched and rose, but still with a sense of being rooted to a single spot. Then with delicacy and tentativeness, the shape began to explore the space behind and to each side, and, with appealing hesitancy of projected look and gestures, the space filled by the audience.

After a time came a little experimental gliding from the magic invisible root, and in a moment the glidings became more and more daring and exuberant and playful, more free. Arms and legs, hands, fingers, ankles, toes, neck, head, the whole body began to circle and swoop about the newly created space all around. Soon the playfulness, although the sense of space was just as generous, more so, became more serious, more concentrated, more self-absorbed, more dignified and graceful.

The long arms, in one of those sweeping movements, reached to the swirling hem of the white dress, and gradually as the dance continued the dress rose higher and higher, revealing the long, elegant legs and lithe torso of a naked woman. For a moment, with a crescendo of music behind her, she posed stationary, the voluminous gown covering her head, her face, her individual identity, trailing behind her to the ground over her upraised arms, her female form exposed and offered fully to the space around, to the audience.

Then the gown cascaded down around the body again, except that in doing so it had bundled over the waist, and the woman's arms folded in front over the swelling that appeared there. For several minutes now, with a touching mixture of clownishness and dignity, which sent ripples of amusement through the audience, the dancer mimed the movements of her new role, travelling about the stage with increasing awkwardness and heaviness in walking and stooping and reaching, until she grew stiller, and eventually lay motionless on the stage with her feet towards the audience, the swelling shape at her waist obscuring her head.

Again the electronic music rose in intensity, and the woman's body began to writhe, and subside, and writhe again, knees lifting and spreading, arms reaching high. The rhythmic struggles grew faster and faster, until with a final high arching of pelvis and spreading of knees they abruptly subsided.

After a long stillness, the reclining form began to stir again, arms now cradling what had been the bundle of the white dress below the waist. In a little while, surprisingly quickly, the cradling arms had carried their care and tenderness all around the stage and then right to the front of the platform, as if the dancer were going to dance from art into life.

It seemed to Donna, when the arms held out an imaginary gift, it was to the very spot in the audience where she was. In a moment the dancer whirled, as if receiving the gift back with one hand, and dancing gaily with it and above it, playfully, around the stage again.

Thelma Dean squeezed Donna's hand tightly, as if she were trying to communicate more feelings than she could contain. "You see," she whispered into Donna's ear, "she's carrying Garth's child."

A kind of quiver went through Donna's body as she stared at the dancer, and continued to experience the strong awareness of Garth's physical presence so close beside her.

Meanwhile the dancer had sent her little imaginary companion off into the distance, and had entered a new role. She was growing more sedate, quieter, perhaps even tired and a little discouraged, a little sad. Visibly the graceful, vital gestures gave way to more ragged, almost ugly stops and starts. Before long, what had once been the essence of youth became the most concentrated condition of halting, crippled, despairing age, awkward and grotesque and pitiable.

The motions of the dancer grew slower, the space in which they were performed more circumscribed, until the very spot in which the original life had once taken root now received and held stationary the declining of the old. There was some diminishing spasmodic quivering until the angular, astonishingly old and ugly seeming body lay completely still, as if laid out in the coffin.

What an unbearably sad way for it all to end, Donna was thinking, when abruptly, with no warning but a split second rise in the musical accompaniment, the white shroud burst into life. The body leaped into the most exuberant, uninhibited, wild activity, surging through the available space, leaping, and swirling in crescendo after crescendo of abandoned movement.

The long white gown sailed higher and higher until it swept completely into the air like a cloud off the body, off the high-reaching fingers of the young woman. It seemed to hover in the light above for a moment as the woman

F. W. WATT

danced ecstatically in complete overwhelmingly beautiful nakedness under it. Then it settled in front of her, or she pulled it down, to fill her arms and cover her body from shoulders to ankles, as she stood motionless, staring out over the audience.

The music abruptly stopped. The young woman bowed deeply, sending her hair cascading downwards to the floor, the light gleaming off her naked back. Then the light went out, and the audience broke into cheers in the darkness.

The clapping, stamping and cheering went on for a several minutes, as gradually cigarettes were lit in the darkness and talk started on all sides. No one got up to move or go. After a few more minutes all the lights in the barn went on, and there was some movement from the back of the audience. A group of people was coming down the aisle.

"Our Chief of Entertainment", Garth said to Donna over his shoulder, as he turned to watch the arrivals following their leader.

The Chief of Entertainment received some applause and cheerful heckling as he came to the front row and addressed Garth and the audience.

"May I present our performers for this evening, Garth, and friends. First, Roberto, artist of a work called 'Time and Space'. Second, Eric, author of a poem called 'Words for Earth, Heaven and the Future'. Third, Tara, who danced 'The Story of Woman'. Last but not least, Carl and Juanita, who composed and played all the music, including their 'Synaesthetic Symphony Number One'. We hope that you and all our friends enjoyed the concert."

Garth stood to greet the performers, who were now in their ordinary clothes, as though to demonstrate their sense of merging back into the community. As he shook hands with each and gave each a hug, the crowd cheered them again in turn, especially Tara, whom Garth kissed on both cheeks.

Garth, the Chief of Entertainment, and the performers stood before the audience as Garth boomed out a kind of ritual benediction in a deep baritone from his great height.

"My friends, from you and from me I give thanks for this evening. Peace and happiness be with us all. Goodnight."

Gradually the barn emptied while Donna stood with Thelma on the edge of a group at the front of the room. She was a little down from where she'd been, a little tired, perhaps, but she felt wonderfully at ease. She was coasting.

In a few minutes, as Donna watched, Garth kissed Tara on the cheek again, and turned away from the performers and those who had remained behind to talk to them. Garth led Donna along with Thelma and Don Planter to the doorway.

"I'll show Donna the river," Garth said to Planter. "Will you take her back up back up the hill tonight?"

"Surely," Don said, linking arms with Thelma. "We'll be together at the Elm Cottage tonight. Whenever . . . . "

Donna didn't object to the sense of being handed about. Everything at the Farm seemed so easy and good. She let herself be led by the hand down to the river bank, where people in couples or groups or alone were strolling or sitting. At a little covered fisherman's hut, furnished with a long wooden bench and open to the river side, Garth paused, lit another cigarette for Donna and himself to share, and drew her in to sit down.

He had been talking about the Farm, who lived there, how it worked. He had told her all about the dozen chiefs. Like Indian chiefs? she had asked, as a joke. Kind of, he had answered, whether seriously or not, she couldn't tell. The Chiefs of education, of security, of trades, of health, of field crops, of transport, of fruit and vegetables, of business, and of entertainment.

"And you," Donna said, still not sure how much of his description was mock solemnity, "you must be the Chief of the Chiefs."

"I am," he said. "I began the Farm, I live out my life on the Farm."

He then began to speak with great eloquence, as if now the heart of his message was to be unveiled. His voice, coming out of the shadows of the hut, lightened and softened and took on a rhythmic, almost incantatory quality.

He told her it was an experiment in living that they were carrying out on the Farm. If the world was to survive, if people were to go on wanting to survive, they had to learn all over again how to live together in small groups relating themselves to their natural environment, relating themselves to each other, relating themselves to the powerful natural forces that moved through human and animal and vegetable nature. They had to rediscover how to be creative and loving, how to take care of each other and how to have fun. How to work and play together in harmony. How to give of themselves freely and generously, and to rise above petty fears and jealousies and personal vanities.

"We have to learn how to be young and beautiful again," he almost chanted in her ear, "we have to find out what it is to be truly human, to be man and woman."

For a long time they sat side by side looking out over the moonlit river. Donna was conscious of nothing more than a quiet yearning to be part of that experiment, part of that lovely world. She was drawn as if by a giant magnet, and had no will to resist. It must be like this to be hypnotized, she found herself thinking: it's the one who's being hypnotized who wants hypnosis most.

Garth turned to her as if re-discovering her there beside him, after his eloquent sojourn in the ideal. He got to his feet and pulled her up.

"Donna," he said experimentally, "Donna," trying the sound of her name on his lips and looking into her eyes to find Donna there. Then he bent down and touched her lips with his.

She shut her eyes as he drew near. Then she opened them when his lips left hers.

"Why did you do that?" she said softly.

"Because I wanted to. Because it felt good."

They were silent for a moment, as she looked up at him.

"Do you mind?" he added.

"No . . . . No. I guess I've been wanting you to do that all evening."

It didn't sound too brash to her own ears, even though he immediately stooped and kissed her again. "Would you like to be my woman tonight?" he asked, holding her at arm's length and looking down at her.

She returned his gaze directly. "Does that mean you want to be my man?"

He put back his head and laughed to the sky. "It does, it does," he said over her head, squeezing her shoulders and still laughing.

"Well, then . . . . I don't see what's so funny."

Garth obviously had no intentions of telling her. He put an arm around her waist and led her back along the river side.

"Where are we going?" she asked, "To your house?"

"I don't have a house."

"How come? You're the Chief of the Chiefs, aren't you? Where do you live?"

Then he explained. He had no house. As Chief of the Chiefs, he called nothing his own on the Farm, and yet in a sense everything was his. He could go where he wanted and stay where he wanted, use what he wanted – as long as his friends were happy for him to do so. He had never found a door closed to him. There were no enemies on the Farm. He was at once the host for everyone and the guest of everyone.

"Here, I'll show you," he said, turning down a long lane with her, and walking in the shadows cast by shrubs and a Chinese elm hedge at its end.

When they got to the door, Garth stood and whistled the song of a bird Donna had never heard before. It was a mixture of twirls and chirps that sounded like nothing a human being could make, piercing the shadows sweetly. In a moment the door opened. It was Thelma Dean, standing in the light of the kerosene lamp, wearing an old-fashioned flannelette night-gown down to her ankles.

"Garth. Donna. Come in," she called into the night. "We're in the back bedroom. Sing out when you want us to take Donna up the hill."

She left the lantern sitting on the hall floor while she turned and walked away to the other end of the cottage.

Garth pick up the lantern and led the way up the stairs. On the second floor at the front was a bedroom with a four-poster bed under slanting rafters, and an old wooden bureau and a writing desk, all rough-hewn in pioneer style.

Garth hung the lantern on the wall hook. Without a word he began to take off his clothes, standing in the middle of the room. Donna walked over to sit on the edge of the bed. She tentatively loosed a shoe. His movements as he undressed were so natural and generous and candid that she gradually lost her shyness, and watched with the same frankness.

"Now," he said, turning towards her, with the light glancing off the bronzed muscles of his shoulders and thighs, "you can see the Chief of the Chief of the Chiefs."

He spread his arms in front of her and almost obliged her eyes to drift down his chest and belly and thighs, pause there for a powerful moment, and then rise up again to his bearded face. He stepped forward, pushing her firmly back on the bed. He began swiftly and efficiently to take off her clothes. It was all so much quicker and more direct than she had expected. She moaned a little when she realized how urgent he was, but she was ready, and she received him into her arms with rushing eagerness after her first hesitation.

Only afterwards, as he lay sleepily and heavily on her breasts did she think of the fact that she was overdue for her annual pill, and when she did she brushed the thought aside as too petty and narrow for such a moment.

She had felt the urgency and strength of the Chief of the Chief of the Chiefs, and she had almost, in the heat and wildness of it, met her man on the height of an ecstasy that sent him writhing and groaning and thrusting blindly. Never had she been closer with anyone else, or nearly so close. It was like having a door open to heaven, and glimpsing what was inside, and having it shut again, but feeling that another time it might let you swing it wide and rush through.

That's what made men so tantalizing. You could do some things for yourself, but for that – for that you had to be with a man. Donna only hoped that she would not get old and tired before somewhere, somehow, there would be that man, or men, who could help her bring that experience into reach and keep it close for a long, long time. Could this be the one? Well. . . . Right now, she wanted to get Garth's heavy body off hers so she could breathe.

"Garth," she whispered, running her fingers through his hair and beard buried deep against her shoulder. In sleep his face was terribly sad. "Garth, I've got to go. They'll be waiting up for me at the Lodge, I think."

Abruptly, Garth was wide awake. "Of course, Lovely," he said, sitting up and kissing her glancingly on the lips and breasts.

He stood beside her and helped her into her clothes, putting nothing on himself. When she was dressed he went to the top of the stairs and called down quietly, holding the lantern for Donna to come out on the landing beside him. In a moment Thelma appeared below. Looking up at the naked man and the fully dressed young woman she said warmly, "Is it time? Come down then, Donna, we'll go. Don's getting the dog from the shed."

Donna took a step from Garth's side, but looked back at him enquiringly, perhaps a little sadly. He folded his arms over his naked chest. "Go with Thelma, Donna. I never go up the hill. Even for you. We'll meet again, if you're parents decide to stay. If not, happiness be with you."

Despite herself, the tears grew quickly in Donna's eyes, as she walked alone down the wooden staircase, passing from the light of Garth's lantern to the light of Thelma's. Thelma could see them clearly. She put an arm around Donna at the bottom of the stairs.

"Oh Garth," she called up softly, "she's so young."

The note was more teasing or coaxing than reproving. He answered in a voice not too different from hers. "So were you, Thelma my love, so were you."

"Go back to bed, Garth, you can be so unkind," Thelma said, as she led Donna out of the house, but her last words were mild: "We'll get you up in the morning, early – sleep well."

On their way to the hill by footpaths and lanes unknown to Donna, Thelma walked hand in hand with her, and Don Planter brought up the rear, calling their lively and inquisitive sheepdog back from time to time as he raced under fences and across fields in the dark. A few hundred yards along, Donna had dried her tears, recovered, helped by her sense of having made a fool of herself in front of Thelma and Garth.

"I'm sorry , I was so silly," she said at last.

"Nothing silly about that," Thelma answered at once. "You're not the first person to cry over Garth Hamilton, believe me."

"Is he . . . . Does he always. . . . ?"

"Oh, Garth is always the same. Except when he's sad – then he's as sad as a person can be," Thelma said, again with more fondness than criticism. "We all love him, Donna, sad or happy. Love him and spoil him. The Farm wouldn't be the Farm without him. After a while, if you come here, you'll understand. You know it's true, you are very young."

"I don't want to get older then, if that's what you mean," Donna whispered fiercely, "I want to be just as I am now."

When the time came for the visitors to leave Notlimah and fly home in Hamilton's helicopter, they had their first good opportunity to compare notes. It didn't take them long to discover that everybody, though obviously not all for the same reasons, wanted to move to Notlimah. Of course a future there seemed all very rash and new and strange. But once it was agreed upon, they were all determined to make the move as quickly as possible.

For the two doctors, the problems of transplanting their experimental and clinical work were greatly reduced by the energy and efficiency of the Hamilton Medical Research Centre staff. They were quite prepared to begin at once to duplicate the conditions enjoyed by Dr. Hornby and Dr. Shearer at the Carter-Trudeau, down to the last detail, if the doctors wanted it that way, and to make whatever improvements were requested. In fact, they dispatched a pair of technicians to follow the visitors to their home base as soon as the decision was made, to take charge of the practical aspects of the transfer. The offer of a generous donation to the Carter-Trudeau's research fund by Chad Hamilton helped greatly to smooth over any administrative and diplomatic wrinkles that might have arisen, as a result of such a rapid development.

One serious difficulty remained on the clinical side. For a handful of patients still undergoing injections of the Hornby-Shearer serum, it was a matter of continuing the treatments for the last weeks of the doctors' stay, and if necessary thereafter having the therapy continued under the supervision of colleagues, with regular forwarding of records and reports. But the case of Faye Delisle was somewhat special.

Faye Delisle was no longer able to sustain herself without the support of a kidney machine, and constant monitoring of her erratic cardiac patterns. Although Chad Hamilton had assured the doctors that they were welcome to bring along with them any patient they might wish to take, it was obviously too traumatic a prospect for Faye Delisle, in her present state, to be dealt with in that way, even if she were willing.

Despite careful preparation, Faye Delisle broke into tears when the two doctors visited her room to tell her their news. They had in any case not been cheerful about the prospect of explaining the matter to her. The usual involve-ment of doctor and patient in extreme situations was even more exaggerated between them.

"How can you?" she sobbed. "I thought you would be here until . . . . I didn't think you'd leave me after all this time."

John Hornby stood near the door, fumbling with his fingers in the pockets of his white coat, shifting from one foot to the other. Norman Shearer, seated at the young woman's bedside, let her first outburst subside before he tried again. Then he spoke to her quietly and slowly and clearly, as if she were a child.

"Faye, we're just as sorry to have to leave you as you are to have us go. We wouldn't even consider it, if we thought you wouldn't be taken care of just as well with us gone as you are with us here. You see, we had to make a very dif-ficult decision. But we're both convinced that if we are to go on developing our way of treating cancer, and if we're really going to be able to help people like you, we've got to take this opportunity. We don't want to go, but we must. We do want you to understand."

Faye Delisle wiped her tears and smoothed back her long blond hair from her forehead. It was done up in pigtails behind, to leave it easier to manage, making her look especially girlish. She took hold of Dr. Shearer's hand in both hers, and with a deep sigh, began to receive the decision differently.

"I'm sorry to make such a scene. I cry a lot these days, not because I'm unhappy, I just don't seem to be able to control myself."

She smiled up at Dr. Hornby, as she continued to hold his friend's hand tightly. "As I've been telling my diary," she said, nodding to the recorder on her bedside table, "I find myself behaving more and more like a little girl, almost a baby. One minute I'm happy as a clown, next minute I'm weeping my eyes out over some silly thing that doesn't matter in the least."

"Not," she continued with a rush, "that this is one of the things that don't matter in the least. It matters a great deal. I don't know how I'm going to get along without my visits from you two."

For a moment she seemed near tears again. Then she went on in a composed and determined way. "But I won't be silly about it again. I know . . . . I understand what you're saying. You're scientists – Dr. Hornby told me what that means long ago – and you have to go wherever you think you can do the most good. As long as you don't just forget all about me . . . . Out of sight, out of mind."

This time she said it with so much warmth to both of them that they knew she was confident it wasn't too likely. There was still a touch of the mature woman in her attitude, even at her most uncontrolled, as there was obviously, finely, in her physical presence.

"Faye," Norman Shearer said, not only to reassure her but because she was still their richest source of information about the results of their therapy, "you must go on using the recorder as often as you can. We'll arrange to have the recordings sent to us, along with all the latest reports on your progress. We'll never be far from how you're getting on. And of course," he went on, improvising quickly in an area he and John Hornby hadn't had a chance to discuss yet, "we'll be coming back again in . . . in the first week in October to see you and our other patients."

He had tried to pick a date that wouldn't be so close as to get them into immediate embarrassments, and yet not so far away as to seem beyond Faye's range of hope and expectation, in her declining state.

As he talked he could see that Faye was becoming more and more reserved, turning in on herself, shoring up her resources perhaps. It was astonishing how quickly patients in these late stages learned to exclude anyone – friends, relatives, other patients, staff – who wasn't in the small intimate circle of fear and need. Which, of course, was how she came to be so dependent on the two doctors in the first place. There was nothing childish about her now. It made him feel a little uneasy, but it was all to the good in the end, and there was nothing he could do about it.

"You're very kind to me, Dr. Shearer, both of you are – as you've always been. I appreciate more than I can say the care you've given me. So you have to go, and that's all there is to it."

Her face brightened and she released Norman Shearer's hand to wave her arms languidly, histrionically, striking the appropriate dramatic pose for the attentive audience of two. A last charming comic-erotic performance for their sake.

"It's been a lovely affair, you dear men. And now that the time has come to part, let's be good friends. Farewell, Farewell. Go, and don't say another word."

Often they had left her room joking and laughing with her to the last minute. She preferred it that way now as well. Norman seized a hand and squeezed it as he got up, obediently silent, and John Hornby gave a brisk, self-mocking gentlemanly bob from the waist as he turned to lead the way out the door.

They walked side by side down the corridor to the elevator without speaking, knowing that they might hear her voice on the recordings later, but would in all probability never see her again.

For a few weeks both Hornby and Shearer had been commuting frequently between the Hamilton Medical Research Centre and the Carter-Trudeau. Finally they were able to claim that they were established in Notlimah. Although Alice Devers was involved in the daily operation of the Centre, and they met with her frequently, Chad Hamilton had not appeared again since their prospecting visit. They were happily aware from the start that neither Hamilton nor the officers of the Centre had any inclination to inhibit the rapid re-organization and development of their work in the new situation.

Their work to begin with was largely confined to the laboratory, since they had refused the invitation to bring their own patients along with them. They had elected to spend a few months with that orientation and emphasis, relieved only by shared clinical rounds with their new colleagues, who were conducting their own treatments, all of a highly advanced and experimental character. The time for them to undertake clinical trials of their own again would come whenever they wished.

The two colleagues resumed their regular laboratory conferences, reviewing experimental results and information that was still flowing in to them about their patients in the Carter-Trudeau. The case which continued to absorb them most was that of Faye Delisle. Every detail, every statistic, was of deep interest.

"Are you sure that's accurate?" Norman asked during their first review at the Centre, pulling an information sheet from his friend's hand. "How can she possibly weigh only ninety-seven pounds and look so great? Damn it man, she was 38-24-36 when she first came to us."

"Well, my friend, you'll have to face it," John said sardonically, "now she'll be more like 32-24-34."

Norman continued to read down the sheet, checking with his own eyes what Hornby had told him was there. "She came to us with a body of a thirty-year-old . . . ."

"And a mind as old as Cleopatra's," Hornby broke in.

"And now she's more like a fifteen-year-old. Even her bone structure seems to have lightened and shrunk."

"And yet," Hornby took over, "apart from deterioration to primary organs, none of which can readily be attributed to the effects of the serum, she's like a perfectly normal adolescent."

Norman read through to the bottom of the sheet, before he corrected his companion. "She's not menstruating anymore. She had a few months of considerable menstrual pain, and then the cycle simply stopped."

Hornby chose to take the common sense view, to give it voice, as it were, in discussion.

"Yes, but considering the mental stress she's been under for the past several years, it's not surprising. Lots of woman cease menstruating for smaller reasons than that."

"Not Faye Delisle," Norman said emphatically. "She told us long ago that she's been as regular and reliable in that department as the moon, ever since adolescence. Except for the occasional pregnancy. Three of them, to be exact. One by her first lover at fifteen – an accident. One by an actor she mistakenly thought she'd like to live with forever. One by a candidate for a governorship. She had that one aborted, if I remember her story rightly, when he lost the election."

John offered a small smile for his friend's not all that embellished résumé, and at the pleasant memories it aroused of Faye Delisle at her most entertaining. Then he turned his chair to talk soberly to him about the essential question in both their minds.

"We really can't be sure where this is going to end. Are we still justified in going on with those massive doses of serum for her?"

Norman nodded grimly down at his friend's face, enquiring, earnest, reflecting his own feelings exactly as they grappled with the old dilemma. "Twice we've cut her off or reduced the amount substantially. Twice the carcinoma flared up again with even more malignancy. There's no way it wouldn't terminate quickly without this form of therapy. I don't see what other choice we have. There are these extraordinary, unpredictable, perhaps in the end disastrous effects on her body, and on her mind – but at least she's still alive. We *are* keeping her alive!."

They might have gone around the whole subject yet once more, familiar as the pattern was, perhaps this time switching roles with Norman doing the questioning and John the reassuring. They were interrupted by a sound of bells close at hand, like a miniature campanile.

"What on earth is that?" Norman asked, looking around.

John Hornby made a face and gestured to the corner of the room with his thumb. "It's the hot line."

"The what?"

"The hot line. There's an attachment to the telescreen in every laboratory and office in the place. A direct line between the Centre and the Lodge. I heard it one day when it was being tested. I pushed the receiving button on the set when I heard the bells and found myself looking at Chad Hamilton's Lodge manager on the screen. He told me Mr. Hamilton wouldn't be bothering anybody, but he just wanted to be able to get in touch quickly if it were necessary. I imagine it's the same thing now."

"Well don't just let it ring, do something," Norman said in exasperation, "it's driving me crazy."

"Why don't you? It's your turn," John suggested imperturbably, pointing his friend bodily in the right direction.

As Norman stepped over and pushed the button, both were surprised to see Chad Hamilton's face suddenly fill the screen of the telescreen, and to hear his familiar booming voice.

"Norman, glad you're in. Is John there too? I want to talk to you both, if you can spare a half hour."

It was typical of Chad Hamilton to give the impression that he was the one with all the time in the world, and the wish to fit into someone else's schedule.

"Whenever you like, Chad," Norman said, still using the first name a little experimentally, but remembering Hamilton's insistence. "Would you like us to come over to you?"

"No, if you can be there I'll come by right now. After all, it's medical business I want to talk to you about."

"What do you suppose this is all about?" Norman asked rhetorically as the screen went dark.

"He's going to fire us," John suggested. "After all, we've been here a month and we haven't come up with a cancer cure yet."

"Hardly," Norman grinned, "In that case he'd have had to fire everybody in the place."

The two friends sat contemplating each other's worried expressions for a few minutes, both with the same thought in their minds, the same theory explaining Chad Hamilton's sudden visit. Neither of them wanted to put it in words.

"Well, we'll know soon enough," Norman said, glancing involuntarily towards the door. "He should be here any minute."

Although his face on the telescreen screen looked thinner and more tired than they remembered it, Chad Hamilton's actual presence gave the two doctors an immediate impression of physical decline they hadn't prepared themselves for. He walked into the room briskly enough, and shook hands with them both firmly, but it was as if his habits were carrying him along beyond the reach of his present resources.

"I've had two months of those damned cobalt treatments," he said immediately, by way of answer to the unexpressed reactions his appearance produced in them. "That's it, no more. They make you feel sick as hell and they don't really do anything for you. The doctors admit as much themselves."

"There have been some interesting successes with cobalt therapy," Norman said, not wanting to argue, but looking forward already to a later stage in the discussion.

"Well, not in my case."

Hamilton dismissed the subject with a wave of his hand, like a man accustomed to treating the business agenda in his own way at his own pace. He sat down, slumped a little in fact, in a chair, and gestured the others to join him. "I want to talk about what you guys are doing. The time has come for you to take me on."

Dr. Shearer and Dr. Hornby looked at each other, neither wishing to speak. The nub of the matter had been reached as both had feared, but more quickly and directly than they would have expected. At last Norman chose to began their answer.

"I'm not sure you'd say that if you really knew what it is you're asking for."

"Try me," Hamilton snapped.

"O.K. The serum we've developed has simply no clinical evidence of success. None. It's at far too early an experimental stage to be considered, except in extreme cases."

"That's me, or soon will be."

"There are many unanswered questions, particularly questions about side effects and complications which we have to face before we can consider any proposal for clinical application."

"Look, Norman, let's cut through the bullshit." Hamilton dismissed it all with a sweep of one hand crossing over the other. "You've got a serum which you think can beat cancer. You've tried it on mice. You've tried it on people. You're going on with it. It may or may not be the solution, but there's some hope. Right now, I've got no hope. Zero. It strikes me it's a pretty easy gamble on both sides."

At this point John Hornby, who had remained uncomfortably silent, tried to come to his friend's rescue. "Norman, I think maybe we should tell Mr. Hamilton about our recent clinical experience with the serum."

"Fire away, let's hear it," Hamilton said, easing back in his chair, waiting with half closed eyes.

Norman began an account of the history of the Hornby-Shearer therapy at the Cater-Trudeau, touching briefly and easily on most of the cases – almost all terminal – in a version of the style he had used often enough in staff conferences and other semi-public occasions. He saved Faye Delisle, whom he called Miss X, for special mention.

Miss X had given them the best opportunity so far to study the efficacy of the serum and its potential side-effects. It was true that in her case advanced malignancy had in fact been controlled, strikingly so. But it was also true that after the several years she had been receiving various kinds of cancer therapy, certain developments were taking place which were possibly attributable to the Hornby-Shearer serum, and which could have serious negative implications.

In fact, in the period they were talking about, Miss X had an extensive and radical cellular reaction which seemed to involve a reversal of the normal pattern of development in cell growth. She came to the hospital with the normal bone and tissue cell condition of a thirty-year-old, except for specific areas of carcinomatous activity. Now, although the carcinoma had been arrested, the woman's body was changing in many respects into that of a teen-ager. At the same time there were some adverse effects on the nervous system and the cardiovascular system that hadn't yet been fully assessed. The reversal process in the cells appeared to be still in full flow -- the reversal of normal cell aging.

"Well I'm damned," Hamilton exclaimed when Norman was finished, open eyed, his brow still furrowed from the effort of concentration he'd made to follow the doctor's account. "But she's still alive, this Miss X. *She's alive.* And without your drug, she'd be long gone. Isn't that right?"

Hamilton looked from one doctor to the other for confirmation.

"In all probability," Hornby said.

"So how do you explain it?" Hamilton asked.

Norman took up the question, familiar enough to himself and his friend, since they had been wrestling with it for years in various forms, though rarely in the blunt open way of a layman.

He would tell Chad Hamilton as best he could what they believed to be the case. It went back to the roots of molecular biology and the continuing struggle to break the genetic code – to discover how, through genes and chromosomes, living organisms developed from impregnated egg to complex mature animals and humans. To know in detail how the blueprints for the full growth were carried out was to know, perhaps, what to do when the mature creature grew in flawed or self-destructive ways, and to prevent that from happening.

Scientists had long understood that the nucleic acid of all cells contained the blueprint of the entire organism which was formed by their division and multiplication. In theory it was recognized that by splicing genes from different organisms, it was possible to program the growth of organisms unlike anything in nature, combining characteristics from different cells. The big problem for the scientist was the infinitesimally small and complicated nature of the blueprints – how could you be sure you were creating, in the laboratory, the specific new organism with the exact program you wanted for certain results. Obviously there were a lot of gambles, for the individual and for the environment.

The Hornby-Shearer serum was a man-made substance which combined common harmless bacteria, found in the intestinal tract of human beings, with a special restriction enzyme. The aim being to produce a corrective gene, one which would then attach itself to and control the growth of the carcinomatous cells. The theory was simple enough. If the genetic program of cancer cells could be impaired or corrected by modifying the nucleic or informational acid of the cells, a cure for cancer would follow.

Laboratory and clinical evidence to date led the two doctors to believe that their serum did, indeed, have a strong effect on the genetic program of cancer cells. Retarding or eliminating malignant growth was clearly indicated. But it appeared, from the same evidence, that normal cells were also reacting to the bombardment from the corrective enzymes.

"The fact is . . . ," Hornby broke in, as he could see that Norman was uncharacteristically flagging in the course of the long explanation, and was beginning to back off from the startling conclusion they had arrived at between themselves: "It looks as though our serum, at least when given in doses large enough to have an impact on the carcinomatous cells, is telling all the cells of the body the same thing."

"What do you mean, 'telling them the same thing'?" Hamilton asked, his brow still wrinkled in the strenuousness of his efforts to follow the explanations.

"He means," Norman came in again, having caught his second wind, "that whereas the normal genetic code in a human organism gives orders for cells to divide, multiply, and produce the particular complex differentiations of function that make up the mature human being, our serum gives orders to . . . recombine, simplify, go back to origins. Where there were eight cells, let there be four, where there were four, let there be two."

"Where there was a woman," Hamilton said slowly, with a realization of what they meant dawning on his face, "let there be a girl, where there was a man, let there be a boy. Good God, what have you two done?"

The three men sat silently for a few moments. It was the first time, for Hornby and Shearer, that their theory had met the response of anyone outside of a select and well-prepared and on the whole healthily skeptical scientific audience. They were well aware of what sort of science fiction madness they might be accused of by a general public crudely informed of the nature of their work and its present results.

"You two doctors were looking for a cancer cure, and you found the secret of youth."

Norman and John both started to speak at once, to stifle this kind of inflammatory conclusion. Norman's tongue as usual was quicker.

"Far from it, Chad. The fact is, we're not sure we're near the first, let alone anything like the second."

"Maybe I'm naive," Hamilton insisted with rising excitement, "but can't you figure out just how much to give a person to kill the cancer cells, or correct them, or whatever it is you say, and keep the patient young at the same time?"

Hornby and Shearer exchanged smiles.

"You're not naïve in the slightest," Norman said, "just a little behind us in our experimentation. The problem is one of threshold. If the dosage isn't massive enough, the serum has no effect whatsoever (except a loosening of the bowels). If it's massive enough to affect the carcinomatous cells, it sets up a powerful reversal program affecting the entire body."

They went round the whole subject several more times before Chad Hamilton was willing to leave it. Then he came back to the place where he began.

"O.K.. Now I think I understand a little better what it's all about. The options for me personally seem clearer. Either I let this growth in my guts kill me . . . ." He clenched his fists over his trim front. "Or I give you guys a chance to cure me. And if you don't kill me even faster, which is a likely possibility, I may spend a few months, even years, getting younger and younger. Christ, what a thought. Wait till I tell Alice about this. She'll have to be prepared --if you make me into a young stud again."

Having rushed abruptly from the serious to the crude and comic in a single breath, he slapped his hand flat on the table and laughed uproariously. The two doctors watched for a moment in amazement, and then, finding his laughter impossible to resist, were soon chuckling along with him. When all three had subsided, Chad Hamilton moved them swiftly towards a conclusion and agreement, in deadly earnest.

"I don't want to put you two on the spot," Hamilton said. "My lawyers will draw up an agreement between us that will relieve you of any responsibility for the consequences of your prescribed treatment. And they'll also write up a long-term contract for you with the Centre, so that in the event of my death, the trust that administers this place will keep you on as long as you're happy to work here. Now, what about it? Is there anything else that's worrying you?'

"What's worrying us," Norman said chuckling again in the gallows humor mood of a minute before, "is that we're not used to working with such an expensive guinea pig."

"That's the most flattering thing that's been said to me since I got mixed up with you guys in the medical profession," Hamilton said, with a wave of both arms to encompass the whole complex of the Centre around them.

Then they got down to business again. Serious business. It was necessary for the doctors to emphasize again to Chad Hamilton that the serum to be administered to him was a potentially hazardous substance. Not only to him but to others in contact with him, once he began receiving it. It could only be given in a carefully controlled environment.

"The bacterium on which the serum is based is very common," Norman explained again. "There's always the chance, though we think it's remote, that it might be passed along, in the recombined form we've developed, to the general population. Take on an independent life. Start an epidemic, to put it bluntly."

"An epidemic of youth," Hamilton boomed.

"Or whatever," Norman said wryly. "Anyway, to avoid that kind of risk with our serum, we've always carefully followed the Environmental Hazards Committee's regulations governing research in molecular biology and genetics. We must continue to do so, even more rigorously, in the clinical context. We've developed certain protocols for the handling and control of it."

"Of course," said Hamilton. "We can have them set up whatever is necessary at the Lodge – make a kind of annex of the Centre. Because that's where I want to be, for better or worse."

F. W. WATT

It was from that time on that Norman Shearer and John Hornby established regular access to the Lodge, and as a further consequence a deeper connection with the Farm.

If it hadn't been for his bi-weekly trips to the Lodge, Norman might have been quite content to live no closer to the Farm than the Shearers' home in the Circle. He might have been content to leave it to his daughter to explore the life of the young people's commune. On the other hand, he might not. He was never very happy about Donna's relation with the Farm from the first night she returned from the place in a noticeably involved state of mind. And the more he learned, the unhappier he became.

The Shearer home, like most of those in the Circle around them, was a ten-acre estate, but with a modest, easily-managed, pleasant split-level house set in the midst of evergreen trees. It was conveniently located near the collector road that led to the Centre. On one side it abutted on Chad Hamilton's private golf course, which Circle residences could use, except on named occasions, occasions which were occurring with less and less frequency. Norman hadn't yet had time to play a round of golf, and Ella was still preoccupied with settling arrangements in the new house. It was Donna who got the most out of the surroundings, walking through the evergreen trees, sitting quietly in the garden, and venturing forth daily to enjoy the varied and lively activities on the Farm.

"What does she do down there all day?" Norman asked Ella when, a few weeks after they had arrived, his mind was free enough of his own preoccupations to begin to wonder how his family was adjusting.

"She's taking art lessons – a sort of course," Ella replied, with a touch of vagueness Norman didn't appreciate.

"What sort of art lessons? Who's giving them?"

"Why don't you ask her yourself?" Ella answered, knowing from his tone nothing she could say would satisfy him.

"I'd like to . . . . In fact I will. If I ever get to see her. She spends more time at the Farm than she does at home"

"And you spend more time at the Centre than you do at home . . . .Anyway, if you could drag yourself away from your Blue TV in the evening, you'd know she's home every night soon after dark. She says that on the Farm, except for weekends and concert nights, they go to bed with the sun and rise with the sun. It's very natural."

"Not to mention healthy and wholesome," Norman snorted.

Ella had been sitting at the picture window of their living room, looking out over the shadowed garden as the day grew to a close, and waiting for Norman to go to his study so she could put a movie on. Now, hearing him sounding so querulous and sarcastic, she suddenly decided the time had come. There would never be a good time, so why not choose the worst?

"Norman, Donna's pregnant."

She watched as the words sank in like an axe blow. Norman stared at her in disbelief, going quite pale. Then the colour returned along with a rush of confused anger and indignation. He came to tower over her where she lay stretched out on the sofa, nursing her nine-month belly.

"Jesus, Ella, I hope you're joking. You've got things mixed up, you're the one that's pregnant."

"I'm a lot pregnant," Ella smiled up at him with infuriating sweetness, "Donna's just a little bit pregnant."

For half an hour Norman raged at her, questioning. No, she didn't know who the father was. Yes, it was true that if they considered dates it had to go back to about the time of her first trip to the Farm. No, Donna didn't seem to be very worried, or to be considering an abortion. Yes, she spoke as if she intended to have the baby, and keep it.

"For God's sake, Ella, the girl's barely eighteen."

"I was sixteen when I had Donna," Ella reminded him.

"But you at least had a man, you had me. Who the hell's she got? It looks as if she's been going around like the neighborhood bitch."

Ella, turning away from his angry and contorted face, could see Donna approaching the house along the short-cut from the Farm, a footpath leading right to the garden.

"Norman, I do wish you'd stop playing the heavy father. You're at your worst when you're like that." Before he could break out again, she held up a hand and shushed him. "Simmer down, for goodness' sake. Donna's coming in now, there's no need to upset her."

"Upset her?"

Norman was still speechless with indignation at his wife's attitude, when Donna came into his sight and waved at him through the window. He couldn't bring himself to wave in return. But he felt a deep twinge of complex emotion, as he saw her lithe, athletic looking figure, intensely young and feminine in the long, flowing peasant-style dress she had taken to wearing, her auburn hair spreading loose over her shoulders. There was a lightness and gaiety in her step and movement of arms that seemed to contradict the mood he had endured, created, in the living room for the past hour.

"I can't talk to her now," Norman said, "but you tell her I want to have it all out with her before bedtime tonight." With that he stalked off to his study.

"Hi, Mom," Donna said, arriving in time to get a glimpse of her father's back going out the other doorway. "Is Dad in one of his moods again?"

There was an edge in her mother's reply that cut both ways. "You could say that. I had to tell him your little secret."

"Oh God," Donna groaned, with a mixture of exasperation and boredom. "I suppose it had to come out sooner or later." She looked down at her mother's grossly pregnant form, and at her own still slim belly. "Didn't it?" she added with a laugh, catching her own unintended meaning.

Suddenly both women were laughing helplessly. Donna fell to her knees and buried her face, tearful with laughter or relief, in her mother's breast.

"You awful girl," her mother gasped, gradually getting control of herself. "He's so angry. He wants to talk to you tonight." She smoothed Donna's hair tenderly, looking down at her slight, vulnerable shape showing through the loose folds of her cotton dress.

"He'll ask you questions, you know. What are you going to tell him?"

"That I'm happy. That I want to have a baby. That it was an immaculate conception."

She lifted her head and wiped her tears dry with the backs of her hands. "I'll think of something . . . . Anyway, what right has he to be angry? It's none of his business. I'm seventeen, after all."

"You'll have to do better than that, my dear," her mother said, giving the girl a last stroke on the head before she stood up, adjusting her long dress. "Remember, he's a man and a father. When a man gets to that age, he's forgotten what it's like to be young. And a father has special feelings about a daughter and . . . and all that."

"Don't I know it," Donna moaned. "Well, what I think I'll do is . . . take the initiative. Catch him off-guard. I'll go up and see him right now."

Before her mother could consider the wisdom of that tactic, she was running up the stairs and calling, "Father, father! I've got something I want to tell you."

Three hours later, the father and daughter emerged separately, Donna with tear-reddened eyes, Norman with the blackness of his mood even more deeply established. Without a word to his wife, Norman pushed past her and out the door into the growing darkness. Donna slumped in a chair near her mother's sofa.

"He's hopeless, Mother. I just can't get through to him. I think he's drunk. He's gone off in the most terrible mood and I'm afraid he's going down to the Farm to do something awful."

"He's not a fool, Donna. And he may have had a few drinks, but he never really gets drunk. He's not going to take a shotgun to anybody."

Ella was speaking rationally, as much to encourage her own faith as to communicate it to Donna. Still, Norman for all his size was hardly a man of violence, and however he might talk at times it was true, he wasn't a fool. "Besides, where's he going? What did he say he was going to do?" Ella asked.

"He wouldn't say." Her daughter's voice rose almost to a wail. "He just said he was going to find out what kind of place the Farm really was. And things I wouldn't like to repeat about screwing young girls and taking no responsibility and all sorts of crazy things like that. I don't know how I'll ever face those people again if he goes down there and . . . and . . . . ."

Gradually as the two talked,they comforted each other. It was a comfort in itself, as her mother told Donna, that they both should be pregnant more or less at the same time, peculiar as it might seem under the circumstances.

"I'm especially glad," Ella said, finally, submerging her own fears for her daughter, to make up for her husband's roughness. "Our babies will grow up together."

Then they decided not to sit around waiting for Norman's return. Whether they liked it or not, he was gone. They could hardly know for how long.

The only names that Norman got from his daughter were those of her art teacher – Robert, Roberto as he was called affectionately. And no, Roberto was not the man who had got her pregnant. And Garth Hamilton? Was it likely that she could have got pregnant from Mr. Hamilton's son, the Chief of the Chiefs, of all people? In any case, it was none of his business. Norman was determined to make it his business. He strode along the paths and lanes in the light of the moon, driven by anger, and by churning emotions more complicated than that, and too subtle to give a name to.

What exactly he would do, he wasn't yet certain. But first he would question Roberto, and then the Chief of the Chiefs, Garth Hamilton.

The walk had a calming effect on him, despite his determination. Certainly the exercise thinned the alcohol in his veins, though he had drunk more than usual in his anger and frustration. He rehearsed a dozen versions of his line of approach, discarding each in turn, before he actually met anyone. Then it was a trio of young women in peasant-style dresses, chatting under the twilight sky on the pathway to a stone cottage. They called out 'good evening' so casually and cheerfully and unsuspectingly, that he swallowed his black feelings for a moment and returned their greeting, going on his way deeper into the territory of the Farm.

Now, upon reflection, he altered his strategy mentally. Obviously these young people had their own way of seeing things. They were very different from his own generation. Probably rather different from other young people who hadn't chosen this kind of communal life, whatever it might turn out to be. He would have to be more cautious, perhaps a little cunning, or he might find himself helplessly shut out, a foreign elder, not even able to get information, let alone being able to communicate his indignation and his insistence that they should take responsibility for their actions.

By the time he reached the river side, and the largest cluster of buildings assembled there, he was cool enough to deal with strangers effectively, he felt sure.

"Good evening," he said, approaching a young man who was pumping water to fill a couple of large pails, working an old-fashioned hand pump with an easy graceful movement – though it seemed to Norman that the well he was drawing from was fitted also with a modern pipe and pump system.

"How are you?" the young man answered, not breaking his stroke. "Are you from Heaven?"

"What?" Norman said, startled despite himself. He had had qualms about the sanity of this community before he arrived.

"From the hill. Hamilton Lodge?"

"Ah. I'm from . . . ." Norman resisted an answer reflecting his state of mind – Hell. "I'm from the Circle. From . . . . "

He was going to identify himself further as Dr. Shearer of the Hamilton Medical Research Centre, when he thought better of it. He'd rather not give too much away at this point. He was a long way from finding out who'd done that to his daughter.

"From over there." He waved vaguely in the direction he thought his house must be.

"I wonder," he went on, "could you tell me where I'd find a man called Roberto? an artist?"

"Roberto," the young man said at once, warmly. "He's usually on the river at this time of night. See that bridge?" He pointed to the wooden bridge a hundred yards away, beyond the cluster of buildings. "If you go out in the middle of that bridge and look downstream, I'll bet you'll see Roberto's punt moored there. Just give a call down to him. He works all night, you won't wake him."

Norman thanked him and walked towards the bridge. He didn't want to stop long enough to ask what kind of work Robert could be doing at that time of night in the dark in a punt on the river. Standing on the creaking boards of the bridge, Norman could make out the long motionless shape of a punt anchored in mid-stream, water rippling quietly around it. And in the stern cushions of the punt, the shape of a man stretched out to full length, both hands over his face.

Norman stood for a few moments, absorbed in the sense of stillness emanating from the boat, the river, and the motionless shape of the man. Finally he leaned down and called softly, feeling a little embarrassed at doing so. "Robert."

His call had no effect whatsoever. He waited a few minutes, and tried again, a little more loudly. "Roberto."

Dimly in the shadows below he could see the man take his hands from his face and slowly raise is head. Now he was looking straight up towards the bridge.

"Roberto, I'd like to talk to you."

The man raised himself still farther until he was leaning back on his elbows, his head and shoulders off the punt cushions. Norman started to walk off the bridge, intending to come on to the river side nearer the boat. Before he could take two steps Roberto spoke.

"Man on a Bridge. Don't move. Stay just as you are."

Norman stopped, turned back to the railing, and leaned over as he'd been doing. The man remained in his position on the punt, staring at him, silent again.

"I'd like a word with you, please," Norman said.

The man took his right hand and passed it over his eyes slowly, holding it like a shield for a moment, and then putting it down so he could stare again.

Norman's impatience rose sharply. "What are you doing down there, anyway? Will you talk to me or not?"

The man sat upright now, pulling his knees towards his chest, and leaning his chin on them. His voice came quietly and calmly over the water.

"I'm reading you, Man on a Bridge, I'm soaking you in. I'm making you mine. It's all there. Space. Time. Eternity. A bridge, a man, a river. What else is there?'

"What on earth are you talking about?"

"Man on a Bridge, I'm going to paint you . . . . I think I have you. I think I do. I'm finished now. I've had my moment. Are you going to come aboard?"

Norman said nothing, hardly knowing how to speak to such a man, but quickly walked off the bridge and down to the river side. When he got there Roberto had the punt turned in his direction and was standing at the stern with the punt pole in his hands. A few thrusts with the pole send the punt's bow up onto the bank at Norman's feet. He stepped gingerly aboard. As soon as he began to move forward and the bow lifted again, Roberto thrust off with the punt pole and aimed the boat downstream.

As much for self-protection as anything else, Norman sat down, with his long legs stretched towards Roberto, who took his seat again too, setting the dripping pole down along the side of the boat. They glided with the slow movement of the current.

"Man in a Boat, talk," Roberto said, smiling so that Norman could see his teeth gleam in the moonlight through his full beard. His hair, Norman could see now, was shoulder length, held back by a bead brow-band.

"I'm Donna's father," Norman began, dropping all his subtle approaches to the subject.

There was a pause, which Norman was trying to assess. Then he had to break the silence himself. "You're giving her art lessons."

"Art lessons. Art lessons."

Roberto's tone was a little exploratory, a little incredulous, as if the term was only vaguely familiar to him, and certainly nothing of immediate import. Then came a murmur of recognition. "Ah, Donna. The Lamb . . . . She's been coming to paint with me."

The Lamb, Norman thought bitterly. Sheared. To the slaughter. His anger returned in full force as he looked at the man's body draped casually over the seat and floor of the punt, a picture of ease and self-assurance and youth. "Is this where you do you're painting? Like tonight?"

Roberto's answer out of the shadows was calm, quite free of defensiveness or antagonism. "Not here, all this is preparation. You have to do your preparation by yourself, in your own peace. It's when you bring it all together to express it that you can work with others present, alongside you or receiving you. The Lamb must do her own preparation in her own way, the way that's natural for her. She has to work by herself, just as I work by myself."

"Do you call this work?" Norman snorted, waving an arm to encompass the boat and the river and the banks and the bridge and the whole dubious scene of which they were a part.

"Man in a Boat," Roberto said almost coaxingly, "you seem so uptight. Why don't you let the water do it for you?"

He dropped a hand into the river where it lapped the punt side, and lifted it again, allowing the water to fall through his fingers. Norman bit off his first angry reply and kept his silence. Before he attempted to speak again, Roberto continued in his quiet, husky tones.

"The Lamb is learning. She was all technique, all materials, all execution. She wasn't prepared. Now she's getting a better balance. She's spending a lot of time working by herself, preparing, and then when the time comes to execute, the execution takes care of itself. Do you follow me?"

"No," Norman said in quiet exasperation, "I don't understand a word you're saying. Are you giving my daughter art lessons or aren't you?"

Roberto let a long, slow, sympathetic hiss of breath escape from his mouth before he answered. "Man in a Boat, you are so . . . obsessed. You're going to go up like . . . a volcano. Like a . . . ." Roberto eased his head back on the cushions and looked straight up to the stars.

"Like a supernova."

Now he trailed both hands in the river, one on each side of the punt.

"I don't give the Lamb art lessons. I don't give anybody art lessons. That's nineteenth century. That's vanity, obsession with self and time. People trying to perpetuate themselves through their pupils and their products. Teaching each other how to make immortal works of art, so their childrens' childrens' children will know that once they were alive on this earth and were famous people. The Lamb doesn't really want that. Nobody really wants that, if they think about it. I work alone at my thing and then I sit with other people and I execute. And she comes and watches and tries herself and we talk a little, and then I execute, and she executes and other people execute."

"What do you mean, execute?" Norman said almost in despair, clutching at any possible clue.

Roberto lifted his hands from the water and held them up in front of his face, making a little lifting, shelling out movement with them.

"Execute, put it out, share it. For me, right now, it's the electric glass and screen. For you, for the Lamb, for me another time, it might be something else. Technique is nothing. Technique is vanity."

A light was beginning to dawn for Norman. Putting aside his fears and suspicions a little, he was beginning to understand and believe Roberto.

"Electric glass and screen, what's that?" he asked, a touch of courtesy creeping into his manner, and even a little curiosity, however lined with contempt, thinking that his daughter must have sat and listened to this kind of thing from Roberto many times.

"The quickest, most direct way I've yet been able to find to get it all from here . . . ."

Roberto bunched the fingers of one hand over his eyes, and as he went on, gestured with his other hand and arm to the wide world. ". . . . To there."

He lay back for a moment with both hands trailing in the water again, as if the mere reflection on the effort involved to get it from here to there temporarily exhausted him. Then he explained further.

"If you've never seen it, it's a system worked out by me and my friend the Chief of Machines and Technology. He used to be with IBM before the Government took them over. The glass is electronically activated, so the paint glides, and every tincture and grain gets picked up and projected instantly and exactly, but enlarged to whatever scale you want with all the movement and flow, just as it's set loose. It's the closest thing to immediate mind-projection an artist has ever devised. I love it. . . . . But of course, you've got to be prepared. It shifts the whole balance. Hours, weeks, months of work in the mind for an instant execution. Instead of all that time in the studio, on the canvas, laboring over technique, materials."

"I begin to see what you mean," Norman commented after a long pause. "And are you pleased with the progress of . . . of the Lamb?"

"She's got soul, enthusiasm. She's learning how to free it all up. I think she'll come along. The Chief of Entertainment was talking to Garth about letting her perform at a concert night. If she does, you'll have to come."

"Garth," Norman said, his mind closing on the name like a rat-trap. "Garth Hamilton. Is he around somewhere tonight?"

Roberto shrugged his shoulders. "Our man is always around. He never leaves the Farm. I think he's down at Bullrush Cottage. Do you want me to drop you there?"

They didn't speak again as Roberto drove the punt into the middle of the stream and down-current a few hundred yards farther. Here and there along the banks, groups and couples and solitaries could be seen, or sometimes only their glowing cigarette ends. Occasionally someone called out quietly, "Roberto, Roberto," recognizing him or his boat on the moonlit water.

As he stepped out of the boat and onto the shore at the closest point to Bullrush Cottage, Norman had a qualm of conscience for his surliness. "My daughter seems to like working with you very much, Roberto."

"Well I'm glad, Man on the Shore, I'm glad," Roberto called after him. "We have a saying on the Farm, 'when two are together, what one likes the other will like.' That's how I am with the Lamb." With a wave he thrust the punt into mid-stream and headed back towards the bridge.

Norman glanced at the illuminated dial of his watch before approaching the cottage. It was almost twelve o'clock, and he was considerably more sober than when he started out on his explorations. But there was still light showing through the cottage windows. Even so, Norman hesitated on the path. Now that his anger had cooled – or perhaps hardened would be more accurate – he began to be more conscious of how he might appear to others. He hardly knew what Roberto must have made of him, not that it seemed to matter.

Before he could decide whether to advance or retreat, the cottage door opened and a laughing couple stood in the lamplight to say goodnight. The young woman, obviously well advanced in pregnancy, as her silhouette showed, wrapped her arms around the neck of the tall strong-looking bearded young man who was leaving, and kissed him warmly on the lips.

"Come to dinner Sunday, Garth," she said to him, turning to slip back into the house. There was tenderness, solicitude, perhaps even a little concern for him in her voice. "My sister's arriving from Seattle, remember? You'll love her."

"I'd like that," the young man answered, blowing another kiss. "Sleep well, Tara."

He didn't seem especially startled when, as he walked away from the closed door, he almost bumped into Norman on the path.

"Hello," he said, trying to see into Norman's face, "you're from the Circle, aren't you? The Chief of Security told me you were walking in tonight. Welcome."

Norman's anger flared again at the easy confidence of the man, as much as at the knowledge that his own movements hadn't gone unnoticed. "What is this, some kind of military camp you run?"

The young man sent a peal of laughter towards the stars. He took Norman by the elbow in the friendliest way and began to walk towards the river. "That's very good. I'll have to tell the Chief of Security. He'll be flattered. No, you see, we have to be a little careful. A few years ago, we used to just let everybody come and go without worrying, but more recently we've had to keep track. Let's face it, there are some crazy people in this world."

"You're Garth Hamilton," Norman said accusingly, stopping in the path and removing his arm from the man's grasp. It infuriated him to be pulled into this man's camp, united against the crazy people of the world.

"That's right," Garth answered. "G. C. Hamilton the Second."

Standing face to face with Norman, overtopping him by an inch, he spread his arms widely and raised them slowly to the stars. "And you . . . . You're the most, well, obsessed man I've met in months . . . . Can't you relax, my friend? On a beautiful night like this?"

"Look, Hamilton, somebody's said that to me already tonight. I've come all the way over here to have a serious talk with you. Can we go somewhere where there's some privacy?"

"Why surely, friend. Privacy is free for anybody who wants it at the Farm. Come on, we'll go to Roberto's cottage, he's hardly ever there till dawn."

Garth Hamilton strode off into the shadows leaving Norman to follow and keep up as best he could, not always easy to do with the twists and turns of the footpaths. At last they came out onto an open moonlit field, and in the middle of it, without a tree or shrub within a hundred yards of it, stood a one-story building with a door and a window and a sloping roof. They approached it walking side by side.

"House in a Field, Roberto calls it."

Garth disappeared indoors, and in a moment was holding a lantern to show Norman the way inside. The single room, amongst its simple furnishings, had a bed, a table and two chairs. Garth put the lantern on the table, placed a box of cigarettes beside it, and also pulled a bottle and a jug of water and a couple of glasses from a wooden cupboard.

"You'd rather drink than smoke, I'll bet," he said, holding the bottle up to the light. "It's wine of the country, my friend, fortified, very nice. Have some?"

He filled two glasses, leaving room in his own for a dash of water. Norman was suddenly in need of a drink, he realized. He sniffed his glass suspiciously, then took a sip. It was a little foxy, but left a surprisingly pleasant aftertaste. He took a long swallow. Garth lit a cigarette from the box, blowing some sweetish smoke to the ceiling, and pushed the container over to Norman. Norman ignored it. Taking a firm hold of himself, Norman was about to begin when Garth Hamilton spoke first.

"So you're the man who's going to kill my father."

Norman choked on his wine. Wiping his chin, he gasped out his question. "What do you mean? Who told you a thing like that?"

The shock that ran through his veins was mainly due to hearing so unexpectedly what, in his heart – in their hearts, he and John Hornby – he was almost driven to admit was the truth.

Garth continued to blow smoke up to the ceiling of the cottage. He eased back in his chair and lifted a leg across the corner of the wooden table. "Not to worry, Dr. Norman Shearer. There's little about the Farm or the Lodge or the Centre that I don't find out about sooner or later."

"What did your father tell you then?" Norman demanded.

"Nothing. Nothing at all. My father and I are on excellent terms. Have been for ten years. We're in perfect agreement. But we never see each other. Never talk to each other except by telescreen. It's a splendid arrangement."

Norman was beginning to recover from his first shock. There had to be a simple explanation. The problem was, he didn't know how to pursue the questioning. "What makes you think . . . . How did you know I was involved medically with your father?"

"Alice Devers. Alice is the golden link between my father and me these days. She's my step mother, in a manner of speaking. Before that, there was someone else. And before that another one. There's always been someone. Alice is the best of them all."

"Then you must know," Norman burst out angrily, "we're not trying to kill your father, but to . . . to save his life for as long as possible."

"Of course, of course," Garth said, making calming gestures with both hands. "But you will admit, even so, that in the end you'll probably kill him."

Norman was speechless again. The impudence of the man was breathtaking. How could he possibly answer such a question. Garth sat quietly and let him fume. At last Norman felt he could make the effort of discussing the matter seriously. And after all, this was Hamilton's son.

"There are dangers involved in any experimental treatment. Your father knows exactly what's involved, and he personally insisted – insisted is too weak a word – demanded . . . . "

"Oh, my father knows how to demand."

"Well, he demanded to be put on this course of treatment, despite the risks. He has formally resolved anyone from responsibility."

Garth shrugged his shoulders as if to indicate that he was not inclined to disagree with Norman about the trivial details.

"And furthermore," Norman went on, "the therapy is being conducted under rigorously controlled conditions and the most careful monitoring. We wouldn't do it any other way."

"Wouldn't you?" Garth hissed across the table, leaning towards Norman, and grinning in the lamplight, his teeth gleaming in the heart of his rich beard.

"No, of course not," Norman howled in anguish.

He threw back the rest of his drink and pushed his glass forward for another. He could feel the heat of the alcohol in his veins. His mind was in turmoil. Why should he sit here being cross-examined, defending his credentials as a doctor, defending his own sense of responsibility, when it was this man's irresponsibility that should be under attack. This wasn't at all his idea of the way the conversation should be going, what they should be talking about. But he couldn't think of a method to get it back on the right track.

"Supposing," Garth said, in a most reasonable, sympathetic, thoughtful voice, putting both hands in front of him, their backs down on the table, and looking into the palms for the words, "supposing you had an opportunity to experiment with that serum of yours . . . . Supposing you had an opportunity to experiment on a . . . a perfectly normal healthy human being. Now wait," he went on, holding a hand to silence Norman's immediate reaction.

"From what I hear, you're on to something, well, incredible. Something that could change the course of history. The way the first nuclear bomb changed the history of the world. You've discovered how to make people grow younger. Literally. Physically."

Norman leaned forward and buried his head in his arms. What could he say? The whole situation had got completely out of hand. It was obscene, like dropping your trousers on international television, or saying shit and fuck on Cross-Continent Telescreen Call In. It was stunning for Norman to hear a virtual stranger say it out loud across a kitchen table. Even John Hornby and he hardly dared to speak out to each other in the laboratory. They buffered the facts in the most sophisticated scientific terms.

Garth Hamilton's eyes were lit up with the amazing propositions he was uttering. He talked on with wild spurts of energy. He bounded from quiet gloom to exuberance. When the spirit was in him, the man was obviously a born preacher, a demagogue. Everything became so vivid, so exciting when he talked about it. Norman Shearer continued drinking his way through the bottle, as the prophet described the world that might be, if the possibilities of the youth drug could be realized.

"And I," Garth said at last, his enthusiasm ebbing a little to allow him to return to the present, "I will give my body to you to put it to the test."

"What are you saying? You? Why?" Norman asked thickly across the table, at this first chance to speak in half an hour. "Can you tell me why you would think of offering yourself as a guinea pig? You're mad. If we're going to kill your father, we're going to kill you too."

Garth Hamilton's high spirits were clearly gone. He was slipping lower into despondency. His face was taking on the look of a bearded martyr.

"Because I'm twenty-nine years old." Garth said, stubbing his cigarette firmly in the ash-tray, and picking out another from the wooden box.

"And I'm thirty-nine. So what?"

"Oh you," Garth said with a sad smile. "You're motivated."

"Yes, motivated" he went on. " As my Daddy taught me years ago when I sat on his knee. . . . There are only two kinds of people in the world. Those who are motivated, and those who aren't. You are, I'm not. I discovered that about myself when I was eighteen. I tried to commit suicide then, and failed. My father talked me out of trying again. It was a brilliant idea on his part. He knew that I wasn't motivated – of course he is, to the nth degree. But he figured out a way to fake it for me. Unmotivated people only go along from day to day because of inertia, or on the pleasure principle. If life isn't fun anymore, unmo-tivated people turn into vegetables or animals in a herd, or cut their throats. But my father, who understood all that perfectly, had a solution for me."

Garth Hamilton inhaled deeply, and then blew out slowly in a long streamer of smoke to the ceiling shadows. He seemed to be relishing the memory in a melancholy way.

"My father had this social theory, maybe he still has it. He believed that the world in the future would divide even more rigidly into two classes, the motivated and the unmotivated. The motivated would struggle for power and authority and for all kinds of success in every line of endeavor. But they would be a smaller and smaller minority. The great herd of unmotivated people would grow. They would drift about aimlessly, cushioned more and more from the harsh necessities of former ages – you know, the struggle for survival, the biggest and strongest motive of all. The masses would become more and more the appendages of the communications and entertainment and advertising businesses, moved only in the search for pleasure, even their pleasures being defined by the motivated. There would be an astonishing reversal of history, my father believed – and the evidence in the last ten years probably supports him – he believed that the old dream of the mass of mankind, to achieve the heaven of leisure, would become a reality very soon. A reality in which the masses wallowed in motiveless leisure, while the privileged few worked like hell. Worked like hell."

Garth burst out laughing crazily at his own paradox. And Norman, despite himself, joined in, though at some level of his mind he was standing aloof and passing the judgment 'manic-depressive, manic-depressive' on his companion's behavior. He was beginning to realize that he was himself rapidly getting drunk, but he no longer cared.

"So what was it? What was your brilliant father's . . . your father's brilliant idea?" he said, slurringly, reaching for the bottle to fill his own glass.

"My father suggested to me that instead of cutting my throat in a fit of depression and lying down with the vegetables, I try a little experiment. Just for a year. Build a leisure world for yourself, and for others, a community in which people get together to do whatever they want, to enjoy themselves, to have fun. Let them work a little if they want, but only as long as it's entertaining. Let there be no boredom. No drudgery. Let freedom and spontaneity be maximized, let everyone be leisured and pleasured. Have all the money and all the resources you want to sustain that community, and you Garth, he said to me, you be the chief of that community. You'll be able to have all the pleasure you want yourself, which is motive enough for a motiveless man, a young man anyway, and at the same time you'll show how the world will have to be managed in the decades to come. Then, my father said, and this was how he won me over to the idea finally – when the year is up, if you've had all the pleasure you can stomach, if you don't want to go on, I'll help you cut your throat."

The two men sat silently over the table, except for the sharp intake of Garth's breath as he pulled at the cigarette, and the clink of Norman's glass when the bottle touched it.

Garth's bearded face looked solemn, almost saintly. Tears glistened in his eyes. Then a smile touched his lips and he gazed directly at Norman's flushed face.

"What more could a father do for his child?" he asked. "And so you see," he went on, "the beautiful simplicity of it got me, the arbitrariness of the choice – to live or to die. For a motiveless man, what difference did it make?"

Norman applied his mind as best he could to the question. Shaking his head slowly back and forth to clear it didn't help. He had no answer. Garth was talking on past him in any case.

"My father and I are in exactly the same position with respect to your medical discovery. We've got a limited time, each of us. His by necessity, mine by choice. I went past that first year. It's been ten years, now. Soon I would be thirty if I could see myself going on at the Farm into middle-age. There's no way, impossible. I'm going to die before I'm thirty. I refuse to drift into old age. The Farm is for the young. Keep me young and I'll stay here, live on in my motiveless way. If you can't, or won't – it's all over anyway. I mean that. I've been here before."

Norman's head felt as if it had been subjected to a jackhammer. Somewhere beneath the fog and pain, the original reason for his coming to the Farm throbbed. He knew it was there, but he couldn't quite take hold of it. He stared across the table at Garth Hamilton's downturned face knowing that he intensely disliked everything about the man, even while warming to him in some inexplicable way. He was the kind of corrupt, spoiled young man people were always trying to take care of. The kind who couldn't take care of themselves.

"My daughter," Norman blurted out, remembering with a rush of energy and anguish. "Donna. She's only seventeen."

Garth appeared to be unmoved, or not to comprehend. He shrugged his shoulders a trace, and smiled not unsympathetically at the father's agitation, but said nothing.

"It was you, wasn't it?" Norman insisted, leaning forward over his glass. It was clear to Norman at once. Chad Hamilton's answer showed he knew exactly what the question meant.

"Does it matter who? Me. Someone else. These things are bound to happen. That's what being young is."

Norman didn't want to stay in this man's presence any longer. He pushed himself to his feet, and stumbled towards the door. Garth didn't try to stop him. When he reached the doorway, Garth called. "Will you do it? Will you give me the serum?"

Norman stood weaving in the doorway, peering down from his height at the calm, sad, handsome young man who had held his daughter in his arms, who had done that to her.

"I just might do that to you, Garth Hamilton. I just might do that to you."

In weeks that followed Norman Shearer remembered that night with shame and bewilderment. How could he have behaved that way, thought those thoughts, however much the people at the Farm deserved to have the worst thought of them, the worst done to them. How much of it was drunken imagination, how much reality? Had he really contemplated for a moment the possibility of experimenting with a human guinea pig? It was like one of his fever-dreams, hallucinations that came during thermotherapy when body temperature went above a hundred and one. Gradually, as the vividness of the memories faded, he was left with nothing but a more subdued and reserved pain at the growing evidence of his daughter's pregnancy.

Meanwhile, however, his feelings were wildly confused and re-directed. His wife Ella, with surprising ease for a woman producing a second child so much later than usual, gave birth to a fine, healthy boy of five pounds ten ounces. Small, but perfect, was the verdict of the attendant obstetrician. A darling, was Donna's response to her baby brother. She hoped to have one as beautiful.

The birth drew mother and daughter closer together. They rarely quarreled now. And they spent more and more time in each other's company, to the point where, once she was up and about again, Ella began to go with Donna on her visits to the Farm. At first they left the baby with a neighbor, and then when he grew strong enough, they carried him with them, passing the burden back and forth for both to share and enjoy.

Norman had said nothing to Donna and Ella about his night at the Farm. But one day soon after that traumatic visit, he had dropped a remark to Chad Hamilton and Alice Devers, when he came by the Lodge to do his tri-weekly check-up.

"I met your son the other night."

Norman threw it out in the most casual way, keeping his own feelings well out of sight, but observing Hamilton and Alice Devers carefully. Hamilton occupied a large bed located in the middle of the huge Lake Room. He'd had that area set up as the hospital annex, where he could be treated as required, but at the same time lead a life, day and night, as close to normal as possible. A young staff doctor from the Centre was in residence at the Lodge, as well as four suitably young, efficient and attractive nurses, one of them male. If Hamilton was going to be ill, Norman realized, he would be ill in style.

"Don't let yourself get mixed up with Garth and that Farm crowd, Norman," Chad Hamilton said in a jocular tone, and then, turning to Alice: "Dangerous company for Norman to be keeping, don't you think Alice? Garth's a notorious seducer and corrupter."

Although it was eleven in the morning, Alice Devers was still in lounging pajamas. With her long black hair around her shoulders and the elegance of her pose across the foot of Hamilton's big bed, she looked more like something out of a harem, or a Blue Network story, than an executive officer of the Hamilton Medical Research Centre. An increasingly active partner in Hamilton's business affairs. She was stroking Hamilton's feet with one hand under the covers. Obviously at this stage in Hamilton's illness, the two had no intention of veiling their intimacy from a regular visitor like Norman. She smiled at the trace of embarrassment in the doctor's manner.

"Ignore him, Norman," she said, "it's those injections you've got him on. He's high on them and he's getting sillier every day."

"Nonsense," Hamilton boomed. "It's quite true, though, give the guy credit. Garth's lured some extraordinary people down there. From all parts of the country. He's got more talent and brain power in that one commune than there is in the whole of the Ivy League put together."

"Chad," Alice interrupted with a dose of reality, "the entire population of the Farm is a hundred and fifty people, man, woman, and child."

"O.K., percentage-wise," Chad went on, demonstrating how reasonable he could be. "My God, the Chief of Health or whatever he's called down there would have been an asset to any hospital staff in the world. Then there's the Chief of Business. Graduate of the Harvard School, the first woman to lead the class since my Alice here took all the honors. I'd have hired the woman myself, even though she isn't nearly as brilliant, or well, as beautiful as this one here. The other guy who's first-rate down there is their Chief of Security. He's a drop-out from the CIA, one of the brightest young men in the outfit. You can bet they lost some sleep when he walked out on them, with all he knows about intelligence operations and electronic surveillance and that kind of thing. Now of course, they realize that on the Farm he's as safe as if he were committed to a mental hospital. I'm the one that has to worry. He's probably got the whole place bugged . . . . Garth," he suddenly boomed out, looking up at the ceiling, "are you eavesdropping on me, you crazy son of a bitch?"

Alice turned over on her stomach on the foot of the bed and looked towards Norman's bedside chair, shaking her head at Chad's childish behavior.

"You see what I mean?" she said.

"Never mind," Chad resumed in his normal voice, "they may have their organization down there, but mine's even better. This place is a hell of a lot more sophisticated than most people realize." He reached out with one hand and patted the large mahogany case at the head of the bed, with its array of buttons and dials and screens, somewhat resembling the cockpit of an airplane.

"Garth has got his toys, and Chad has got his toys," Alice said, beginning to get to her feet like a woman who has more important things to do than lie around gossiping.

From the beginning, Norman admired the way Alice Devers managed her relations with Hamilton during the course of treatment he was undergoing. It was not always easy to follow the procedure established and required for anyone coming into close proximity with the Hornby-Shearer serum or its recipients. Fortunately Alice was not the kind of person who needed any reminders or supervision. He and John Hornby were treating her as an equal in this respect.

"But you still love us both, don't you honey?" Chad said, reaching down to catch her arm.

She let him pull her towards the pillows, so that she was sitting beside him. Then, after a moment, getting up again, she kissed him on the forehead, gave him a maternal pat, and walked away. Norman immediately began his examination of the patient.

"I have to report to you, Doctor, I'm feeling great," Chad said with energy and emphasis. "You didn't tell me that stuff was going to affect me like a . . . like an aphrodisiac. I haven't felt so . . . so horny since I passed my fiftieth birthday."

"I'm glad for you," Norman murmured, with as much wryness in his tone and expression as he could risk, putting his stethoscope to Chad's tanned chest.

"The trouble is," Hamilton went on, "someone should have explained it to Alice. She thought she was taking on an impotent old man who wouldn't bother her except maybe once in the fall and once in the spring. And now you're turning me into a young buck."

Chad burst out laughing at his own double caricature. Then he went on, quite seriously, with the kind of candor and intimate revelation people seem to save for their private doctors.

"You know Alice Devers is an amazing woman. She's as gorgeous as a beauty queen, anybody can see that, can't they?"

"Oh yes," Norman nodded, reaching for his medical bag to cover his embarrassment.

"But she's hard as nails for all that. The most efficient, the shrewdest, the most enterprising guy I've had doing business for me for many years. If Garth had had half of her toughness and ambition and all round ability, he and I, well, we could have . . . . "

Even Chadwick Hamilton wasn't able to find the words to describe what a success such a combination would have been. His mood changed abruptly. "Well, what the hell. It's over now." For a moment Hamilton's face looked tired and lined and old, and then it lit up with energy again, like a young man's. "But listen, Doctor, you'd better start giving some of those shots to Alice. What's the point in a fellow feeling the way I do when all his woman wants to do is talk about business?"

Later, when Norman returned to the Centre, he gave a full account of his examination to John Hornby, including his sense of Chad Hamilton's psychological state.

"Faye Delisle all over again?" John asked finally.

"Evidently. Though he's got a few years to go yet, and there's a certain difference in personality."

"And in appearance," Hornby conceded.

"Indeed. . . . Shall we hear the latest recording from Faye?"

Despite their joking, the news from the Carter-Trudeau was not very cheerful. Faye Delisle's weight had dropped to eighty-three pounds, and her energy had faded to the point where she was sleeping a good deal of the time – like a child who'd outgrown her strength, only in this case it was the opposite of growth. However, when she was awake, and with the Hospital support systems helping her main organs, she was remarkably happy.

For the most part, Hornby and Shearer had been enjoying her chatter, and learning from it as well. Long ago at the Carter-Trudeau one of their psychiatrist colleagues, hearing a little about the recordings they were collecting, suggested that they might like to let him use the serum experimentally on some extreme schizophrenia cases. At the time they were able to brush aside the notion, but they were well aware of the potential interest for psychiatry of a drug having such an impact on mental states.

Faye's recorded voice was even more like a child's than before. She talked about the hospital routine and her present doctor and a number of trivial matters that they let pass. Towards the end they focused their attention more carefully, and even replayed a few sections. Faye was beginning to talk more and more frequently about her father and mother.

I haven't thought about them much for years. They've been dead for so long. I was seventeen when they were killed in a jet crash. My mother never liked the idea of my trying to get into acting and films and that kind of thing. My father was secretly proud of me, I think. He pretended to agree with Mother about me showing off my body, but he liked the attention I got. I suppose it's just as well they didn't live to see me make a career on the Blue.

I've still got a big panda bear my dad won for me at the country fair when I was twelve. I used to sleep with it every night. I'd cry if I couldn't have it in bed with me. What would my psychiatrist have to say about that, I wonder? Sometimes I just lie and close my eyes and remember those days, and I think so hard about them that when I open my eyes I expect to see Mom and Dad coming in the door the way they did when I had my tonsils out. You know, I'm going to get them to send my panda here from home. I know exactly where I put him, he's in a cardboard box in a cupboard. He'll be so good to hug and I'll bet after all this time he'll love it too . . . .

The recording didn't really finish. As was happening more and more often, Faye had simply forgotten to turn it off, and it went on, picking up the occasional hospital noises, until probably a nurse or somebody pushed the off button.

"Do you think you can get Chad Hamilton to go on record for us too?" Hornby asked, after they heard as much as they wanted.

Shearer had the same thought. "I don't know, I haven't felt it was the time to ask him yet. He's talkative enough when I'm there, I can tell you. Let's wait and see. I'm not really sure how useful it would be as a comparison."

Norman and John were both thinking of the condition Chad Hamilton had reached by the time they began him on their therapy. He was not as extreme a case as most they had taken on, but he had undergone a considerable variety of treatments, from radiation therapy to hormone injections. It was probably these last that decided Hamilton, when he elected to turn to Hornby and Shearer, even more than the trial with cobalt treatments.

"They were trying to make a bloody woman out of me," He complained when he described this phase of his case history to the two doctors.

And it was true that there was the likelihood of some occurrence of female characteristics from extended hormonal infusions of the kind he would have been receiving.

"Let's face it," Norman said a little disingenuously to Hornby, as they brooded on the nature of the clinical cases they had so far, and on the difficulty of conducting useful research with what they had to work on. "We need a few normal, healthy human beings to give us the right kind of clinical evidence."

"Are you volunteering?" Hornby asked drily.

His testy tone provoked Norman to say more than he had really thought of saying, or at least drove him to put it more bluntly. "No, but I know someone who has."

Hornby looked up at him sharply. Although he had gained a little more weight around the middle since coming to Notlimah, John Hornby to the eye of the casual observer had changed very little. He was the kind of man who might remain more or less as he was, portly, comfortable looking, for many years. But as always, on the subject of medical research he could be quite sensitive, certainly alert. It was clear to him that this was not one of Norman's jokes.

"What do you mean by that? Has somebody around here been talking too much?"

They had lived for years with a chronic worry about sensational public disclosures of the nature of their work, as indeed did most other researchers in the cancer field. They had winced often enough at the plight of fellow researchers around the world who, in trying to give an accurate and positive impression of their own work, had fallen victim to an enterprising journalist or broadcaster, and had to cope with a barrage of public interest, even public hysteria. This was to be expected, now that cancer in the kind of environment the modern world offered most people, had so far outstripped all other killer diseases. In their own situation, Hornby and Shearer increasingly felt as though they were sitting on a keg of dynamite.

Norman took pity on his friend at the flare of concern he saw on his face, and didn't continue the suspense. "I think it's all under control," he said, "but at least one unauthorized person knows a good deal more than he should."

"Who?"

"Garth Hamilton. He wants to be a guinea pig for us."

John Hornby whistled in astonishment. Norman watched silently as a parade of reactions passed over his friend's round, normally serene face. Disbelief, grudging acceptance of the fact that Norman meant it, concern, serious interest, and something approaching a kind of guilty – even greedy

– curiosity to know more. The very feelings Norman himself had entertained on the subject at one time or another, though he had one or two more as well.

Norman quickly sketched in his understanding of Garth Hamilton's attitude, sparing no details that might dramatize the manic-depressive tendency of his personality. When he was finished John said nothing, but sat tapping his pencil on the table, lost in meditation.

"Of course I told him," Norman concluded, modifying the facts a little in retrospect, "it was absolutely out of the question. There's the simple matter of medical ethics. There's the fact that there are environmental regulations that have to be observed. There's the danger of contamination, with a man living the kind of life he lives down there on the Farm. The inescapable element of risk and danger for others. . . . He's a very stubborn man, though, just like his father."

"He doesn't want to take no for an answer?"

John Hornby was still deep in his brooding. His reaction surprised, even agitated, Norman, who had fully expected him to dismiss the story quickly. At most he thought John might feel a twinge of temptation, longing for forbidden fruit. He had not expected John to be interested from the beginning, and grow steadily more so. "Of course, from the scientific point of view it would be a wonderful opportunity. And I for one believe it when Garth Hamilton says he's going to kill himself before his thirtieth birthday. A completely wasted life, if he does."

John didn't want to change the subject. "The suicide rate in the Western World has gone up three per cent every year for the past ten," John said, producing the fact as if it were a footnote to a report.

"Do you really think . . . ," Norman began, after another pause, and then hesitating, wondering if he might be going too quickly, "should we think seriously about this crazy man's offer?"

As they sat staring at each other, neither of them choosing to answer the question, Norman realized that John Hornby had already gone past that point. He had been thinking seriously about the possibility ever since Norman raised it. Thinking hard. Now he was plunging ahead into the details, with all the energy of someone in flight who has leaped over the first most awesome obstacle, and is eager to skim those beyond.

"There's the personal risk for Garth Hamilton," John said, going back over the facts again," and there's the risk of contamination and contagion. From what you say, Garth wouldn't consider some experiments here under our controlled conditions. Wouldn't let himself be admitted to the Centre?"

"He claims – they all claim – he never leaves the Farm."

John continued to push the subject. "Impossible to do anything outside of a properly regulated environment."

Norman caught up to and passed Hornby at this obvious first stop. Plans rushed recklessly through his mind. The Farm's Chief of Health, a medical drop-out but a Johns Hopkins man, undoubtedly well enough trained before he rebelled against Pentagon policy and threw up his public career. An isolated cottage on the Farm? Surely that could be arranged. Electronic communications, recording of data. It all began to seem very practicable. What more secluded and protected environment could they find in which to place a scientific experiment than the Farm? And what more likely volunteer than a more or less idle young man of retiring way of life and with a history of suicidal intention?

There was, of course, the question of professional ethics.

"Do you think you could live with your conscience, John, if we ever did a thing like this?"

"I'm a scientist, not a moralist," Hornby replied, with a wry grin.

It was clearly too late to retreat. They were both psychologically committed beyond that point already. The frustrations and limitations of the past few years had built up a powerful need to go on at whatever cost. It could almost be said that they were both prepared long ago for such a venture, if anything remotely possible presented itself to them. After the initial qualms, they plunged in deeper and deeper, their inhibitions having evaporated.

"We should contact Garth Hamilton right away," John suggested. "Despite what you say, he may have backed down by now. If not, the sooner we start the better."

Norman was torn between a revulsion at the thought of having to make arrangements with Garth Hamilton himself, and a worry that, by asking John to do it, a last-minute hitch might develop.

"He won't back down, I'm sure. But if you wouldn't mind, I'd appreciate it if you would work out the details with him. It's just a personal thing with me. Between me and Garth."

John looked at his friend with considerable curiosity and a little concern. He was on the point of pursuing the matter further, when abruptly he decided not to open the subject beyond the point it had reached. He wanted no last-minute hitches either, evidently.

"Surely," he said, "I can do that easily. I'll try and get in touch with him by telescreen this afternoon . . . . If we're fully agreed."

He stood up in front of Norman. It was obvious that he wanted to make the agreement a formal moment. They stood three feet apart, the one lean and athletic and towering, the other portly, firm to the ground, dignified. They read the full implications of what they were doing in each other's eyes. Simultaneously each put out a hand. Their handshake was warm, firm, and short. Then each went about his business.

In the afternoon John Hornby asked the Centre office how he could get in touch with someone at the Farm. Call the Farm business offices, listed in the directory, was the answer, what could be simpler. In the privacy of his apartment, John rang through to the number he found.

"I'd like to speak to Garth Hamilton, on a personal matter, if I may." John said to the young woman in the t-shirt and Afro-hair style, looking not at all business-like, who came on the screen.

"Half a minute," was the cheerful answer, "I'll see if he's available. Can I tell him your name?"

"Dr. John Hornby, from the Medical Research Centre."

The screen darkened for a few seconds, during which John could still pick up the audio. The young woman's voice was calling to someone else. "Can our man take the telescreen? Tell him it's personal, from the Centre."

Hornby was beginning to feel uncomfortable. Already the connection between Garth Hamilton and the Centre was more public than he thought was wise. But almost immediately the face of the bearded, friendly young man came on the screen and the situation lost all traces of awkwardness.

"I was kind of hoping to hear from you people one of these days. Is it time to get on with it?" the young man asked, his eyes searching the electronic connection on his side as John Hornby's were on the other.

John hesitated a moment. It crossed his mind that there could be the makings here of a gigantic misunderstanding. He might have to be fairly explicit.

"I believe," he said, "that you are still seriously considering a certain form of medical treatment for an illness from which you're suffering? A chronic illness?"

Garth Hamilton's brow furrowed for a moment and he was silent, obviously baffled. Then abruptly his mouth opened wide in his rich black beard and he burst out laughing.

"I am, I am," he roared, sounding very like his father in the same kind of exuberant mood. Then more soberly, "I'm damn glad you called. My chronic illness, as you so aptly put it, is getting more serious every day."

"You're fully aware of the nature of the treatment we're talking about?'

"In general, yes. I know what I'm getting into perfectly well, if that's what you mean."

"Then I'd like to arrange the details with you. Can you . . . . can you come in to the Centre?"

"No. No, I never leave the Farm. But my Chief of Health will come. He's very good – and very discreet."

Between them they arranged for the Chief of Health to come to John Hornby's town house adjacent to the Centre that evening. Looking down from his low balcony at the appointed time, eight-thirty, John was bemused at first when he saw a long-haired, straw-hatted young man, wearing patched blue jeans and carrying a canvas knap-sack on his back, come cycling around the curved driveway towards the town house row. Having located the right address, and seeing John on the balcony, the young man waved and approached to park his bicycle at the entrance. He then stood under the balcony and swept off his hat. He had a round, cheerful, friendly face, a younger, trimmer version of John Hornby's own.

"Dr. Hornby, I presume," he said, in a clear tenor.

"And you must be Dr. Crossland," John said, hardly believing it, but leaning down and offering his hand in any case.

After a quick handshake, the young man prevented Hornby from leaving the balcony to open the front door by taking hold of the rose trellis and quickly swarming up it to stand on the balcony beside his surprised host. He unhooked his knap-sack and slid it to the floor.

"No one calls me Doctor at the Farm. It's Allen, if you like."

Soon the two men were sitting side by side in the waning light, drinking a cordial glass of bourbon.

"Is everything that informal on the Farm?" Hornby asked, with a touch of perfectly conscious and deliberate priggishness, letting his eyes drift down to Allen Crossland's knap-sack on the floor. "No black bag even, the rural doctor's trademark?"

Hornby was hoping to discover as quickly as possible whether there was any likelihood that the proposed medical experiment could be carried out properly. He had no intention of allowing it to go ahead without at least the minimum of controls with a properly qualified and conscientious medical authority overseeing it. He was more than a little dismayed at his first impression of the Chief of Health.

Allen Crossland smiled at him imperturbably over his glass. His manner implied that he understood very well what was going through Hornby's mind.

"When I first came to the Farm," he said, "I was straight out of the system. I took it for granted I'd be saluted, literally and figuratively, every time I turned around. It was a very strange experience to come to a place like the Farm, where established roles mean nothing. I came as an assistant to the then Chief of Health, and I remember the shock I felt when I first met the woman – it was a woman then. I discovered that it was the same with all the roles on the Farm. There's absolutely no mystique, there's no separation. If you've got a skill, fine, use it. But don't expect anybody to treat you as a special kind of human being. The knap-sack belonged to my predecessor. She gave it to me when she left, saying, you'll find it a lot more convenient for bicycling than the traditional medical bag. She was right."

Without meaning to, Hornby found he had started Allen Crossland on a long digression. With the same serene expression on his face he told Hornby how the Chief of Security, a former CIA man brought up in the sternest schools of intelligence and military discipline, after he arrived at the Farm, came to accept the role of protector of the community from crime and violence without having to stand apart from his neighbors. And the Chief of Business, who once expected – was expected – to go into corporate enterprise on the highest level, wearing the latest, most expensive one-piece pin stripes, handled the Farm's affairs with the ease and casualness of the neighbor on the other side of the fence.

"Artist, teacher, carpenter – doctor – each role at the Farm appears for the sake of its function, but once the function is completed the individual merges with the group again," Crossland explained, with the enthusiasm of a convert. "No classes, no castes, no professional cliques. It's tremendously refreshing to be taken by people for what you are, instead of stamped by some prearranged conceptions about the category you belong to."

John Hornby was not an argumentative man, but he was sufficiently provoked by Allen Crossland's serene confidence to give the obvious answer.

"It's usually felt," he said quietly, "that the desire to earn the respect of your fellow man is a spur to creativity in the human race."

Crossland looked blank for a moment, as if someone had spoken to him in a foreign language. Then he caught the polemical acid in the apparently bland statement.

"Oh, there's lots of creativity at the Farm," he said, "it's just that it's not a matter of personal vanity. We're interested in what's created, not in the fact that a particular person did it . . . . Come and see for yourself. You'd find it quite interesting, I'm sure."

John considered that the time had come now to get down to brass tacks, and leave behind this ideological digression. "I will come, if for no other reason than to see what kind of arrangements you make for our experiment."

As if a button had been touched, Allen Crossland dropped his serene spiritual manner and became crisp and efficient. It was a medical consultation – and Dr. Crossland proceeded to show that on his side he was well enough prepared and qualified.

"As I understand it, this is a live vaccine you're using," Crossland said, "developed through gene-splicing with an intestinal bacterium. Presumably you've worked to date under Environmental Hazards Committee guidelines?"

"We have."

"What kind of controls have you built into your virus, then?"

Precisely the most important question for the supervising doctor to ask. John Hornby dropped all his reservations about Crossland for the moment, and began to explain fully what he should know to make use of the Hornby-Shearer serum with reasonable safety from contagion and contamination.

As for the built-in controls, the bacterium on which they based their serum was chosen and cultivated for its relative innocuousness. In the recombined form, the virus would only survive within a temperature variation of one point seven degrees above and one point nine degrees below normal body temperature for human beings. In the laboratory, they were able to render it inactive outside of that range within three to four hours.

"So the possibilities of transmitting the virus from one person to another, if they aren't in actual physical proximity, are minimal."

F. W. WATT

"With normal precautions, minimal."

"Transmission would require close proximity or contact between transmitter and recipient, and a maintaining of body temperatures within the prescribed range?"

"Correct. And of course we have ready means of dealing with cases of accidental or unwanted exposure: thermotherapy. In these instances, and for termination of the effects of the treatment, we simply raise the body temperature artificially for a brief period, until we're confident that the virus has become inactive."

"A case of the 'flu would have the same effect.? Well, quite a fine safety and control feature. Would that more medical risks could be managed so easily."

John was pleased to discover how quickly Allen Crossland grasped the essential principles. By the time the evening was over, and Crossland had climbed back on his bicycle to return to the Farm, it seemed that the experiment was in good hands, not nearly so hazardous and unpredictable as it had appeared to be, when his confidence level was at its lowest.

It was agreed that Crossland would personally conduct the special travelling case containing the serum, at its controlled temperature, from the lab at the Centre to the isolation cottage at the Farm, which Crossland would set up and staff. There were no difficulties on that side because, as Crossland pointed out coolly, Garth Hamilton and others from the commune had from time to time over the years gone into retreat for weeks or even months – "To try our own experiments," as Crossland put it with a smile. One of the responsibilities of the Chief of Health was to supply various kinds of drugs to anyone who wanted to try them, under conditions of reliability and safety.

"We won't have to do much explaining about Garth," Crossland said. "People will just think our man has gone off on another extended trip."

"So it's all systems go," Norman Shearer said, when John Hornby brought him up to date the next morning.

"Blast off," John replied, sharing an ironic grin with his friend.

"Too late to back down?" Not that Norman doubted for a moment.

"Too late," John confirmed instantly, with a finger tap on his wrist watch.

Norman Shearer sat on John Hornby's laboratory table, looking down fondly at his friend, swinging a long leg idly. There was something about crime that drew people together. And it was a crime, punishable, as the two doctors were well aware, at the very least by removal of their license to practice, at worst (however unlikely) by an extended term in prison.

"Come over to the Circle and have dinner with me tonight, John, we'll celebrate," Norman said.

John considered the invitation for a moment. He had the same sense of wanting to close ranks with his friend. Old habits kept him from seeing much more of the Shearers socially then before they had moved to Notlimah. Even less in recent months, with Ella Shearer in the last stages of pregnancy, and then giving birth to a son.

"Don't you think you should consult with your better half?" John suggested, with a bachelor's superior concern about the realities of domestic life, over that of a complacent husband.

"I'm baching for a few days, John. Ella and the baby and Donna have gone down to the Farm for a break. I'll cook you a steak, we'll drink a bottle or two of my best red wine, and we'll end up with Blue Television –there's a new series, not quite up to Faye Delisle, but nice just the same."

John Hornby accepted without further delay or argument. The mention of Faye Delisle, however, prompted him to make this conference the occasion to hear the latest recording from her. In the excitement of the decisions and preparations of the last day or two, it had sat on the table unopened, though John had read the accompanying report from the Carter-Trudeau.

"This may very well be the last she'll do for us," John reminded his friend.

He had already passed on the gist of the written report. Faye Delisle's weight was down to seventy-three pounds. She was conscious for only a few hours each day. Although her organs were still functioning, she was surviving on the simplest, most easily digestible kinds of food, and with the constant help of the kidney machine. The staff was impressed by how long beyond expectation her cancer ridden body was still functioning.

The recording began to play. At first the two doctors heard the usual extraneous hospital background noises they had grown accustomed to. The piping voice coming in and out of the voice-leveling range of the machine was obviously that of Faye Delisle, developed still further in the direction they expected. It started, and broke off, faded away and came back in with startling brightness.

Doctor says I should talk to you, but I'm sleepy, so sleepy. It's cozy here in bed. I've got Pandy in beside me. Doctor didn't want me to have him here, but I cried and cried and cried and finally they said, let her have her bear. That's silly, isn't it? I was really ashamed of myself, but I did want him so much . . . . Pandy, Pandy, I love you. Oh Pandy! Nurse! Pandy fall down. Pandy hurts. Nurse! Please. Please. I want my. . . . I want my Mommy. I want my Mommy. I want . . . .

John Hornby switched off the recording. Norman, who had been leafing through the accompanying medical report as it started, as the voice of the young woman began to be audible, put the report down on the table and stood up. His face was tense, drawn, shocked despite himself.

"I'll look at this tomorrow, John," he said grimly, "let's listen to the rest and talk about it later."

That evening the two friends drank themselves into oblivion in front of the television set. Neither said a word about their work or their professional life. It was as if, with their experiment entering a new, critical phase, they wanted to breathe freely and relax at least once more together, before they got in any deeper, or beyond their depth.

Early in the following week, John Hornby received a hot-line call from the Lodge. It was not from Chad Hamilton, but from Alice Devers. She wanted to arrange an immediate conference between Dr. Shearer, Dr. Hornby, herself and Chad Hamilton. She gave the impression that the conference was more her own idea than Hamilton's. When John passed the news onto Norman, his friend was not unduly surprised.

"Alice has been spending more and more of her time at the Lodge. She's hardly ever here at the Centre in normal hours, as far as I can tell. She's taking on the bulk of Hamilton's business responsibilities – and understandably she's getting worried about where it will all end."

"What do you think she wants to do about it?"

"I don't know," Norman answered wryly, "but you can be sure she's got a pretty clear idea herself."

When the two doctors arrived at the Lodge and were ushered into the Lake Room, Chad Hamilton, enshrined in his huge bed in the centre of the room, looked up in a slightly bemused way.

"You remember, Chad," Alice said smoothly, "I told you Norman and John were going to drop in to have a talk."

She was dressed in a slim-cut hostess gown, though it was only four in the afternoon. The soft rose material enhanced her black hair and blue eyes and gave her an unusual feminine air. Even so, she conveyed the impression of an actress who has temporarily taken on a role well within her powers but not her natural choice. Chad Hamilton was holding her bare upper arm, so that had she wanted to stand up from the edge of the bed he could have prevented her.

Seeing the eyes of the two men absorbed in the spectacle of himself, bed-ridden, and the beautiful woman at his side, Chad made a typically blunt and direct comment.

"She's gorgeous, isn't she, gentlemen? I'm a lucky man to have her with me for my last days."

In a maternal way Alice patted the hand that was holding her arm and smiled at him coolly. "Don't you think you should leave it to the doctors to tell you whether or not these are your last days?"

Chad Hamilton gave her a playful push away from him. His voice boomed out at the doctors in the old way as they drew nearer. "Isn't she the toughest girl you've ever seen? How cruel can you be to an old man on his death bed?"

Norman ventured a remark, looking down at Chad Hamilton's healthily blooming face and neck and hands. "Perhaps no one sees you quite as an old man. In fact, you're looking ten years younger than when you started this therapy."

"Exactly," Hamilton cried out. "I feel it. Not ten years, twenty years. Christ I'm a man of thirty all over again. Expect for the palpations," he concluded a little lamely, rubbing a hand over his chest.

"Which brings us to why we asked you to come and talk to us, both of you," Alice Devers broke in. She had pushed chairs over for the two doctors to sit down around the bed, and she selected one for herself.

"You, you mean," Hamilton corrected her vehemently, "you're the one that wanted to talk to them. Of course," he went on, directly addressing the men, "I'm always delighted to talk to you, but this is all Alice's idea."

"Why don't you let me explain, then?" Alice said, trying with considerable firmness to hold onto the direction of the meeting.

"What for? What's there to explain? Why don't you just let them have it?" Hamilton rumbled on, with a mixture of amusement and anger they couldn't quite fathom. "The fact of the matter is, Alice wants to get me off your damned drug."

"That's putting it a little too simply," Alice said tenaciously.

"Well, isn't that it?"

"Perhaps now," Alice said with an icy graciousness, "you might let me say something."

"Say away, say away," Hamilton finished, waving his hands to dismiss his part in the talk.

His expression was that of a hurt boy. He remained silent while Alice figuratively took the floor, as if she were conducting a shareholders' meeting requiring great delicacy and great force, combined.

First, she summed up the patient's medical history to date with a precision and economy which showed how well she had learned how to deal with the medical world. No doubt her time with the Environmental Hazards Committee and with the Centre was paying off. She knew exactly the state of Hamilton's treatment prior to undertaking the Hornby-Shearer therapy, and she knew in considerable detail the progress of the patient as a result of the latest attempt to control a disease which had seemed well on the way to a fatal conclusion. She knew the degrees of success of previous therapy, and the variety of side-effects which these treatments entailed. She recognized that the Hornby-Shearer serum administered in massive doses for several months had in fact, for the first time, retarded the carcinomatous malignancy to a remarkable degree. But she was also aware that Hamilton's general condition, whether from the advanced stage the disease had reached, from the most recent attempt to cure it, or as an accumulated result of previous treatments, was in a state of dangerous decline, despite the buoyant state of mind of the patient. In particular, several of the principal organs along with the cardiovascular system were demonstrating malfunctions.

Hamilton had been listening with increased interest, coming out of his sulk, as Alice drew to a conclusion. "Isn't she great?" Hamilton broke in. "What

F. W. WATT

a mind, what a tongue. If I'd met a woman like this thirty years ago and we'd teamed up, we would have . . . . God knows how far we could have gone! What we could have . . . ." Hamilton's imagination again seemed to fail at his attempt to describe the scope of their potential achievements.

"Let me finish, Chad, please."

"Hell, Alice, it's perfectly clear to these guys. Do you think they're stupid?"

Hamilton turned directly to the two doctors who had been waiting uneasily for the climax. "Alice thinks your dope is changing me so much – I don't mean physically – mentally, that it's not worth the candle. Isn't that it, Alice? Come on, let's have it straight out."

Alice showed no signs of being flustered. It was clear that nothing was likely to perturb her if she chose not to let it. "I simply want to re-examine the treatment you're getting, and assess the results, just as you've done with every other form of medical attention you've had to date. I think the time has come. I think you agree with me, too."

This was the first direct challenge from her to him. In making it Alice turned her face towards Chad Hamilton and refused to let him avoid her eyes. After returning her look for a minute in silence, Hamilton abruptly shrugged his shoulders and slumped down against the pillows. "Go ahead, talk me over. I'm just the bloody carcass."

"Chad's angry now," Alice said to the two doctors, as if Hamilton were no longer in the room, "but he knows what I mean. The psychological effects of this therapy are more disturbing than the physiological . . . . "

"Not to me they aren't," Hamilton muttered, "I like them."

"He likes them sometimes," Alice continued, "but at other times he finds them as distressing as I do. He's extraordinarily unpredictable, going into childish tantrums one minute and becoming his old self again the next, making some irresponsible or silly decision today, and tomorrow swearing at me for carrying it out."

Norman interjected a question. He and John Hornby had had far too little opportunity to evaluate this aspect of Hamilton's reaction to the serum. "Is it your feeling, yours and Chad's, that there have been consistent directions in the effect of the therapy, you know, in regard to moods and mental states?"

"Yeah, of course, as I keep telling you," Hamilton boomed from his pillows, "I've felt younger every day, and I've behaved more and more like a young man. Christ, let's face it, Alice is mad because nowadays I care more about sex than business. It's ridiculous, when I think about it. I'm like some young broad prematurely married to a middle-aged executive on the way up. Alice is all the time negotiating, making deals, buying and selling, when all I want to do is make her."

He guffawed loudly at his own remark, and then subsided into silence again.

"It's not a matter of sex, or business, or any of those things," Alice said, without a trace of discomposure, "it's a matter of personality, character – what this treatment is doing to the nature of a person. In view, that is, of what it is or isn't likely to do for physical health."

"Don't beat around the bush, Alice," Hamilton interjected. "What you mean is, if these guys are going to kill me anyway, you don't want me changed in the meantime."

"If you like," Alice said, smiling for the first time in minutes at Chad, "I want you as you are."

"Or was."

"Both."

John Hornby, sitting as far back as seemed polite, was embarrassed beyond speechlessness by the way the conversation was going. Norman Shearer was able to take it more easily in his stride, partly because of his nature and partly because he had seen more of Alice and Chad together. He was intrigued by the personal revelations, despite the impact this kind of collision might have on their medical relationship with Chad Hamilton. Both of the doctors found it possible to agree with Hamilton's analysis. It was the old comedy of the young wife, wanting sexual attention and fulfillment, while the older husband pursues his career and achieves his gratification through his work. Only in this case, the sex and age roles were reversed. Through the magic of medicine, Alice Devers and Chad Hamilton were passing each other going in opposite directions.

Listening to them, Norman quickly concluded what the best line to take with them would be.

"You will remember, Chad, that it was you who approached John Hornby and me about receiving the therapy we're developing. At that time we told you everything we knew about its nature, at this early stage in our experimentation. As far as John and I are concerned, there's nothing in your reactions to the serum that entirely surprises us. We were aware, as we told you, that certain retarding and reversal effects in the physiological sphere were likely to be paralleled, even more noticeably perhaps, in the psychological sphere. We've assembled enough clinical evidence to show that this is likely to be a common pattern."

He paused a moment to look from one to the other, followed by a brief glance over his shoulder for support from John Hornby, who sat in silence, nursing his grave unease.

"The dilemma we're faced with," Norman continued, "is that if we reduce or take you off the serum injections, the carcinomatous cells will become active and malignant again immediately. If we keep you on the present high levels of dosage, you're bound to go on experiencing these extraordinary rejuvenating effects, and maybe others we can't yet even predict."

There was another pause while Norman reviewed in his mind whether he had put the case fairly and fully. A glance from John Hornby reassured him on that score.

"So there you are," he concluded. "In the end, of course it's your decision."

For the first time Alice Devers began to look distressed. She left her chair and went over to sit on the edge of the bed, beside Chad Hamilton's pillows. She took one of his hands in both hers. The icy grace had faded, leaving her looking tired and frail. Chad responded to her mood by slipping an arm around her shoulder. When she spoke it was quietly and simply, without her usual elegant formality.

"I just wonder if it's right to change a person so much. You know what I mean, Chad," she appealed to him. "You said yourself that above all you wanted to keep your dignity. That's why you came off the cobalt treatments. That's why you wouldn't go on with the hormone injections. It's all so difficult. Is it going to be worth it? Do you two know?"

To everyone's surprise, it was John Hornby's voice that broke the silence. He had said nothing to that point, as was so often the case when he was in a group. The result was that everyone gave him full attention. He was at once shockingly blunt.

"By the most informed medical opinions, Mr. Hamilton has at most about a year to live. Everyone in this room knows that."

John paused a moment to look around, as though allowing objections or reservations. Of course there were none. He went on calmly, with the same bluntness.

"No one else but Mr. Hamilton can decide how he wants to live that year. He could, with certain forms of treatment, degenerate rapidly into a vegetable. He could, undergoing the present form of therapy, suffer a cardiac arrest at any moment – we're not quite sure why he's having heart palpitations, but it's not the first time we've observed these symptoms. Almost certainly, under the present form of therapy, he will continue to experience startling and extreme psychological effects – call them rejuvenation if you like – while the disease he is suffering from is at least temporarily controlled. These will cause him to revert to earlier patterns of behavior, while he still retains his mature consciousness a good deal of the time."

John paused again to give Hamilton a moment's wry scrutiny, to see how he was taking it so far, and then continued in the same tone.

"I don't know what Mr. Hamilton was like as a younger man. If I knew, I would have a better idea of how he might behave in the future. But in any case the circumstances are so complicated that no one could really predict. So when Norman here says that the choice is yours, Mr. Hamilton, he's offering you an alternative which has a considerable element of mystery. You'll have to choose between a reality whose limits you more or less know, and an undetermined possibility. Between the known and the unknown."

"Good for you, John Hornby," Chad Hamilton burst out as Hornby finished and sat back in his chair again, like a Buddhist statue. "I love a man who can lay it all out on the table. Now let me ask you one question. When I've listened to advisors – and I've had many of them over many years – when I've let them have their say, I've always asked them the same question at the end. *What would you do?"*

He was clearly going to wait for an answer, however long it was necessary. Hornby sat smiling for a moment, looking at Hamilton first, and then meeting the curious and attentive eyes of both Alice and Norman Shearer. Norman was very glad it was John, not he, who was being confronted so relentlessly. He would have been hard put to know what to say, and he was highly uncertain what John might answer.

At last John spoke, and not in any way Norman could have expected.

"For me, that's an easy question. With these alternatives, faced with a choice between the known, and the unknown? I would always go for the unknown."

No one said anything further, as each digested this somewhat enigmatic reply. Then he added a further remark that made Norman Shearer gasp.

"You see, Mr. Hamilton, last week I made arrangements to begin giving a course of serum injections – just like the ones you're receiving – to a normal, healthy human being, in the interests of exploring the unknown."

If Chad Hamilton was surprised, Norman was even more so, sitting motionless, paling, filled with consternation at the unlikely prospects of John Hornby telling Hamilton about his son. About they're making his son a human guinea pig.

"Who the hell is it, John? Who would be crazy enough to let you do a thing like that?" Hamilton asked incredulously.

John Hornby smiled at all three again. He seemed to be enjoying himself in an unaccustomed role, as if he were an amateur actor appearing for the first time on the stage and discovering the excitement of holding an audience's attention. Norman was beginning to recover from his first shock. He leaned forward trying to think of some way to bring John back to his senses, without himself giving the game away.

"John, do you think you've got the right to divulge the name?" He added in a weak effort at an in-joke: "Professional ethics and that sort of thing, wouldn't you say?"

John nodded reassuringly to him, knowing that his expression wouldn't really comfort his friend. But then, given a situation in which Norman was actually a lot farther from the facts than he thought he was, it seemed likely that in the end nothing would be much of a comfort to him.

"I think you should tell us, John," Hamilton urged, "having gone this far. I'm sure Alice and I would promise complete confidentiality. I really think I have a stake in knowing who this damned fool is. After all," he concluded with a laughing hug for Alice, "this guy – or gal— we're going to be growing young together."

"I agree," John said, "I think it would help you to make your own decision to know who it is."

Norman groaned and put a hand over his eyes. He could hardly imagine what Hamilton's reaction would be to discover that his son was taking the serum too.

Then John made his revelation. "The normal, healthy human being I happen to be referring to is . . . myself."

Norman Shearer let out a choking cough, which fortunately was drowned by the exclamations of Alice and Chad Hamilton. Norman, hand over his mouth, continued to stare at his friend in disbelief, as John answered the questions and half-questions from the other two. Eventually everything that seemed necessary to say got said, and there was nothing more to do but for the two doctors to leave.

Chad insisted John come over and shake hands with him on their departure. Of course there was no longer any doubt that Hamilton himself would continue with the Hornby-Shearer injections for the time being. He was clearly amazed but, even more, exhilarated by the turn of events. He sent the two doctors on their way with a volley of jokes, and assurances that they would be comparing notes again soon and often. Whatever her feelings were, Alice recognized that there was no point in her pursuing her earlier arguments now.

Norman could hardly wait until the moment they were out of Hamilton's earshot, on their way to the Centre, before taking John roughly by the arm and wringing the truth from him. They were in the back seat of one of the Lodge's electric limousines, with the young driver on his side of the glass window pretending not to hear. But Norman took no chances. Whatever were the facts, he wanted nothing further to get back to Chad Hamilton.

"For God's sake, John," he said urgently in a half-voice, "what was all that about? Who are you trying to play games with, them or me?"

John turned in the seat to face his friend. His face was tired and a little sad, almost as if he felt sorry for Norman. "Maybe with you, Norman. I really didn't mean to play games with anybody. I was going to tell you once matters were confirmed. After all," he added with a smile, "I'll need your cooperation as attendant physician. But I didn't want to get into any hassles with you by raising the question before it was settled, before I'd made my plans for carrying it out."

"But why, John, why? You did it because of . . . ." Norman was going to say Garth Hamilton's name in his agitation, but glancing forward to the driver's seat he thought better of it. "It's because of the other volunteer. You felt you had to run the same risks, or you wouldn't do it for him. Right?"

John Hornby shrugged his shoulders. Looking out the window at the rural landscape of the Farm they were passing through, he seemed to grow even more serene and philosophical than usual.

"Perhaps. Only in part. I've been thinking about it for quite a while, as a matter of fact. I thought I might do it, but try to make it seem an accident – a case of accidental exposure. But I'm too vain a scientist to let anybody think I'd get myself into that kind of pickle. Then when you came along with your . . . volunteer . . . I made up my mind to start too."

Norman had been growing more and more restless at his side. He could hardly contain his feelings. At last he sputtered out his reaction. "That settles it then, John. I'm going to do it as well! Tomorrow morning I'm moving out of the Circle and joining you. We're in this together, as we've always been."

John Hornby had begun to shake his head slowly from side to side as soon as Norman started to talk, knowing what he was going to say. He continued to express his total opposition in this exaggerated way right to the entrance of the Centre, which they were now rapidly approaching.

"No, no, no, no, no, no, no. No way Norman. It just can't be. You're a family man. You have to go on with your normal life. You have to see to your wife and daughter and baby son. You can't ask them to make that kind of sacrifice. Any other way would be too great a risk for them, however you might get along with it yourself. Besides, there would be explanations, and the whole thing would blow up in public. No, Norman, you've got to be careful and patient and go on doing the job as if nothing has changed."

By now they were entering the laboratory. Inside, with the door slammed shut, Norman could rant and shout to his heart's content. He strode back and forth on his long legs in front of John, who was taking off his jacket and slipping into his white smock as if for an ordinary working day. With it half-buttoned he sat down, and at last there was a chance to interrupt.

"Now look, Norman, you're the one who has the hard part. You've got to continue as if nothing unusual was happening, keep up all the necessary pretences, give all the difficult explanations, ensure that the arrangements here at the Centre and at the Lodge and down at the Farm go smoothly. And you've got to make sure the records and reports are kept up to date and are accurate and fully useful. You've got to do what you can, living up to your Hippocratic oath, old man, to preserve life and health for all of us."

Hornby provoked a snort from Norman with this typical bit of irony. But he went on immediately to his most earnest statement. "Above all, you've got to learn everything that can be learned from these experiments, and be ready to go ahead – alone if you have to. Otherwise all the years we've been working together could be a terrible waste."

By the look on his face, Norman obviously considered the affair to be open and in debate still. John decided that the time had come to end that impression.

"Listen to me. If you don't do as I say," Hornby threatened, "the whole deal is off. Everything comes out in the open, everything, and we all take the consequences. That's my final word."

Norman collapsed into a chair and stared in amazement at the round face of his friend. He had never heard that tone of voice from him before in all their dealings over the years.

"You silly devil, you," he said, "I think you've already begun to react to the mere idea of the serum. You're behaving like a bloody pig-headed reckless adolescent."

Hornby grinned cheerfully in reply. He could see that with this outburst of abuse, Norman had truly given up. Then he got to his feet and became business-like.

"You're the only person I'll be in proximity with during my course of injections. For the foreseeable future I plan to move back and forth from my house, which is set up for complete isolation, to the lab – where with our usual restrictions, there will be no problems – at night, and at night only. I've already given explanations to the staff that sound plausible enough for the purpose. As far as you're concerned, you'll have to increase the standard precautions for yourself, in view of the kind of exposure you'll be getting."

As part of their standard practice, and in the context of their larger experimental and research concerns, they had regularly made use of thermotherapy to ensure their own protection from the laboratory-created virus. By now it was well-established that several harmless drugs could effectively raise body temperatures for the desired purgative results. Without secondary reactions, apart from slightly more active sleep and dream patterns which were certainly less extreme than those induced by, say, a case of influenza or other minor feverish aliment. It's safety was, from the earliest stages, a major successful achievement in their program.

Having said all he wanted to say on the subject, and having extracted reluctant guarantees from Norman that he would go on taking thermotherapy and other precautions conscientiously, John Hornby simply left him. He walked into the second room of the lab, where he could begin administering the serum to himself under clinically acceptable conditions.

Norman sat in the outer room for a moment, staring at the door closed in his face. Feeling alienated, shut out, as he had never been before in his relation with John Hornby and their work. Then he got up and strode away, expressing his frustration with a slam of the outer door loud enough to startle a pair of lab assistants talking at the other end of the corridor.

In a little while Norman was back in his house at the Circle, an empty house with Ella and Donna and the baby still away at the Farm, and seeming all the more so to his lonely mood. Preparing himself for bed, he slipped the needle containing the temperature-raising injection into his left arm and lay back on his pillows, taking full advantage of the unusual privilege of doing this at home, instead of having to be closeted for hours at the lab.

After a few minutes, during which his informed mind knew he was only imagining the inching up of his bodily heat so soon, he became impatient. He took a pillow from his bed, clutched the eiderdown to his chest, and stumbled downstairs to the television set. Easing onto the sofa in the way he had seen his wife do so often, he touched the remote control button and tuned in his favorite station, the Blue.

It was never quite the same any more, without new episodes starring Faye Delisle, but often the station was wise enough to play re-runs of the beautiful lady in her most torrid roles. He lay back on the sofa, prepared to spend the night there dozing and waking and dozing again, enjoying as he usually did the slightly euphoric state of mind thermotherapy always put him in.

Deep in the middle of the night Norman woke abruptly with a sense that someone was moving about in the house. He lay still, bathed in sweat, listening, curious in a rather dreamy way, but prepared to lie there and wait. First there was some quiet activity in the kitchen, and then he heard soft steps that he imagined were familiar coming along the hall.

"Dad, what are you doing up at this time of night?"

Donna stood in the doorway, surprise the most lively feature on her face, looking tired and bedraggled in her peasant dress, trailing her shawl along the floor.

"I could ask the same thing of you, my dear," Norman said sleepily.

Then his eyes opened wide and he sat up. He remembered why he was lying on the sofa in that state. His family was supposed to be gone for a week or so longer. He hadn't considered the possibility of being interrupted in the middle of thermotherapy.

"Listen, Donna my love, don't come in here, don't get any closer. I'm ... I'm kind of feverish, a touch of the 'flu, I think."

Donna stepped through the doorway and started to walk towards him.

"I'm not worried, Dad. I'm sorry you're feeling rotten. Let me take your temperature."

Norman stirred with a flare of panic. He had to stop her, but he couldn't tell her the truth. In the past he and John Hornby had shielded other people, especially Ella and Donna, who didn't have to know the risks of their work. Always before it had been possible to take the necessary precautions without giving anything away. It was a bit late to spring it on Donna now.

"Please, Donna, stop right where you are. I just don't want you to catch this thing. Think of the baby."

Donna stood a few feet away from him and looked down with a trace of mild outrage on her face at that suggestion. "It's funny to hear you coming on all grandfatherly all of a sudden. I didn't know you cared."

Norman ignored the reference to his feelings about her pregnancy. He had no intentions of getting into an argument about that now. "Just do as I say, Donna. Damn it all, I *am* a doctor. I should know what's sensible and what isn't."

Donna sighed and slid down on the rug at the side of the sofa. Norman found himself almost shrinking back to keep as far away from her as possible. He hardly had the strength to hold out against her stubbornness any longer.

The fever made him drift away from what was immediately important. But after a moments further thought, he realized that by now he was well out of the infectious stage. His temperature was back nearly to normal.

He could sense his mind wandering off to irrelevant matters, such as the fact that his daughter looked sadder and more tired than he had seen her in months. And the fact that, even so, she was a lovely child – not so much a child either, any more. Much more mature in body and in expression than he realized. Perhaps it was just the result of not having looked at her carefully for a while.

"What are you doing home now anyway?" Norman asked abruptly, as his mind clicked back into the present again. "Where's your mother? I thought you were going to be down there on the Farm for another week or so."

"Mother's there. With the baby. I decided to . . . I felt like coming home."

Norman rose higher from his pillow. His brow warmed again, as he focused on what she was saying. "You left your mother and the baby down there all by themselves? I don't understand. Have you two had a fight or something?"

Donna looked up at him sorrowfully. She gave the impression of desperately wanting to be with him, but not wanting to talk about all that. "Couldn't we just leave it for now, Dad? I really don't feel like discussing the Farm or Mother or . . . . It's nice to be here with you for a while."

Through the post-fever haze that seemed to hang like a cloud around his head, Norman peered down at his daughter with uneasy interest. It was puzzling to hear her talk to him in that tone. It was so out of character that it made him even more worried and suspicious.

"You haven't got into some trouble, have you? It's all very well for you not to want to talk about it, but there's your mother down there all by herself . . . ."

"She isn't all by herself," Donna said impatiently, perhaps even spitefully.

"You two *have* had a fight, haven't you?" Norman persisted.

He wasn't very concerned about Ella and the baby, despite his questioning. He had met Thelma Dean and Don Planter, the young couple his daughter and wife and baby were visiting at the Farm, and he thought them a reliable enough pair, as far as he could tell. There was nothing risky about ordinary life at the Farm, certainly, for a sensible adult. In fact, despite the absence of any conspicuous signs of organization and security, it was a virtual paradise of stability and peace. No traffic accidents, no crimes, no pollution, an idlers' dream.

Nevertheless he was surprised to discover that his daughter and wife could be on such bad terms all of a sudden, after having got along so well ever since they knew Donna was expecting. Norman's anger at that development had only made them draw closer together. And of course once Ella produced a baby boy, the two women became like sisters, competing in the attention they could give to the child.

"Dad, why did you and Mother decide to have another child?" Donna asked, ignoring her father's question.

"It wasn't really my decision," Norman answered with a touch of wryness. "Your mother wanted to. She had you when she was so young, she thought maybe she'd missed out on the real experience. Why do women ever want to have a child? Something to do. Something natural. She was unhappy. I don't really know . . . . Why do you ask?"

Donna sat with her legs crossed under her, picking at the threads of the shag carpet. Sometimes her fingers were quite savage. "I think it was because she's afraid of growing old. That's why she does a lot of things."

Norman eased back on the pillow and looked up at the plaster ceiling. His daughter was growing up. She was beginning to understand what adults were like, what made them tick, what they wanted and what they feared. They weren't just peculiar foreigners to her anymore. Soon she would be entirely one of them herself, not a child any longer, protected by ignorance or innocence.

"Of course she's afraid of growing old. Aren't we all?" Norman sighed. "And there is that great adage, Children keep you young. Not that I believed it. You've given me more grey hairs than all the rest of my troubles put together."

Donna rose to her knees and began to shuffle over to the sofa where his head rested on the pillow. "You haven't got a single grey hair anywhere," she said fondly, drawing nearer and attempting to put a hand on his forehead, on her knees close to the sofa.

Norman shrank away from her. He was still in his medical isolation mode. "Donna, don't touch me, you've got to keep your distance."

His daughter stopped her forward motion and dropped her hand to her breast. Her expression was shocked, hurt. Then she jumped to her feet and ran to the door. When she turned in the doorway, her face was already beginning to stream with tears.

"You're so cruel, father. You've always been so cruel, whenever I've really needed you. And you need me too, but you just won't admit it. That's why you're so alone. You don't know it, but you're very alone. . . . Alone."

She dashed out of the door, hurling the last word at him, and ran up the stairs to her room.

Sweat began to pour down Norman's neck again. He found himself breathless, weak, and almost giddy. He staggered to his feet and into the kitchen for another long, cool drink. His mind couldn't cope with this kind of uproar. He hardly understood what it was all about. What did she mean, you're alone. Alone.

He bundled himself up again on the sofa and brooded on her words. She was so angry, and yet so pitying at the same time. What was it all about? Where was his wife, and why had Donna come home by herself?

Towards dawn, having worn himself out with tossing and turning, he dropped into a deep sleep. The sun was shining fully into the room by the time he gradually surfaced to find himself still alive, wilted, weary, but quite comfortable and relaxed. He went upstairs, showered and shaved and dressed.

Then he walked along to Donna's room to start his talk all over again with her, in the hopes of doing better, memories of what both of them had said in the middle of the night burning confusingly in his thoughts.

The door of his daughter's room was a jar. Although her curtains were drawn, enough light showed through for Norman to be able to see the girl sprawled across her bed. She was in a deep sleep. Her breathing was regular. He took a step across the room to look down at her face. The sadness and tiredness of the night before were gone, though she'd been too weary to bother to take off her clothes or get under the covers. Her expression was peaceful, angelic.

It made Norman think of Ella, as Ella was at sixteen or seventeen. Ella, Norman now remembered, was pregnant at that age too. What was it for Donna? A month and a half, or two months? Donna still looked more like a child herself than a mother-to-be. But she had remained adamant. She was going through with the pregnancy.

After watching her for a few moments, Norman decided not to awaken her. For whatever reason, she was remarkably in need of sleep. He walked out, pulling the door shut quietly behind him.

Downstairs he called the Centre and informed them that he would arrive a couple of hours later than usual today. Then he went into the garden and got from the shed the old bicycle his wife had bought for him in the hopes that he would use it for pottering about the neighborhood with her, and for exercise. Without any very clear plan in mind, he was making his way down the winding and intersecting paths and lanes that led into the heart of the Farm. He wanted to see Ella and the baby. He thought he should, and right away.

He had never quite mastered the geography of the Farm. However, with the landmark of the hill and its invisible Lodge to serve as a general guide, he gradually made his way closer to the larger cluster of buildings which served to focus the life of the Farm. The mid-morning sun made cycling on this early June day pleasurable. He drew in sight of the big wooden barn near the bridge and stream, features of the place which he remembered and identified easily enough.

Here he was held up and obliged to wait as a herd of sleek Herefords were driven across the lane, out of one field and into another. The two younger women in jeans who were driving the cattle gave him their good mornings, and were going on to the other side of the pasture. When one of the young women hooked the gate-chain behind her, Norman decided to ask directions.

"I wonder if you could tell me if I'm on the right track to find Elm Cottage?"

"That's it over there," the young woman said, pointing past him to a clump of trees. "You'll have to go back the way you've come, if you want to take your bike. Turn left at the first chance."

In three minutes Norman was knocking on the green painted door of the cottage, which was half-open, giving a glimpse of its pioneer-style wooden furniture. His knock sounded hollowly down the corridor, but there was no sign of life. As he listened, he could hear from behind the cottage the low hum of a motor. After a few moments, he stepped back onto the path and began to follow it through the grass to the back of the cottage.

The sound was coming from a long cedar shed which had its open side away from the cottage. Norman walked far enough around to be able to see into it. A young woman in a patchwork smock, her hair done up in a bandana, had her back to him. She was turning a leg for a piece of furniture on a wood lathe. Norman watched until she finished the cut, put the calipers on it, found it true, and bent to adjust the lathe setting.

"Hello Thelma," he said above the hum of the motor.

She turned unhurriedly, as if used to having spectators behind her, and smiled her recognition. She touched the switch and turned the machine off with one hand, pulling the bandana from her head and loosening her hair with the other.

"Hello, Dr. Shearer. Welcome to the Farm. We don't see you here very often."

"I've come by to find out how you're all getting along. Mrs. Shearer and . . ."

Norman hesitated a moment, looking carefully at the fresh-faced pretty young woman for noticeable reactions. "And Donna and the baby."

"That's nice," Thelma said with an apparent simplicity and cheerfulness, "I'm making a crib for the baby, see? Ella really likes mine, and this is going to be just the same. Or at least, just as nice."

She held out a side piece for him to examine. He smoothed his hand over the wood and made suitably appreciative remarks.

"There was no answer at the door," he said finally, realizing that she wasn't on the point of telling him where his family was.

Thelma looked as if she were just focusing on his difficulty that moment.

"Oh, of course," she said "I've been with Don for the past couple of nights. Nobody was around when we came back this morning. I'm not sure where they could be."

She pursed her lips as she considered the possibilities. None of them seemed too certain, evidently. "I know they've been spending quite a bit of time with Roberto. You could try him."

"Both of them? All three of them?"

"Yes, all three," Thelma said with an amused air. "Roberto has been working on a Madonna and Child idea. Or as he says, 'Me, Donna, and Child'. Isn't that a terrible pun?" she concluded, screwing her face up and groaning her disapproval of that kind of humor.

Norman grinned indulgently. He was not at all amused. In fact, the utter casualness of life on the Farm had never infuriated him more than now. These people seemed to take it for granted you could wander back and forth from one establishment to another as the will drove you and opportunity allowed.

He had disliked the idea of Donna and Ella and the baby getting mixed up with them any more than they already had. But Ella had been so restless, and so curious to get a first-hand look at how they did things down here, that he could hardly say no. He could hardly, in this age of liberalism and enlightenment, keep wife and family under lock and key. Still, he had counted on a certain amount of normal discretion and common sense, on Ella's part if not on Donna's.

"Thank you, Thelma, if you could point me in the right direction for Roberto's place, I'll go along and see if I can catch up to them there."

He was soon bicycling off to find the House in a Field, having left a message with Thelma so that if she saw his wife and daughter (he kept up the pretence that he didn't know where she was) before he did, Ella should call him at home later. The route to Roberto's house took him over the bridge and along the river path. At one point, a young man, shirtless, deeply tanned, a reddish beard to match the hair on his chest, approached from the opposite direction, jogging bare-back on a Percheron type horse. As they exchanged good mornings, Norman took the chance to check his directions.

"I'm looking for Roberto. Am I going the right way?"

"Yes you are," the young man said jauntily. "I just left that devil climbing into his hammock over there."

He pointed down the lane and to a clump of tall trees in the field to the left.

"You'll see a gap in the hedge," he added, as he jogged off, before Norman could ask anything further.

Although he was a little puzzled, Norman turned in through the gap in the hedge, wheeling his bike. He was realizing that the conflict in direction was because the footpath led to where Roberto himself happened to be at that moment, whereas the lane must lead to his home.

The path opened up into a small clearing shaded by half a dozen immense oak trees. Suspended from the spreading branch of one was a hammock, and stretched out in it, hands dangling on either side, one foot hooked over at the other end, was the young man Norman had first seen, looking much the same, but reclining in the bottom of a boat. At the jangle of the bicycle drawing near, Roberto lifted his hat from over his eyes, and gazed up at the visitor.

"Man on a Bike," he said, raising himself on his elbows, "You look worried."

With experience to teach him, Norman was determined not to get distracted.

"I'm looking for my wife and my . . . children. I understand you might know where they are."

"My wife. My children. You see what happens?" Roberto said, lying back in the hammock again, and fanning himself in long easy sweeps with his large-brimmed hat. "When people are possessions, they get lost like possessions. You can be deprived of your possessions. Trapped by your possessions. It's a terrible thing to have possessions."

"An interesting theory," Norman said drily, leaning on his bicycle wearily. "At the moment, I'm rather anxious to find out where these people are. Can you help me? I was told they might be at your house."

"Ah," Roberto said, resting his hat on his breast and staring hard at Norman. "That might well be."

"Don't you know?" Norman asked impatiently.

Roberto studied him for a moment again before answering.

"I haven't been to the House in a Field for . . . . "

He counted silently to himself, putting out the fingers of one hand and closing them again several times.

"Eleven nights."

"So you haven't seen them for eleven nights?"

Roberto shook his head.

"Yes, I've seen them, all three of them, many times. Here, at the river, other places. We've been working together. *Your* wife, *your* daughter," he went on emphasizing the possessive pronoun with a cheerful irony, "they have a great need to express themselves, to free themselves. They learn quickly. I think it's been good for them to work with me. They've been good for me, to me, that's for sure."

He smiled warmly at Norman, inviting him to share in this mood of appreciation and generosity generated by the relationship with his family. It was hard to be sour in face of such geniality. But Norman succeeded.

"So you don't know where they are now? They're not at your house, anyway?"

Roberto shrugged his shoulders. Clearly his mood was too self-contained and happy to be disturbed by someone else's.

"Perhaps they're at the House in the Field. I doubt it, but perhaps they are. Our man is living there now."

For a moment the remark went past Norman without effect. Then he gripped the handlebars of his bicycle so fiercely he lifted the front wheel from the ground.

"Do you mean Garth Hamilton?" he thundered.

Roberto seemed oblivious to the agitation in the visitor's face and voice.

"Garth wanted to be by himself. Everyone does from time to time. What better place than the House in the Field?"

"And do you have any idea," Norman said evenly through gritted teeth, "why Garth Hamilton wanted to be by himself?"

Again Roberto shrugged his shoulders. It was clearly not his concern. According to his philosophy, nothing could be more normal. It was neither necessary nor desirable to probe for reasons. "Maybe a special trip?" Roberto suggested. "A very special trip. It's nice to go away sometimes," he went on, a little dreamily, as if remembering similar occasions in his own life. "No one would disturb him at the House in a Field if he put out the sign. He could come back when he was ready."

Norman had lifted his bicycle by the handlebars and turned it back in the direction he had come from. His tone was still icily controlled. "Would it be likely, then, that anyone would visit him there?"

Roberto raised both his hands, the one holding the brim of his hat and the free one, expressing the openness of the possibility. "Only if our man wanted company, not otherwise."

Norman was off and peddling, churning with agitation so strongly he didn't know whether he had or hadn't offered a goodbye or a thank you over his shoulder. In a few minutes' brisk rolling, he reached the long lane that led up to the House in a Field. Half way along it, was a set of picket gates ajar. Hanging from the gate latch by a chain was a small wooden sign with the word PEACE etched in it. Evidently the Farm's equivalent of No Trespassing or Do Not Disturb.

When Norman got to the door of the one-storey building, he dropped his bicycle on the grass and knocked loudly, again and again. Despite his attempt at self-control, he found himself pounding with his fist.

"I think he's flown the coop," came a voice from the lane behind him, as he dropped his fist and tried to peer into the window. A bearded young man with a knap-sack on his back and astraddle a bicycle had obviously just arrived behind Norman. He had a worried look on his face, as Norman whirled to confront him.

"Where's he gone?" Norman demanded.

The young man put down his bicycle and come to stand beside Norman.

"I'm afraid I don't know that. I've been out asking around, and nobody seems to have seen him. He sent the overnight nurse away last night after supper. Convinced her he felt fine and was going to sleep late. I came right over as soon as she reported to me this morning.... You're Dr. Shearer, aren't you?"

He looked up into Norman's startled face and put out his hand. "I'm Allen Crossland, Dr. Crossland."

"How did you know who I was?" Norman asked, still taken aback by the other's rushing words.

"Who else would know about this Garth Hamilton business? There's only John Hornby, me, and the staff here, yourself, and Garth. Unless he's gone and done something stupid."

With Norman hard behind him, Crossland stepped up to the door and pushed it open. Inside, the kitchen utensils looked as if they had been put in use recently, and the big bed had its covers strewn about as if it had just been rather energetically slept in.

"I've already had a good look around this morning," Crossland said. "I'm sure Garth was here last night, but it's this note that worries me."

He handed Norman a folded sheet of paper taken from his trouser pocket. "It was waiting for me on the table."

Norman unfolded it and read the careful, round, boyish hand that half-covered one side.

"I have to go somewhere, Allen. I'm not sure whether I'll come back. If I don't, call the chiefs together and elect a new Chief of the Chiefs. Ask Business to fill you all in on the Trust, etc. Nothing to worry about financially. As for me? I'm happy, in a sad sort of way. Thanks for everything. Peace, my friend. Garth."

"What the hell does this mean?" Norman asked, turning it over in his hands several times as if to find further clues.

"I really don't know," Allen said, perching on the corner of the table and tugging thoughtfully at his beard. "I never expected this. But for the past few days his moods have fluctuated even more than usual. Of course he's always been moody – a little on the manic-depressive side, if you put any stock in those labels. But this was different."

"In what way?" Norman asked, despite his wide-ranging worry, voicing his curiosity about the clinical evidence.

"For one thing, the fluctuations seemed quicker and more extreme, from mature to adolescent and back again. He was talking about his father a lot the past few times I was here, as if he were. . . . ."

"Reverting? Reverting to an earlier phase of their relationship?" Norman asked, held for a moment by the fascination of yet another case history.

Either his accuracy of insight or his absorption in the topic obviously surprised Allen Crossland. He looked up at Norman with considerable interest showing on his round face.

"Yes, a good way of putting it. That's exactly how it struck me."

Suddenly Crossland leaped off the table and ran across the room to a corner. He pulled a cloth from a small table to look at what was underneath, and to show it to Norman.

It was an audio recorder.

"I forgot about this," Allen said, as he bent over the machine and examined it. "It's been used quite a bit. Garth was being very conscientious about this experiment, though you wouldn't think so now, maybe. He wanted to do everything you and Dr. Hornby asked. For the benefit of science, as he always put it. I wonder if we might get some idea about what's going on from the recorder."

Norman strode over to look down at the machine.

"It's run right out," he said, pointing to the indicator. "That's odd. It wasn't turned off."

Crossland picked up the machine and carried it to the kitchen table. There they both stood looking at it again, each waiting for the other to speak.

"Shall we listen to it now?" Crossland said at last. "At least just the last bit?"

Norman slumped into a chair at the opposite side of the table and nodded by way of answer. He put a hand over his eyes, as if to concentrate better on the voice. But at first there was no voice, just a few indecipherable bumps and knocks and crashes.

"I'll start it farther back," Crossland said, from his chair, leaning forward to make the adjustment.

When it ran again, the next few minutes of sound were undeniably bedroom noises. To Norman it seemed remarkably like part of the sound track of any of a hundred Blue Television episodes. As it proceeded, a look of belated realization appeared on Crossland's face, turned to amusement, and then rapidly gave way a deepening dismay. He stared across at Norman Shearer, who stoically avoided his gaze, keeping his eyes buried in his hand.

The noises increased in intensity, the sounds of bedsprings, the swish of bed-clothes, and above all the moans, not articulating any words, barely identifiable as human, growing louder and longer, rising, at first mostly female and then with hypnotizing crescendos a counterpart of male and female – the two reaching at last the limits of the bearable.

It all climaxed rapidly in an agonizing shriek, neither female nor male, neither single nor double, but some ecstatic fusion of the two. Silence followed. Silence for so long that Crossland leaned forward as if he thought he should turn it off.

Whether it was that greater experience made him a better diagnostician, or that his curiosity was stronger, or for whatever reason, Norman took his hand off his eyes long enough to gesture to Crossland to leave the controls alone. Then the hand went back over the eyes again, and he resolutely sat motionless as a statue until the last evidence of the recording was heard.

It had begun to give out sounds of movement again. Stirrings, quiet stirrings. Sighs. Then, for the first time since they started listening, audible, comprehensible words, fragmentary phrases. Exactly when Norman positively identified the woman's voice as that of his wife, he didn't indicate overtly in the slightest degree. At no time did Allen Crossland show any signs of recognition either, whether because he didn't know, or because not to know fitted his idea of a gentleman.

Ah, good.

Very good.

You're sooooo . . . .

You.

That was . . . crazy. Put your hands here, I can still . . . . Here.

Christ.

Don't swear in front of the child.

Ha, do you mean him or me?

Funny man.

Did we wake him?

Sleeping like a lamb. It would take an earthquake.

Wasn't that an earthquake?

Bomb.

Hurricane.

Tidal wave.

Are you always . . . ?

Are you?

Never.

Me neither.

Don't lie.

Gradually the sleepy voices began to become more audible, to separate more clearly into male and female. To take on recognizable characteristics, personalities. And then gradually the female voice became more silent, and the male voice took over, until it was virtually a monologue. An eloquent, lyrical, absurd but fascinating monologue. A celebration in words, a eulogy of sex, of sex and beauty and youth. An impromptu poem in free verse. It went on and on, until gradually the male voice faded away into silence.

"I should go," the woman said, abruptly breaking the mood.

"Christ," the man said, as if waking sharply out of his own speaking dream, "you shouldn't have been here in the first place."

"Aren't you sweet?" said the woman, with more amusement than sarcasm.

"No, I mean it. I'm not supposed to have anybody within half a mile of me. That's what I told you at the door. Medical regulations. You could get real sick, especially the baby."

"Babies have a great natural resistance to germs. And because of my husband's profession, I'm immune to everything. Besides, what could you do? You couldn't turn us away at the door, could you?"

"No, I sure couldn't," the man's voice agreed throatily. Then with urgency, "But now, you must know, you've got to do stuff, take care of yourself, the baby, you must know all about that thermotherapy stuff . . . ."

Cutting across his voice, the woman's. "Hush, I know all that. I know what to do. Remember? My husband's a doctor."

This was followed by an absence of words, but barely audible sighs and stirrings. Then in the background came the whimpering of an awakening infant.

"What's the matter with him?" the man's worried voice asked.

"He's hungry, of course. Time for his night feed," the woman laughed. "You don't know very much, do you? You're really just a baby yourself, even though you do have a lovely long beard."

"Hey, that hurts," the man's voice cried.

The whimpering of the baby came closer, and then it was silenced abruptly, and for several minutes there were only mother-with-babe-at-the-breast sounds. The man spoke again. "So that's how Roberto gets to see you, Madonna and Child."

"Oh, Roberto. He's very sweet. But all he does is look, he never paints. Is there really anything to this instant art of his? Sometimes I think he's even more of a baby than you are, taking himself so seriously and always talking, talking, talking, never doing anything."

"Ah, but you've never seen him at work in a public concert," the man's voice objected. "It's something you'll never forget. Ask your daughter. He made a convert of her."

"I thought it was you who made the convert of her . . . . You know, this is so cruel. How could we do this to her?"

The man's voice broke through with a new energy and exuberance. He was refusing to join in the mood of worry, guilt, or whatever it was.

"There's no cruelty in loving, none, never. She has to learn, she won't learn any younger. She needed me and I needed her and it was fine. Then you needed me and I needed you – how I needed you – and it was . . . fine. She'll have a thousand lovers before she's as old as . . . ."

The man was silenced in mid-sentence as if a hand had been placed over his mouth. The woman finished the sentence. "As old as her mother? Maybe. But I don't think she'll forgive me very easily. Or you."

"Oh, well, forgiveness . . . ," the man murmured.

There was another long pause, and then the male voice started again in a different tone, moodier, more thoughtful, more in turned.

"What is she? Sixteen? Seventeen? My mother died when I was seventeen. She was killed in a car accident. Afterwards my father had some kind of sex fit, I guess. His own form of nervous breakdown. He began to screw every woman within reach – and he had a very long reach, right around the world. I never used to know what woman would be coming home for dinner or slipping out of the house the next morning. Some of them tried to be nice to me . . . . I guess I was a little bastard. I know I took the whole thing pretty hard. My father and I never spoke to each other again really – except once, a couple of years later, when he talked me into starting this commune. Yeah, the Farm was his idea to begin with. Daddy's best toy for the boy who has everything."

"Garth," the woman said pityingly. "I've never heard you sound so bitter."

The man's voice came back at once more brightly. "I'm not bitter, really, not any more. All that's in the past. But right now, maybe it's this damned dope I'm on, I find myself thinking a lot about those days. I guess, inside, I realize now that I abandoned my old man as much as I used to think he abandoned me. More so probably. After all, he was a man whose very success made him a kind of a loner. For all the hangers-on who leeched onto him, or tried to. I'd like to think we could talk to each other now. Despite the fact that we're so different – in attitudes, ideas and in age of course . . . . He's the most motivated man I've ever known, and I'm completely without motivation. But we're family. I guess that's all there is to it. Blood. It seems ridiculous, I don't believe in family, blood. I believe you can have a genuine relation with anybody – or not have one – just as you can with somebody you happen to be connected with in that way. But even so, I keep thinking of the son of a bitch. I like him. And now he's going to die."

As if reacting to those words, the baby's voice rose to a sharp wail. The woman began to make soothing sounds. For a little while there was the confusion of the infant being passed back and forth and changed and settled.

"There, there, he'll be alright now, won't you, little man," came the woman's cooing voice. "Garth, why don't you just go and see your father? If you feel that way, I'll bet it's just the same for him."

The young man snorted derisively. "You don't know Chadwick Hamilton. Can you imagine what he'd do if I ever walked in his front door? He'd say, 'What the hell brings you across my threshold for the first time in ten years?' I haven't seen him anywhere face to face for four or five years, except on tele-screen. I've never been inside that crazy place he's built up there on the hill, though everybody seems to think it's the greatest thing since the Taj Mahal. Before that, do you know we used to have a little cabin up there, a shack really, and he'd take me swimming in the lake. Not that he'd remember that, now that he's ruined the place. Anyway, one thing he's not, and that's a sentimentalist. The last thing in the world he'd want would be a death-watch."

"Garth, don't be so fierce. You're only hurting yourself. Come here."

There was the sound of stirring and bed-springs moving.

"Yes, just put your head here. There's room for both of you. You won't disturb him. He's already in dreamland. That's why a woman is given two breasts, so there's always a place for another baby. Yes, you are a baby. I think that's why you wanted me, really. That's what you wanted. What's another woman's body to you? You've had so many women, haven't you? But a mother. You really do need a mother, don't you? Yes you do, you do, don't you? You do."

The sound of the woman's voice went on, repeating again and again, soothingly, abandoning the meaning of particular words. The tone became softer as it became less articulate, rhythmical, hypnotic. Then without any real transition it lifted gently, lifted into song, a wordless humming, a lilting of vowels and consonants, a lullaby without form but drifting sweetly on and on. Gradually it grew softer still, quieter, until all the recorder could pick up was the faint sounds of breathing and sighing.

For several minutes the two men sat at the table in the House in a Field, listening to the silence of the room as it had been a few hours earlier. Norman, with his hand over his eyes, was able to disguise the fact that they were wet. Crossland had shifted sideways, so that he was gazing across the room, at the unmade bed, and out the half-open door. He avoided looking around as Norman got to his feet and stepped out into the open air. After a minute he turned off the recorder and followed the other man as far as the doorway.

Norman was standing with his hands at his sides looking up to the hill that could be seen catching the mid-day sun.

"I guess that's the best bet," Allen Crossland said, nodding towards the hill. "One of us should go and check it out. Maybe if you would do that," Crossland continued, since Norman showed no response, "control the damage up there, to anybody, and I could take care of this place. Make sure it's decontaminated and tidy things up and look after the serum and arrange to have it and the recorder sent back to you and Dr. Hornby."

With a shake of his shoulders, Norman Shearer seemed to take hold of himself enough to concentrate on these practicalities. He turned to face Crossland.

"Yes, of course. I think that's the best plan. There's no use keeping this place set up any longer. If we do find Garth Hamilton, we can't go on with the experiment. After all this."

"Will you call me from the Lodge? I'm in touch with the Farm switchboard."

Crossland tapped his hip pocket to indicate the electronic bleeper he had there for emergencies, so typical of the Farm's combination of rustic and technologically advanced. Norman nodded, and turned to pick up his bicycle. On second thoughts, he faced Crossland again. He held out a hand to the young man and shook with him gravely, looking down into his round face, which was touched with concern.

"I hope we meet again in slightly pleasanter circumstances," he said, managing a trace of a wry smile.

He cycled down the lane, glancing over his shoulder once at the picket gates to see Allen Crossland still standing in the doorway of the House in a Field. Then he began the long circular ascent which would take him to the Lodge.

For several hours Chadwick Hamilton had been lying awake in his big bed in the Lake Room. He liked the early mornings there especially. If the night were outstandingly bright, the floor of the quarry lake, which was also his ceiling, would remain light enough for faint shapes and glimmerings to be constantly in movement above. Then as the sun rose gradually, even more gradually than the dawn itself the dark tints lightened, and the movements became more articulated. It was like the steady growth of experience, intelligence, consciousness itself, spreading and becoming more detailed and richer. Chadwick Hamilton owned many expensive works of art by many great artists, living and dead, but nothing pleased him so much and so often to look at as this spectacle, always changing, always the same.

He had been using the early waking hours, when he was alone, in his typical way, these last few months. To review his condition, to be sure he was in control of his life. When the first news of his illness had been broken to him by his personal physician, and confirmed by the best cancer experts around the world, his immediate thought was -- at all costs he had to retain control of his life.

The cancer might kill him, if the doctors were right it certainly would, but as far as possible the manner and moment of death would remain in his own hands. He had seen too many acquaintances drag themselves or be dragged ignominiously into oblivion, disgusting physical relics, unrecognizable personalities, to be willing to tolerate that kind of fate for himself.

Practically speaking, his main worry was not to let the end creep up on him, so that he might find his powers of decision and action atrophied before he realized it. That was why the Hornby-Shearer serum seemed the best treatment of last resort. It held out the promise at the very least of burning out in a bright, intense, youthful flare.

This morning was both deeply worrying and pleasing to him in a strange way. Pleasing, because as he lay back on the pillows and watched the light broaden across the bottom of the lake above his head, he was confident that he could see things clearly in his own life and was capable of deciding and acting. Deeply worrying because, with that clarity, he knew that the moment was drawing very close.

For three years he had been happier with one woman, Alice Devers, than he could remember being ever before in his entire life. It was an unexpected discovery at his age, long after he had ceased to take sex seriously as a shared experience for two people exploring the possibilities of a continuing relationship. Last night it became obvious to him, no doubt to her too, that the golden epoch might almost be over. If that was finished, it was hard to appreciate anything else that might be left.

Last night had followed the pattern they had agreed on, and it had gone by reassuringly in the usual way for most of the evening. When Chad had first decided to go on the new therapy, there was the problem of Alice. Did it mean he would have to forego any kind of intimate relations with her for fear of infecting her? That would have been intolerable.

So they arranged for Alice, on most days and nights of the week, to take all the clinical precautions that anyone dealing with the serum and its applications had to take to ensure sterile conditions. Avoiding close physical proximity, of course. But in addition – and Chad appreciated the delicacy with which Dr. Shearer made this perfectly clear, without innuendo or prudery -- if at any time Alice were to be seriously exposed to risks, she would have to resort to the most effective form of thermotherapy to ensure her protection.

At first Chad had reservations about the dangers, and about the unpleasantness of overcoming them. But he was reassured when he discovered that thermotherapy was relatively easy to undergo, and had as its most notable consequences a brief period of dreaming or hallucinating. It was Alice who convinced him privately that as far as she was concerned, this was not a matter of importance.

"It's just like birth control," she teased him over their wine glasses, "it's always the woman who has to take the precautions, whether the man does or not."

Once a week, after a week-long elaborate and rather delightful game of aloofness and delicate distance, Alive Devers stepped through the medical barriers separating them so tantalizingly, and slipped into his arms. For Chad these occasions were like his early days with Alice, when she was employed by the government committee he agreed to serve on, and she was waiting for a divorce decree to come through, and they could only meet secretly and far less frequently than they wanted. Chad became a young man again, except that he had all the experience of three or four decades of sexual plundering behind him.

Whether it was physical characteristics that matched, the right angles, the right thresholds, the right words, or whether it was because for the first time in his life Chad was making love to a woman whom, despite her youth and inexperience, he thought was his equal in all the abilities that had brought him to money and power – whatever the reason, with her he was a deeply satisfied man.

As for Alice? He didn't feel he had to ask questions that went too far below the surface. She was flourishing, that was obvious. Flourishing in ways that he had made possible, as no younger, less successful man could have. In the world of business, he opened up areas for her to move in that she could never have moved in without his help, and she proved herself daily. It was tremendously challenging and exciting for her, and exciting for him to watch and teach and applaud. It was like having an ambitious, brilliant offspring taking over more and more of the family enterprise.

And in other ways? Well, how can you ever tell for sure a woman is happy? Alice made jokes about all the women who had preceded her, without showing the slightest signs of jealousy or concern. Henry the Eighth, she called him, when in a particularly affectionate mood. But whether from sustained determination, or out of her own natural magnificence, she eclipsed them all – in vitality, variety, and what seemed her own real hunger.

"You always were an ambitious little girl," Chad murmured into her long black hair, late last night, as she tried again to arouse him.

It was he who had let the side down finally. It was he who, even before his illness, faded a little after the first enthusiasm of three or four years ago – a fading natural enough, in a man in his late fifties, after all, and not enough to worry him at the time. It was he who began to take a more benign view of their sexual enterprises, enjoying earlier memories, though recognizing the less daring and ambitious ventures in the present for what they were.

And it was Alice, naturally enough again, who seemed to grow restless and frustrated, though she emphatically declined his perhaps not entirely sincere suggestion that she should meet and enjoy the company of some younger men.

Then came the shattering news of his illness, and her loyalty to him was no longer a matter she would allow to be questioned, even as a joke.

In reaction to the Hornby-Shearer serum, or perhaps at the suggestions that merely taking it aroused, Chad at first reverted to the ardor of their early days. Alice by then had settled into a cooler, quieter kind of relation, and he soon sensed that she almost resented the belated disturbance. She didn't want the upset and fury that he suddenly wanted to provoke. She had become middle-aged, he had grown young. A ridiculous paradox.

But then last night, as if with repeated attempts the fire had finally caught, Alice came to him in the old, old way. He had felt good, wonderfully surprised and full of enthusiasm and welcome. He was deeply happy to recognize her again as a woman whose powers, emotional, intellectual, sexual, he found irresistible. And giving herself to him with a completeness that was overwhelming, that for the first time in his life, with genuine modesty, he believed he didn't deserve.

He knew that in many ways he still had the body of a man half his age. The malignant tumor had as yet made its presence known mainly by a loss of general condition, from his not leading as active and energetic a life as he wanted to and had always done. He was used to joking about how his magnificent physique was preserving him from the damage the doctors were trying to do to him. There was an element of truth in this picture.

It didn't worry him too much right away, when he found himself ineffectual, lying naked in the big bed in the middle of the Lake Room, with only thin silk separating Alice's waiting, eager body from his own. He had known impotence as a passing experience, caused by recognizable temporary forces and situations, too much to drink, too many women in too short a time, just plain lack of interest with other more important things on his mind. But with Alice there had rarely been anything more important at the moments when they were together in that way.

He tried and she tried. He was determined, and she was ardent, ingenious. Nothing would work. They lay back and looked up at the murky shadows of the lake floor above their heads, holding hands, in silence. Chad gave a deep shuddering sigh.

"It had to be, sooner or later," he whispered hoarsely.

"Don't make too much of it, it doesn't matter," Alice said, burying her face in his bare shoulder. "Rest, sleep, and we'll wake in the night."

"It does matter?" he said loudly, angrily, to the ceiling. "I won't live like that, half a man. It's . . . . it's not worth it. I don't understand, I've been feeling so good."

Alice began to rub his chest over his heart in long slow circles.

"Of course it matters, you're right. But it's not all that matters. Besides, it isn't the first time. Remember at Barcelona – or was it Valencia? – three years ago? You had about as much virility as a wet cabbage leaf. I danced for you every night for a week, and you could hardly raise an eyebrow."

Despite his gloom, Chad laughed at the memory. "Well I was sick, very sick. Damned ptomaine poisoning, wasn't it? Rotten fish. Every time I tried to put a hand on you, I threw up."

"It wasn't very flattering at the time," Alice murmured.

She had become more and more preoccupied with her stroking. The sweeps got slower and moved lower. She explored his firm body with the most gentle yet persistent curiosity, as if she were touching him for the first time. That's when he made his remark.

"You always were an ambitious little girl."

He said it quietly, sighing, relaxing, arms stretched over his head, waiting but not really with much hope. He had given up.

"That's a rather ambiguous thing to say," Alice murmured, continuing her progress over his body.

Gradually, discovering for herself that there was to be no intense focus of interest for his physical presence, but with her generous and attentive movements leaving the impression that that fact was of only passing curiosity in her journey, Alice ventured on all over his flesh with hand and mouth. Your body is alive to me, her touches were saying, all parts equally fascinating and attractive. I expect nothing of it but to yield to and receive my sensuous contact, my massage, my messages.

His breathing deepened. Slowly her movements shortened and came to a soft halt, leaving her close and still beside him. It seemed as though he had slipped into sleep imperceptibly. But then his calm, quiet speaking voice rose into the darkness.

"You must find someone else now, Alice. You're too wonderful to waste."

Her answer was immediate, equally quiet and unperturbed. "Someday, perhaps, my love. A long long time from now. It can never be like this, with you – with anyone else."

They turned to each other and wrapped arms and held on tightly, nakedness against nakedness, close despite the years and the disease that separated them, as tears scalded their faces. Then, after a long while, both slept, unaware of the last glimmerings of the lake floor above their heads.

It didn't surprise or worry Chadwick Hamilton to find Alice Devers gone when he woke. During the past months, medications and treatments had often stunned him into sleep at odd hours and for long periods of time. Alice came and went whenever she and he needed. She was never gone for longer than he could tolerate, and never there for no purpose. On the whole he admired her for keeping to the kind of work that she had been doing before, long and taxing hours, when they were able to be full business partners involved in the day to day challenges and excitements of his wide-spread financial and communications empire. It didn't matter to him anymore, but he was glad it did to her.

But the sense of absence and loss was nevertheless strong upon him, as he lay watching the morning light reach downwards and over the bottom of the lake above his head. In this mood he could understand how some people found the Lake Room oppressive. Of course he could fill it with vivid artificial illumination at the touch of a button. But as much as possible, he preferred to let nature throw what light it was going to. Today, the sun would likely be bright enough, judging by the early indications.

Up above and looking down, a person on the hill would see a sight which everyone assured Chad Hamilton was truly beautiful. The clear water of the spring-fed lake, changing shades from blue to green and back again as the day progressed, was like a deep-set precious stone, embedded in the white rock of the quarry.

Chad lay back on his pillow watching the morning sun shaft its light through the changing facets of that jewel, the one he valued most of the many he owned. His body was relaxed, his mind crystal-clear. An immense sense of confidence flowed through him, as he satisfied himself that indeed he did have control of his faculties, his destiny, within certain inevitable limits realistically assessed.

The experience with Alice was saddening, but it was also comforting in a way. Having it all so clear in his mind was a source of great strength. In the near future he might lose some of that secure mastery, but he was sure that he would retain enough to be able to act when the time came, not just be acted upon by the fates.

Looking upwards at the waving plants and the movement of fish, Chad found his attention drawn by a disturbance on the surface that was changing rhythms of light cascading through the water diagonally towards the lake bottom.

As he watched, an intruding dark shadow, larger than any of the creatures who made the lake their home could have made, fluttered downwards and then up again, creating chaos among the small fish. Annoyance at having the lake's tranquility disturbed touched Chad's mind at the same time as bewilderment. No boat, no raft – no swimmer – entered these waters without his permission and without his knowing.

He touched the panel at his bedside, and brilliant spotlights shot upwards through the glass and into the water, meeting head on the downward light from the sky, and leaving all objects in their path even more vividly lit. With a turn of his hand on a lever, Chad guided the lights back and forth through the depths, searching. Suddenly the distorted shape of a swimmer swept into view, growing larger as it descended, a naked body with flowing hair, arms and legs waving in the effort to dive deeper. As the lights fixed onto the shape, it abruptly turned upwards again, glimmering, diminishing as it surfaced.

Chad was about to press a button for the attention of his staff when something made him hesitate. A minute later the shape came billowing and rippling downwards once more, following the beam of light from the Lake Room as if swarming down a ladder.

F. W. WATT

Chad watched with growing fascination as the shape reached right to the glass, seemed in fact to be trying to press for entry, to pound – of course with no effect – and to signal. And then Chad thought he could see, in the bright focus of the spotlight beams, a figure he could recognize, a face, even an expression. Imagination, perhaps. What swimmer would dare to trespass in that sanctuary?

Quickly Chad switched the spotlight on and off several times, signaling in return, however ambiguously. The figure shot back towards the surface, leaving a trail of bubbles rising slowly after it.

It would be several hours before any of the staff would normally be in to see him, unless he called. Chad had no intention of waking them until he found out if his wild guess about the swimmer was true or not. He swung his feet onto the floor and strode naked to the far side of the Lake Room. Through the first set of double doors was the dressing room, and beyond it the lock room, empty of water now, just a tiled shaft open to the sky twenty or thirty feet above.

Chad stood naked in the middle of the lock room, stared upwards, and addressed the patch of blue sky high above with a low warbling whistle.

As it echoed up the tiled shaft, Chad found it at the same time strange and familiar to his own ears. He hadn't made that sound for many, many years, probably not since his son was twelve or fifteen. It was an inspired message to the sky. Only one person could understand it. The echoes died and there was silence.

Chad tried again, a little louder, a little more drawn-out. The sounds had barely died when from above, seemingly far, far away, a faint returning whistle found its way down the shaft. It warbled to its end, and then it started up again and went through the same soft melody, coming closer. Chad watched the edge of the tiled shaft, where the lock gate opened into the lake, where the water of the lake lapped within inches of the top. He whistled again, and before he was through, a dripping head lifted over the bulwark of the lock gates and peered down.

Chad stood still in the middle of the shaft floor, hands on hips, head bent back. The face of the other peered down at him from twenty-five feet above, water dripping from hair and beard. And the voice came echoing downwards. "What the hell are you doing down in that hole without any clothes on, Dad?"

"What the hell are you doing up there in my lake, you son of a bitch?"

Abruptly they both burst out laughing, in big booming, identical male voices.

"I heard you lived under a lake, Dad, but I didn't really believe it. How do I get down there?"

"Stay put. I'll send a raft up this way with the water. Just get in and float your ass down here. I'll be waiting for you, you clown, you."

Chad Hamilton shook a fist playfully at the figure of his son, and stepped back out of the lock room. A touch on the switch panel outside sent the machinery into motion with the sound of rushing water dimly audible from outside.

Chad stepped back into the Lake Room and walked slowly back to his bed. He was tired, his head was whirling, but he was exhilarated at the same time. He hadn't spoken to his son in the flesh for four or five years at least. He hardly knew how to react, or what to expect. But under all the mixture of emotions, he was glad. The timing was perfect. He hadn't thought it would happen, he would never have asked Garth to come. But this was a very good moment.

He climbed into bed and pulled the covers up around his shoulders. Several minutes later he heard the lock room doors open. "In here, Garth," he called through the open hall door.

Garth stood in the doorway, a towel he had picked up from the dressing room wrapped around his shoulders, his hair and beard glossy from the water, his feet and legs bare. He peered all around the Lake Room before entering, as if to get his bearing prior to making the plunge. "It looks a little different from down here," he called across the room, stepping towards the bed in the middle, still craning his head upwards, "what happens if you spring a leak?"

"That's my little secret," Chad said, indicating that at the very least the topic had come up before with visitors to the Lake Room. "Where are your clothes?"

"I only had a pair of jeans," Garth said with a grin, slumping down in a chair by the bed and rubbing his head and beard energetically with the towel, "they were so dirty and the water was so clean I thought I should take them off."

"You always did like skinny dipping," Chad said, grinning at him. "You're a little hairier now than you were in those days, though."

Garth stopped rubbing his beard and sat looking at his father, a hand still holding the towel end to his face. "I didn't think you would remember those days."

He gave a slightly ironic emphasis to the phrase 'those days', inviting whatever weight his father cared to put on them. Chad, settled deeply into the pillows, seemed unlikely to react adversely. He didn't know why his son had come. He didn't particularly want to know right now. He was content that it should have worked out that way.

"As a matter of fact, I've been thinking a lot about the past," Chad said. "I'm a sort of semi-invalid now, and you have lots of time to think when you spend fifteen or twenty hours a day in bed."

"You've got Shearer and Hornby working on you now. I know all about that. How is it coming?"

"Oh, hell," Chad said, throwing up his hands, "they're curing the disease and killing the patient."

There was a moment's silence while Garth digested this bit of information. Then suddenly again, together as if on cue, they burst into wild laughter. When the laughter died down, Chad spoke first. "I've been trying to keep a hold on myself. This therapy does funny things to your state of mind . . . ."

"Yeah, it does, doesn't it?" Garth agreed without thinking.

Chad looked at him sharply, wondering if there was sarcasm in this rather odd way of chiming in. He let it pass. "I find myself drifting back twenty or thirty years, doing things, thinking things . . . . It's strange, kind of nice sometimes. But worrying too. These doctors tell me there's a sort of reversal process going on in the cells, so really your body is getting younger all the time. And it's true, crazy as it sounds. I feel in many ways fifteen or twenty years younger already."

Garth leaned his head back on the chair and gazed up at the lake water above him. He had begun to relax into the mood of the Lake Room. All his resistance to the sacrilege of the architecture and engineering that was involved, the assault on the hill and lake as he knew them as a boy, gradually faded. He chimed in again like an echo of his father's voice. "Funny thing, I feel younger too. Like a teenager."

Chad stared at the relaxed figure of his son for a moment. "Are you high on something, Garth?" His tone was not accusing, or angry, as it might have been years ago, but merely enquiring.

"Hell no, Dad, no more than you are," Garth said with a grin, lifting his head to meet his father's gaze.

Chad returned his look suspiciously, and then grinned too. "I never did know what the hell to make of you, Garth," he said contemplatively. "I never really understood what was going on in your mind."

"You understood me well enough to keep me going for the last ten or twelve years. For sure I would have cut my throat again – done it properly – if you hadn't talked me into the Farm idea."

Chad looked pleased to hear these words from his son. "I guess that's the only good thing I did for you in all these years. I made every mistake in bringing up a child that a dumb rich father can make. I gave you everything on a silver platter to the point where you lost all interest and motivation. So it was a kind of desperation idea, the Farm. I figured if you could get mixed up with a bunch of other spoiled kids who had everything and wanted nothing – in a situation where you were responsible – you might be able to work your way out of it."

He stopped, hesitated a moment as if wondering how far his candor should go, and then with a grin continued. "Of course I was counting a little on heredity. I figured you would have enough of my organizational talents buried in you somewhere to want to get a system going. And from what I hear and see, you sure did."

"With your money behind it all."

"So what? It's the world of the future. All the material resources you need handed to you, and the great problem one of organization, organizing the lives of people who haven't got any motivation. Christ, man, you still don't realize it, but you've been serving your apprenticeship to govern the world."

Garth sat shaking his head in amazement as his father reached this absurd height of rhetorical enthusiasm. "Dad, you just don't understand. This has been a good time, an entertaining game. But I have no desire whatsoever to go any further with it. Can you imagine trying to live that kind of life after thirty? It's for the kids, the young people. When they get to that age on the Farm, we send them on their way. And when I get to that age, which is very soon now, I'm going too." He looked almost sullenly at his father, and Chad's expression showed that he knew exactly what Garth meant by 'going'.

Chad stretched his legs in the bed and looked upwards towards the lake waters, through which the morning sun was now sending bright rays. He gave the impression of one who was husbanding his resources, not having much to spare. "I don't think we're all that different after all, Garth," he said at last. "We both want to have control of our lives. We both won't accept conditions just because they've been pushed onto us. Sure, we're different too. Because I've always wanted to do things, to organize, get a business going, open up a new possibility, build a more efficient structure. Ambition, maybe, whatever name you want to put on it."

"Motivation," Garth said. "that's your word. It covers it all."

"O.K., motivation. And you've been the opposite, Garth. Nothing you particularly wanted to accomplish. But you know, opposites sometimes come together. A man who is very highly motivated may not be all that far from a man who is . . . who has no motivation whatsoever, who just doesn't care."

"You've lost me," Garth said, wrinkling his brow, a little uneasy at slipping into the web of his father's reasoning.

"I mean, a highly motivated man like me will do anything, anywhere, anytime, just to be doing something. To satisfy his need for accomplishment. Now a man like you, Garth, with some talents – and you've got lots of talent, I know that – for some reason doesn't think anything's worth doing. But because personally you don't care, you could just as well say to yourself, Instead of doing nothing I'll do this . . . or that, or whatever. It wouldn't make any difference what it was. So you see, what the man who's totally involved, totally motivated, like me, has in common with a man who's totally unmotivated, like you, is . . . what's the word? Objectivity. Impersonality. The ability to get outside themselves."

In the course of his father's extraordinary monologue, Garth's expression changed from suspicion and bewilderment to growing comprehension, doubt, and then grudging acquiescence in the rationality of the discourse. He might not agree, but at least he could see his father still possessed all his faculties. He wasn't merely maundering on.

"Impersonality," he echoed his father. "Not particularly caring about your own self, your own needs. Or lack of needs."

"Right," Chad went on, encouraged by his son's willingness to listen, even to show a hint or two of agreement. "Hell, you didn't start the Farm because you were trying to do something that mattered to you personally. It was a straight choice. Take on a little experiment your old man suggested to you for a trial, or go and cut your throat again, properly, as soon as they released you from the hospital. It was a matter of complete indifference to you personally. You could equally well have chosen either. Once you started on the Farm idea, you got lost in it, carried along with it. You weren't able to be depressed all the time, to become a vegetable. One thing led to another, kept you going. And now that you've pretty well exhausted the work you can do there, you're back with the old objective choice again."

"What old choice?" Garth asked, intrigued by his father's vivid rendition of his complicated past, resisting the crude simplifications but admiring the boldness and clarity of the picture.

"The choice between cutting your throat, or taking on a little experiment suggested to you by your revered father."

The two men sat looking at each other for a long time in silence. Then a slow grin began to spread across Chad Hamilton's face, a kind of challenging grin, and in a minute despite himself Garth found his lips smiling in return.

"What the hell do you have up your sleeve, Dad?"

Chad lifted both hands over the covers and raised them slightly as if to demonstrate there was nothing hidden. "It's obvious, Garth. It's time for you to come out of the Farm environment and conduct your experiment on a larger scale. The problem of our time and of the immediate future is . . . how to govern the people who have everything they need and don't know what to do, don't want to do anything, don't know what to want."

"The unmotivated."

"Right. I own or control the biggest complex of mass media, entertainment enterprises, and communications systems in the world. Here's where the interesting challenges lie. Here's where the shape of the future will be decided. I want you to come in and learn the business and eventually take over. Do that instead of cutting your throat."

"Only son inherits father's corporate empire?" Garth said derisively making up his own newspaper headline.

"Like hell," Chad said genially. "My only son is . . . Alice Devers. She's got more business and financial sense than a dozen guys like you put together. You'll have your share, though, as much as you're capable of using, and as much as you'll need. Listen, before we get into any details, and before you give me an answer, let me say something else."

Garth shrugged his shoulders and settled deeper into the chair. Chad rose higher in the bed and half turned to open a small door in the panel of switches at his bed side. Inside the door was a switch with an illuminated handle.

"Do you see this?" Chad said, looking back at Garth to make sure he had a clear view of the handle. "When I built this Lodge I did it all my own way. The other houses we have were designed by other people to their tastes, your mother, other women, brilliant architects, that sort of thing. This was my own. And I don't intend to pass it on to you or anybody else. Nobody can possibly appreciate this crazy place the way I do. So for that reason and for another reason I'll come to, I've designed it so it can pretty well self-destruct."

"Self-destruct," Garth said blankly, turning his eyes over the immense Lake Room and along the vast expanse of glass ceiling. "Looks pretty solid to me, built to last forever – except maybe for that."

He pointed upwards to the great volume of translucent water suspended above their heads by the sheets of clear plastic or glass or whatever it was.

"That's right, Garth," his father said with relish. "You've hit it on the head. If I were to pull this switch, three things would happen, one right after the other. First, every door in the Lodge would slide open. Second the alarm bells for everyone to evacuate would ring for three minutes solid. And third, charges would go off along the seams of that ceiling, and the whole goddam lake would crash down here and flood the Lodge from stem to stern."

Chad eased back in the pillows to observe his son's reaction. Garth sat motionless except for his head and eyes, which he used to inspect the entire room, the doors and especially the ceiling, assessing the full implications of what his father had said. He could see it was perfectly feasible. Mad, awful, but ingeniously simple too.

"You always did like mechanical toys, didn't you Dad?" he said shaking his head slowly to express his incredulity. "You always used to find the most complicated ones to give me, and then it was you who would end up playing with them, mostly, anyway. This time you've outdone yourself. But don't you think that anybody pulling that switch might find themselves . . . in a bit of an awkward position?"

"Oh, there's a match to this switch up above, at the gateway," Chad said reassuringly. "I had this one put down here by my bed after I got the news about the cancer."

Garth gave up all pretence of thinking it was a big practical joke, a game his father was playing. His face filled with dismay. If it weren't for the rich beard, his expression could have been that of a troubled eighteen year old.

"Christ, Dad, that's crazy."

"Maybe. But it means a lot to me. I can lie here and look up at that lake and know that at any moment, if it all gets to be too much for me, I can finish it easily, instantly, certainly. Nobody can stop me. I don't have to end up some kind of rotten carcass for the medical profession to play with. As long as I've got enough strength left to lift a hand, I can choose my own way, and my own place, a place I love to be in. I don't have to worry about things slipping out of my control."

Garth had got to his feet and was walking about restlessly, his towel flapping loosely about his legs. He stopped a few feet from the bed and glared down at his father.

"There has to be some better way than ending up under a bloody lake. You must have the best medical brains in the world at your fingertips. You've got . . . . "

"Oh sit down and shut up, Garth," his father said impatiently. "I've been through all that a long time ago. You have to face the facts. It's only a matter of months at the most."

Garth's forehead turned scarlet under his deep tan and he shouted back into his father's face. "Then for Christ sake, do it now! Pull the bloody switch. Get it over with. Right now!"

He waved his hand furiously upwards to the swaying, rippling waters lit brightly by the sun. Then he stood, tall, muscular, like a Roman statue complete with toga, exchanging fierce stares with his father. Finally his father looked away, lay back wearily on the pillows, and gazed up at the ceiling. His son remained standing at his bedside, his raised arm gradually slumping to his side. His father spoke with tired tones.

"No luck, Garth. This is my home ground. I get to make my own decision. I don't decide for you, not any more. I'm not making it easy for you."

Garth folded his arms, hugging the towel to him, and continued to look down at the drawn, tired face of his father. Several times he seemed on the point of speaking, but he couldn't get the words out. His father went on gazing upwards. Finally Garth settled on the edge of the bed, almost forcing his father to turn his face towards him.

"You've given me my life to live," Garth said quietly, "once, twice anyway. I could hardly ask you to take it back and get rid of it for me. Anyway, I didn't really come to see you for that. I came to . . . . "

He hesitated as if after all he wasn't sure he could say it right out. "I came to say . . . thank you."

"Thank you?" Chad's tired face lit with a trace of surprise.

"Yeah," Garth grinned sheepishly, "I never was much good at that. Better late than never," he concluded, putting out his hand.

Chad slowly drew his right hand from under the covers and met his son's grasp. Then he began to object whimsically, still holding the handshake. "Jesus, don't start getting sentimental on me, after all these years. I'll begin to think you're not my son."

"Well, you see, that's what I want you to know. I really am your son," Garth said, his voice so low it was almost inaudible. Then abruptly he jumped to his feet.

"Look, Dad, there is one thing you could do for me."

His father looked up in surprise.

"What's that?"

"Lend me a pair of pants," Garth said with a grin, glancing down at his bare legs.

A few minutes later, brushing off all alternative suggestions, Garth was on his way striding down the hill and back to the Farm. His borrowed clothes were a reasonable fit. Norman Shearer didn't notice anything odd about them as he observed the young man approaching him on the path he was cycling up towards the Lodge.

The two men caught sight of each other far enough off for each to prepare himself. For Norman, the flow of bitterness and rage had slackened some time ago, though his first glimpse of Garth Hamilton, tall, easy, handsome, pacing with his long downhill strides, started it up for a moment. He was well under control by the time Garth stopped and stood, hands in the pockets of his father's expensive slacks, waiting to pass the time of morning, and Norman came to a halt on his bicycle.

"I've come looking for you," Norman said, with deceptive mildness.

"Yeah, I've been playing hooky." Garth didn't appear particularly penitent. In fact he seemed to be in high spirits. The effects of the young man's physical well-being, radiance almost, which Norman perhaps misunderstood, was enough to make the older man explode.

"Do you realize you could be infecting the whole bloody country?"

The icy rage in the older man's voice caught Garth by surprise. "I haven't been near anybody – except those who tell me they're immune anyway," Garth said indignantly. "And I'm going straight back to the House in a Field."

Norman glared at him with an expression of anger and disgust. Grudgingly he accepted Garth's statement – not as a matter of fact, but as his genuine belief. "No," he said, having had ample time to go through all the possible ways out of the mess, "you're not going back to the House. It's not the place for you now. Crossland has dismantled the equipment. You've got to go to the Centre."

Garth looked shocked for a moment, started to protest, and then subsided, standing with his hands in his pockets waiting for his immediate future to be decided, as though indifferent.

"You've got to be checked out and treated for the effects of the serum . . . . The experiment is over." Norman added, with brutal coldness to make the point clear, "Over."

He looked hard at Garth to give him time to react. Garth returned his stare without flinching and without comment. He would neither provoke nor be provoked. Plans were formulating in Norman's mind. He continued.

"You walk in the direction of the collector road when you get to the bottom of the hill. You'll be picked up by a car there, and taken to the Centre. I'm going on up to the Lodge now to make some calls and set everything up."

Garth erupted into life instantly, protesting eagerly. "No, don't go up to the Lodge. Look, my Father doesn't know anything about this experiment with me. I don't want him to know. There's no use in his knowing. Why the hell upset him?"

It was Norman's turn to be surprised, not expecting the energy and urgency of this appeal. Filial solicitude from Garth Hamilton. He studied Garth for a minute before deciding how to react. "All right," he conceded, "I won't go to the Lodge. I'll go to my house in the Circle instead. That'll mean the car won't be along for another fifteen minutes or half an hour. Keep moving. Don't let anyone who's not from the Centre stop on the road and try to talk to you. I'll see you when you check into the Centre."

Norman didn't wait for an answer. He wheeled his bicycle around and peddled down the hill at top speed, without looking back.

As he cycled towards his home in the Circle, Norman found himself rehearsing speeches to his daughter and wife. Angry speeches. Bitter speeches. Sarcastic speeches. Worried speeches. Anguished speeches. No words could ever be adequate for his sense of outrage, doubled outrage.

Then as he sailed through the fields and orchards of the Farm, skimming easily along the graveled lanes and over the wooden bridges across irrigation ditches and canals, anger, bitterness, personal pain began to seem irrelevant. Nothing could change the past, no amount of raging and accusing. Nothing could change the earlier years either, the years of confusion and frustration for himself and for Ella, her floundering in the doldrums of a life she didn't know what to do with, him intermittently plunged into the excitements and challenges of his job – both clutching at ways to escape the relentless, pointless slide from youth into age.

When the anger ebbed momentarily, this is what he kept coming back to. How pathetic it was that Ella should try to fend off middle-age by having another baby. How pathetic, really, to be throwing herself at a young man who wouldn't give her another thought, probably, when he went on to the next woman, as pretty or prettier no doubt, younger certainly.

A sense of misery flooded over him. He couldn't go home right now. He couldn't walk into the house, the kitchen, the bedroom, where they had been trying to live together with their limitations and their fears. Later, not now. Later they could try to live together again somehow.

Norman took the turn that led towards the collector terminal and the Centre. He would go all the way to the Centre, get hold of John Hornby, arrange with Dr. Crossland to pick up Garth, Ella and the baby, and Donna too. Bring them all to the Centre, admit them, and make sure all of them were properly checked over and cleared of possible infection in the right medical conditions. Make sure thermotherapy was their physical salvation. After that, the future could begin.

Parking his bicycle in the lot at the Centre, Norman went in the private staff entrance and put through his calls, the last to John Hornby at his apartment. It was rather reassuring to see John's round, serene face filling the telescreen screen.

"John, are you all right?"

Hornby looked a little startled at the abruptness and urgency of Norman's question. "Certainly," he said. "But I may say you don't look all that well yourself. What's the trouble?"

Norman proceeded to explain that the bottom had fallen out of their little illicit experiment. That Garth had left quarantine, was no longer reliable enough to continue with, had contacted several other people and had to be dealt with firmly. Disciplined, in fact.

"What I've done," Norman concluded, "is to have these people all brought in here – they'll be on their way now – and I was hoping that you would come over and give a hand."

John Hornby looked puzzled at this suggestion. "I'm not sure what I can do, Norman. In my present state, I'm more likely to be a source of risk than Garth Hamilton."

Norman plunged ahead with his proposition. He was dreading having to explain too much, but he had confidence in his friend's quickness and consideration in personal matters.

"John, the people Garth has possibly infected are Ella and the baby and Donna. I was hoping that you would do something to make sure they realize what kind of a mess they've got us all in. They have to know the facts now."

"I don't understand," John said, consternation spreading across his face at Norman's half-revelations.

"I want you to be here in the laboratory when they come in. I want you to show them what's going on here. Give them as full a picture of the laboratory side of the experiment as you can. After that they can be decontaminated, and discharged when they're ready. I think that's the quickest way to make them see how serious this thing is. I don't want to talk to them. Will you do it?"

John was nodding his head as the explanation came to an end. He now understood all that he needed to make a decision. As Norman hoped, he had no wish to pursue the puzzle any further, without encouragement. "Of course, Norman. You take care of the arrangements, and I'll be right over."

Half an hour later Norman Shearer was safely barricaded in his office, leaving strict instructions not to be disturbed. From his windows, he could watch discreetly as two electric cars pulled up, one behind the other, at the entrance. Out of one Garth Hamilton emerged, and out of the other Ella, carrying the baby, and Donna with a pair of small suitcases. He waited till he saw the two groups enter separately.

Norman turned to his desk and sat down, attempting to imagine what would happen for the next little while. He trusted John Hornby to do the job properly, to bring home the nature of the fire these people had been playing with, to ensure the continued secrecy of their work, if it wasn't already too late for that. He had his own scenario for how the laboratory visit would go. Something like this.

First they would all be ushered through the admittance procedures with the best care and expedition the Centre could muster. They would be taken upstairs to meet Dr. Hornby in the laboratory, while rooms were being put into the final state of preparation for them in the isolation section. Dr. Hornby would give them his formal dignitaries' tour of the laboratory in his most solemn way. He would spare them nothing.

In here are the glass cages in which the mice are kept for experimental purposes. Yes, they are rather ugly. That's because they are a special breed, skinless almost, developed to be highly susceptible to bacterial infection and sensitive to the effects of drugs and chemicals. Trials are considerably speeded up using creatures of this kind.

Here we have the control group, which is given the same routine and the same feeding formula as those being subjected to trial injections. Over here is a group of specimens that have been exposed to cancer inducing agents and allowed to experience all stages of the disease to the degree we would consider equivalent to a human patient's condition in the terminal stages. As you can see, they are in a conspicuously poor state. Quite right, they are not enjoying this phase of the experiment. Against this wall is a group of pregnant mice undergoing much the same developments.

Now in this next section we have the specimens who are receiving massive injections of the serum Dr. Shearer and I are attempting to perfect. First, in this cage we have the group who began with no indications of cancer – mice we consider to be normal and healthy. You will notice nothing in particular about them, probably, in first seeing them, except that they are by comparison with the others, shall we say, hyperactive. They show signs of unusual voraciousness of appetite, considerably increased sexual activity, and a kind of communal gregariousness which we have tended to recognize in the young of the species.

Yes, you could say they seem to have undergone a kind of rejuvenation, and the process appears to continue as long as the injections are given.

Now in this cage we have segregated a number of pregnant mice. You won't be able to see anything of note from visual observation, except some of the same behavioral characteristics I have just been describing. But the interesting features of the impact of the serum on these specimens is that they seem to undergo consistently a phenomenon known as uterine re-absorption. That is to say, when a female which is known to be pregnant is given substantial and repeated doses of the serum, she proceeds to absorb the fetus or fetuses back into her body. The growth and development in the embryo is reversed, until there is nothing left to indicate that there ever was impregnation.

Now over here are some specimens that have already produced their litters. In this part of the experiment we have injected both mother and offspring.

We're not sure why, perhaps because of the hormonal balance, the impact of the serum on pregnant and mothering females seems unusually potent.

With the offspring, we are encountering what is perhaps the most striking outcome of our experimentation. In young mice up to the equivalent of, say, three or four months in a human being, the retarding and reversing effect of the serum is dramatic. Instead of cell division and multiplication, we get reunion of cells and a steady reduction of tissue.

It has proved difficult to follow this reversal process through to its observable conclusion for several reasons. First, a secondary effect of the serum in massive doses appears to be an impact on the nervous and cardiovascular systems that results in aberrant heart functions. At the extreme, in cardiac arrest. It's possible that the source of this reaction is to be found in cell activity in the nervous system and brain which we haven't yet been able to trace with any exactness.

The second reason is that with the young mice, when the reversal process goes past a certain point, the specimen becomes in effect too young to survive outside its mother's womb. If we were to go on making comparisons with the human parallels, it would be like a process in which an infant of several months of age retreats in its patterns of development until it in effect becomes a premature baby.

With that general idea in mind, recently we've begun to treat these young specimens just like that – like premature births. With incubation and intravenous feedings we have been able to allow the regression to go on to a surprising degree. It seems likely at the present time, that after certain laboratory innovations, we will sooner or later be able to follow the offspring back to the very beginning of their lives.

We have already come very close to sustaining the activity of some specimens to the point where they exist as little more than . . . impregnated ova. Practically speaking, given laboratory limitations, so far what we end up with is a trace of blood, perhaps even sperm, on a microscopic slide. So far the magic moment of union – or in this case disunion – is too delicate and infinitesimal for science to observe. Though theoretically it may be possible, when the right condition can be maintained.

Now I have one last cage to show you. In some ways it's the most important feature of the whole experiment. We've only recently been giving full attention to this aspect of the experiment, and the results are noteworthy.

Here we have a cage in which there are mice without cancer, that is, perfectly healthy, normal creatures like those in our first control group. But we also have in with them a full assortment of mice in stages equivalent to those in all the other cages I've shown you. Yes, that's right. Mice with cancer in advanced degrees. Pregnant mice. Mice with offspring. And of course the offspring themselves. All these are undergoing or have undergone serum injections. These, and the healthy, normal mice not receiving injections, are allowed to intermingle freely, associate, feed together, copulate and so forth.

Now the interesting feature of this cage is that *all* the inhabitants of this particular environment show the same kinds of reversal patterns in cell development.

Yes, that's what I said. *All* these mice are showing the same kinds of clinical reaction, the ones who don't get the injections as well as the ones that do. Indeed, the evidence is very strong from this type of experiment that the serum we are using is, under certain conditions of temperature control and physical proximity of carrier and recipient, highly contagious. Mice which have not been injected display the same signs of cell response and behavioral reaction as mice which have been injected, if they are put into proximity in the right conditions.

Nurse, come at once, Mrs. Shearer and her daughter both seem to have fainted. Mr. Hamilton is suffering some kind of seizure.

Well, with that melodramatic conclusion – a case of wishful thinking pushed too far – Norman woke from his reverie. No doubt it was too much to hope for such a spectacular and salutary shock to them all. But he felt confident that at least John would make them realize the seriousness of what they had been doing. They would leave the lab chastened, willing to be careful and conscientious during their treatment – and maintain confidentiality. With a sense of alleviated soreness of spirit, Norman attempted to bury himself in the paper work that had accumulated on his desk in the last troubled days.

He was still absorbed an hour or two later, when he got the call he was expecting from John Hornby. He immediately agreed to come to the laboratory to hear John's report.

When he entered the room, it was as if nothing had changed over the past few days. John was seated at his table in his white smock, hard at work. He didn't look up as Norman approached and perched on the edge of the table.

"What have you got there?" Norman asked at last.

John eased back in his chair, and handed a folder to Norman. "I've been re-reading it. It's the autopsy report on Faye Delisle. It arrived with a couple of other things of interest in the morning mail. I would have called you at once but I wanted to study it again."

Norman's face settled into grim lines as he started to glance through it. In a minute he was deeply absorbed, and the grimness changed to lively concern. "So it is the effect on the brain cells, then," Norman exclaimed, lowering the folder to his knees and looking at John with dismay on his face.

Hornby's expression was benign as usual. He nodded, as if agreeing to an abstract proposition. "Apparently. We'll get a good deal more when the electron microscopy is completed. But it's clear enough even now to confirm our tentative concerns. Clear enough for the time being, anyway," he concluded with a wry grin that gave his face its most boyish appearance. "I've brought all the clinical work to a halt – I hope you agree."

"All of it?" Norman asked sharply, looking hard at Hornby.

"I've come off the injections myself, as of now," Hornby said, "I've taken off the cases here at the Centre, and sent instructions up to the Lodge to stop them until further word. You took care of the Farm side of things before, anyway, and I've had a further chat with Allen Crossland myself."

Norman got up from the edge of the table and paced up and down restlessly, whistling periodically as the full implications sank in.

"I think," John went on, "we're in the process of decontaminating everyone who's been exposed, accidentally or intentionally. Garth, Ella, Donna and the baby are well into thermotherapy by now. That leaves you and me. We can start whenever it's convenient."

John glanced at his watch to confirm his general reckoning.

"What about Alice Devers?" Norman asked, his mind racing back to their meeting with Chad Hamilton and her, when she so much wanted to bring the Hornby-Shearer therapy to an end.

"Alice will be all right, I'm confident she's been following approved procedures. She's been coming into the Centre with the same kind of precautions as I've been taking. I think she may be here now. My idea was that we should go and see her as soon as possible – thinking not only of Chad Hamilton and her, but of our project's future here at the Centre."

"Call her up then," Norman said impatiently. "Tell her it's an emergency."

Alice Devers' suite of offices was on the top floor of the Centre. It had an open air patio, as well as glass windows on all sides. The view of the surrounding terrain was magnificent, not the least attractive feature being the spectacle of the whole of Notlimah to the east, the spacious estates of the Circle, the dense forest separating them from the Farm, and the hill barely visible in the middle of the rural and agricultural scene, with the glinting lake enshrined on its plateau. When John Hornby spoke to Alice on the intercommunication system and set up an immediate interview, he quietly brushed aside her first enquiries.

"We'll explain when we arrive," John had said.

Alice was seated behind the immense desk covering one side of the main office, with the elaborate paraphernalia of the Hamilton empire's communication network behind her. She was dressed in her crispest, neatest, most business-like one-piece grey flannel suit. The only feature which marked her as changed from the early days when they dealt with her upon arriving at the Centre was her eyes – they were large beyond their usual dimensions, and clearly they had been tearful often and long recently, however much control they might be under now.

"We've had some significant news from the Carter-Trudeau Hospital," Norman announced as soon as the formal greetings were over. He took the spokesman's role naturally. "News of some concern, I think I should say."

Alice composed herself to hear it. In this mood and posture she gave the reassuring impression of imperturbability.

"A long-standing case, the one we've gained more information and clinical evidence from than from any other, is now complete," Norman said, in his best staff conference manner. "The patient has died and an autopsy and further tests have been performed and are still being carried out. Preliminary observations show that the impact of the serum we've been employing is more noticeable and severe in regard to brain tissue than in regard to other types of cells. We now feel that we must call a halt to further clinical applications until we have a chance to assess the implication of this evidence and conduct more new experiments in the laboratory to verify and if necessary compensate for these results."

Normal looked over to John Hornby for his approval of this version of the facts. John readily offered it with his eyebrows and a nod of his head.

Then Norman came to the crux of the matter. "We've contacted the staff at the Lodge, but we wondered if you wanted to break the news to Chad personally."

Alice sat in silence, with no comprehensible expression on her face, observing them both and evidently not having an immediate reaction. It almost seemed as if the news was a matter of indifference to her, difficult as that might be for them to believe.

"Unless," Norman concluded lamely, "you'd rather we did it ourselves."

"No," Alice said, as if waking up to their presence and their need for reassurance. "That won't be necessary. I understand how you both must feel. It's a terrible disappointment at this stage of your work. But of course you'll treat it as a temporary set-back. You'll go on, won't you? You'll learn what you can from these developments, and continue with the work? I know that's what Chad would have – would like you to do."

It was the turn of the two doctors to be silent. They hadn't known exactly what to expect from Alice Devers, but they hadn't really anticipated such a generous and philosophical response. They were saved from having to say anything in reply by a sudden outburst of activity on the communications panel behind Alice. Several lights and buzzers were activated at once, enough to startle both the men.

Alice calmly touched the button of the telescreen in front of her, which had its speaker silenced, and held one earpiece to her head to receive the news that was trying to reach her. It was the Lodge manager, calling from the gate house, in a state of considerable agitation. In a moment, almost before Norman and John could grasp what was amiss from the expression on the manager's face, Alice had him calmed down and launched on a course of action. She ignored the remaining indications on the panel, but sat self-absorbed, looking out the windows.

"Would you like us to go?" Norman ventured after a pause, feeling the irrelevance, if not the awkwardness, of their presence.

Alice turned her large eyes back on the two men, as if remembering they were there. Then she rose to her feet and walked towards the French doors giving onto the patio. Pushing them open she beckoned them to come with her.

On the Centre roof-top the sun was shining brightly. She walked with them to the flower boxes on the east side and slowly lifted a hand to point in the direction of the heart of Notlimah in the distance.

"There's been an accident at the Lodge," Alice said quietly, without a trace of agitation. "A serious accident. The Lodge has been flooded."

The two doctors gasped in alarm, both remembering vividly their first impressions of the lake, and the Lake Room, with its immense spread of glass ceiling and its depth of clear waters overhead, beautiful, but sometimes oppressive. Now as they stepped forward and stared in the direction of the hill, they could hear the distant sound of sirens from below, trucks rushing over the roads and lanes farther away. It was obvious that a great crowd was converging on the location of the Lodge.

"For God's sake," Norman spluttered, "that's awful. What can they do? Can we take you there? Can we go there and find out . . . ?"

Alice turned away from the distant view with tears almost daring to spill a little. That was the only sign of feeling. Her voice was firm. "No thank you, Norman, John."

And then, as if taking pity on their bewilderment and consternation, she added: "You go, if you like. I think you'll find it's too late. I'm sure you will. Some accidents are more . . . unexpected . . . than others."

The last sight of her they had was of a beautiful, dignified, isolated young woman settling behind the big desk into a position of deep stillness.

An hour later, the two men were on top of the hill, standing among the crowd of workers and staff and business associates and police, looking down from the lake edge. Looking down at the clear waters of the lake, on which now bobbed an occasional cushion and wooden table, or other flotsam and jetsam, and which showed, if you peered deeply enough, the edges but not the bottom of a vast crater in the middle, where the waters had plunged through and filled an opening below its former bottom. On the lake itself a number of rafts and boats were plying back and forth, and several divers were at work already trying to explore the depths of the bubbling, murky cavity.

In the next few days and weeks, as they tried to put their lives back together again into something they could describe as normal, neither of the two men mentioned again the long, strange conversation which took place

F. W. WATT

between them on the edge of the lake at that moment, as they watched in shocked fascination.

Perhaps both attributed their experiences to the hypersensitive condition they were in from the strains they each had been operating under. Or to the accumulation of serum and thermotherapy their bodies were responding to. Perhaps they were simply too embarrassed at the intensities that emerged in their conversation at the time of the disaster affecting Chad Hamilton, Alice Devers, Garth, and in different ways themselves.

Norman Shearer turned the direction of their exchanges on that disastrous afternoon, as they stood together, paced restlessly back and forth, stared out at the emergency crews at their work -- by telling John Hornby about his dream the night before.

Often they both dreamed under the influence of the temperature-raising drugs they used. Normally the dreams were rather pleasant, and altogether the experience was hardly any more serious than taking a sauna, a steam-bath, or getting drunk. Talking about their dreams surely had nothing to do with the nightmare scene of devastation they were watching helplessly. But this time Norman implied that the dream he recently had was beyond the ordinary – and then John admitted that he also had something of the same unusual kind to report. Quietly, waiting restlessly by the busy scene at the lake side, the two friends tried to share what each so vividly remembered.

My dream started off very pleasantly, Norman said. He had been watching TV, waiting for the restricted Blue Television Network to begin broadcasting, as it did late at night, in accordance with censorship regulations. He was watching his wife's set, rather than his own, lying on the sofa, since his wife was away. He had just had a painful interview with his daughter, which he was trying to forget. He must have dozed off with the set still playing.

He dreamed that he was watching a video of one episode out of Faye Delisle's greatest Blue series. He'd even invented a plausible explanation in his dream – Faye Delisle, as a last bequest, had given him and John Hornby a complete set of her strictly private records of five years of work for the Blue Television Network. Collectors' items, worth a fortune, if they really had existed.

The episode Norman dreamed he was watching was a porno comedy in which Faye plays the guest conductor of a symphony orchestra. She gets a little more deeply involved with the members of the orchestra than is usual. During rehearsals for a big concert in Carnegie Hall, Faye, who first appears as a bit of a tartar, dressed in a severe black pantsuit, her hair drawn up in a tight bun, looking like an austere Slavic ballerina, gets angry at the inadequacies of the brass section. All males, of course. After reprimanding them frequently, and having to stop the music every few bars to correct them, she calls the rehearsal to an end and orders the brass section to stay behind for a special practice.

The men aren't too upset at the suggestion. In fact, by that time it has been made amply clear that their uncustomary ineptitude was due to distraction. The conductress has such a splendid body, discreet as the costume she is wearing may be, that they can't keep their eyes or minds on their music.

However, when they have to stay behind, one of them with due servility suggests that they might do better with a little sustenance. The conductress reluctantly agrees, and soon a couple of the members of the brass section have returned carrying bottles of wine and legs of chicken and pieces of sausages and bread and bowls of fruit. The spectacle of it all laid out and the men eating and drinking eagerly is more bacchanalian than the conductress has in mind. She soon testily orders the beginning of the practice session, though not before having imbibed a little herself.

The rehearsal room has become warm, so that understandably everyone has begun to discard clothing. The conductress, deeply involved in her music, is herself obliged to make a few trifling decisions about what to discard in order to keep cool. She does so casually, hardly noticing what she's doing. Her decision only serves to raise the temperature of the members of the brass section.

They are keen to make the rehearsal go splendidly, however, so they are performing above themselves. The conductress, taking a moment or two away like the players from time to time to sip and savor the wine, becomes more and more involved in the intoxicating beauty of the music. Eventually she is dreamily, eloquently enacting with her conductress's baton and her arms and body the intricate charms of the score – dressed only in panties and bra, her hair having splendidly loosened from its knot and begun to cascade in all its blond splendor down her shoulders.

By this time the music has grown louder and more ecstatic, as the eager men fix their eyes on her and blow their instruments with intense concentration. The remaining vestiges of their clothing have been gradually dropping from their heated limbs. They have been inching their chairs closer and closer, a maneuver rather more difficult for those with the larger instruments, such as the tuba, but eventually the conductress is tightly encircled, where she displays her musical ardor on the podium, by a group of sweating, exuberant males united in one focus.

Abruptly, as the camera leaves the puffed and beaming faces, burning eyes, and contorted limbs of the male musicians to close in on the shape and face of the conductress, she wakes from her deep absorption – to find herself an almost naked sole young woman surrounded by a crowd of horn-playing but obviously randy men of all shapes and sizes, looks and ages, including the weedy young trumpeter whose instrument is almost touching her bottom.

There is a slowing and running down of brass sounds, as her conducting slows, as realization dawns on her face, and then there is silence. Disbelief. A wry awakening to the reality. An amused half-hearted pretense of searching for

F. W. WATT

an avenue of escape. Then a forward tide of male bodies. A reaching of hands, a holding, a pulling and ripping of the last flimsy garments.

In a moment, the conductress is delectably, gorgeously nude and – within the rather flexible restrictions applied to Blue Television sequences by the censor – about to be joined in sexual congress, the logical climax of all these stories.

In the confusion of glimpses and unusual camera angles that follows, one thing is made amply clear. The beautiful conductress has long since abandoned any show of resistance or fear, and is being swept along to unbelievable heights of orgiastic delight.

The underlying comic motif is nicely maintained through it all, of course – we see the solemn, bespectacled, profoundly serious French horn player, in his underwear, still picking away at his score, professionally ignoring the distractions around him, trying to perfect his part, flat and off-key as the resulting notes might have sounded to anyone else listening.

John Hornby was a bit puzzled at the way Norman retold the story of his dream to this point. It sounded like pure fun, of the sort that Norman, and millions of other North American males, enjoyed night after night on the Blue.

"It seems like one of the episodes I saw at your place last year," John suggested. "What was it? 'The Office Party'? Faye played the boss in an insurance company office, didn't she? Icy bitch who gets thawed out during the Christmas festivities."

Norman shook his head. "This wasn't like that. In fact, it wasn't like anything I've ever seen."

He then went on to describe the last part of the dream, or to be more exact – nightmare. It was a cheerful orgy that turned into a nightmare. First, the comic French horn player, detached from the orgy and absorbed in his music, on closer inspection turned out to have the face that Norman saw at least once a day at the Centre – John Hornby's. It was a shock to Norman, a dampening recognition, not to be himself one of the eager satyrs, but a ridiculous outsider.

The situation worsened drastically when the whole scene took on a different character. Now the bare backs of the randy, fornicating musicians, crowded around and over and hiding from view what should have been the luscious shape of the ecstatic female in their midst, began to slow their pushing and thrusting movements, and to ease into reclining positions on the floor. A space in the centre opened and it was possible to see the focus of their exhausted lust.

Sitting in the midst of the chaos of naked male bodies slipping into satiated sleep around her, was a woman – but not, surely, the beautiful young conductress, certainly not Faye Delisle in make-up and costume. It was an incredibly old woman in a high-backed rocking chair, deep wrinkles lining her bony face, thin white hair tucked under a kerchief, a peasant gown and shawl hiding her scrawny body, her knobby hands holding a piece of knitting in her lap, her hollow eyes ignoring the irrelevant naked male spectacle around her.

As soon as the camera came to focus on the old crone, she raised her eyes from her knitting and looked to where the French horn player – John – was sitting alone. Her eyes, bloodshot and watery as they were, seemed deeply familiar, though he couldn't find a name. The old woman's mouth opened in a crooked toothless smile, and she lifted a knobby hand to beckon.

But it was Norman who was drawn into the scene by the summons. Unable to resist, he rose slowly and came towards her, mildly aware of his underwear, came towards the scarf, sweater or sock that was obviously being knitted for him, obediently willing to try it on as she held it up to him.

But as he approached, he was stopped in his tracks by a sheet of glass, he on one side, the old woman and the spent orgiastic scene on the other. Now it was the glass of the TV screen, and as he began to tap and then to pound it to get through in response to the more and more frantically beckoning old lady, he woke up. His bed-clothes were drenched in cold sweat.

"I think there was a lot more," Norman said when he had finished his description, "but that's all I can remember. Perhaps it's just as well."

"It's enough to put you off thermotherapy," John said with a sympathetic grin.

John was already thinking about his own dream, so very different – just as he and Norman were different in personality and temperament – but with something in common too. He felt encouragement to try and describe it, listening to Norman and recognizing how each was anxious to share his deepest concerns. After all, dreams are an attempt to communicate too, however devious their methods, no one could deny that.

"My dream was more, well, scientific than yours," John said, his smile taking on a little more wryness. "It comes right out of our work."

He didn't say so, thinking it would soon be evident, but it went a long way beyond their work too. John claimed he rarely dreamed, so that he was more likely to dream on the thermo- therapeutic drug than otherwise, and perhaps more likely to try and remember the details, however bizarre or intricate . As the dream went – or more probably, John conceded, as his rational mind tried to make it seem to go, when reviewing the usual sort of chaos and incoherence of a dream – the Woman in the White House had conscripted the Hornby-Shearer team.

"Who, might I ask, was the Woman in the White House?"

"I'll give you one guess."

"Alice Devers?"

"Correct." John rubbed his chin a little ruefully at the success of his partner's guess.

Norman grinned his encouragement. "Well, we could do worse. It could even be possible. I'd give her my vote."

The Woman in the White House placed the doctors' team under the direct authority of her Chief of Staff, who had several faces throughout the dream.

Sometimes he looked like Chad Hamilton, certainly, at other times more like Adolph Hitler, or some other old time political figure like Carter, or Trudeau of Canada.

"I think," John said, "my dream must have been influenced by all those big photographic murals at the Carter-Trudeau."

In any case the medical research team was sent on a special mission to supervise an experiment in Youthadation.

"Youthadation?" Norman asked in amused astonishment. "What on earth's that?"

The two by this time had taken a seat beside the large mounted telescope that was on the highest spot on the hill overlooking the Farm. Under the small round roof of the mounting, they could still observe all the activity of the lake site, while preserving a little peace and privacy for themselves.

"Well, you know," John insisted as if it should be obvious, "Youthadation – like chlorination, fluoridation."

"Ah," Norman sighed, miffed at being so slow to comprehend.

The Hornby-Shearer team was dispatched in military fashion to a certain region where they were to arrange for the infusion of a specially developed variety of their drug, in undetectable quantities, into the water system of the entire population.

"Ah," Norman said again, this time beginning to make sense of the term, or perhaps simply sinking into the flow of the dream without resisting any longer.

The region chosen for the experiment was one of naturally high fertility and large families – the Canadian province of Quebec. The Woman in the White House expected them to report back in five years on the effects of Youthadation. Was it possible to sustain the population's youth by this method, to stabilize it at an optimum point, while controlling the birth rate?

"An interesting question," Norman said drily, as he looked over the stretching fields of Chad Hamilton's devastated empire.

Having organized all the region's water purification plants and got them started, under the pretext of establishing controls against germ warfare, the next stage was to set up observation and reporting units, all of course disguised in various ways to avoid alarming the population. Since Quebec was an isolated, semi-autonomous, foreign language community in the midst of a vast North American continent, the problem of controlling the experiment was much smaller than it would have been with, say, Texas or British Columbia.

Dr. Hornby and Dr. Shearer began their tours of the region – rather like the Environmental Hazards Committee in real life – summoning local doctors and hospital authorities, and exercising dictatorial powers of questioning and investigation. They also visited hospital wards and private homes.

"Don't tell me," Norman said, still naturally enough a little inclined to take John's dream more lightly than his own, "all that happened is that everybody got diarrhea."

"Wrong," John answered, confident in the vivid memory of his dream experience, emboldened by it, "everyone got younger. That is, everybody up to later middle-age."

The population, imperceptibly at first, but then strikingly, alarmingly, to the ignorant masses, divided. Those in the second half of life already continued their inevitable decline into senility and death. Those in the first half of life began a baffling reverse process.

At first there were cries of dismay and grief from those on the older side of the watershed, who saw themselves as losers, the gap widening between themselves and the lucky ones who were saved, some in the nick of time, by what was to them some mysterious source of youth. There were many poignant scenes as couples were parted, imperceptibly at first, and then with sickening acceleration, down opposite sides of the slope.

But then the problems of the other half of the population, the junior half, began to surface.

Having just survived the chaos and frustration of teenage life, having at last arrived at adulthood, young men and women found themselves being gradually sucked back into the confusion and uncertainty and frustration of adolescence. Parents having just congratulated themselves on a successful weathering of the tantrum stage of early childhood found their well-behaved offspring plunged back into the storms again. Couples who had sailed into the comfortable harbor of middle-age were driven out again into open water. Confident middle-aged wives, who had steeled themselves to their husbands' sexual crises, and achieved serenity or indifference, felt the previous decade's bitterness and jealousy all over. Husbands, whose peace had at last been established on the plateau of maturity, after a stormy phase of sexual escape by their bored wives, again heard their mid-day calls to home from the office mysteriously ring on, unanswered, as they used to do.

Boys and girls who had finally, in their twenties, identified their true loves in the same age groups as themselves, began again to part company in the search for mates. The boys, looking to younger teenage girls, or only sticking with the male gang. The girls, disdaining mates their own age (how ignorant, uncouth, boring) and again hankering after those more mature males, three or four years older (how, worldly and sophisticated). Children, who had just stopped sucking their thumbs, stuffed them back in again. And once more they wet their beds, threw food on the carpet, took off their clothes to play doctor.

After a while it became a matter of question as to whether it was better to be in the first or the second half of the population, young or old, as the gap between the generations widened.

Of course it was the women with small children and the pregnant women who were hardest hit, as in any social crisis. Mothers who had just weaned their infants found their breasts flowing with milk again, and their children clamoring for the teat. Infants ate and drank less and less, and the proud parental comparisons and triumphant claims at every ounce gained, turned into cries of dismay as body tissue shrank, toddlers became sitters, sitters lyers, bouncing babies sleeping babies, robust sons and heirs turned into clingers to life.

There were not enough incubators to go around. Infant mortality increased. While the lucky or wealthy and powerful few could draw on hospital resources, they watched the process go on often to a horrible conclusion. Infant after infant diminishing, more and more births still or premature. Nine month pregnancies shrank to the comfort and ease of five month pregnancies. Five month pregnancies became unnoticeable to outside observers, though objectionable to women who had long since stopped throwing up each morning, and now began all over again. Women who hadn't menstruated for six weeks and were worried, were able to relax, discovering that they weren't pregnant after all. Women who hadn't menstruated for six weeks and were filled with hope, and plans for the nursery and playroom, bled and thronged back into the doctors' waiting rooms, begging for help to get pregnant again. The birth rate in the entire region dropped sickeningly towards nil. Was Quebec francophony doomed? There were cries of alarm at the prospect of the extinction of a race and culture that had survived by the cradle.

Emergency meetings. Telescreen consultations with the Woman in the White House. Attempts to alter the consequences by reducing the amount of the Youthadation drug used in the water supply. Discovery that the virus in the water supply and in the humans using it appeared to have taken on independent vitality.

"Of course," Norman said, enjoying now his own ready understanding of the bizarre logic of John's dream. "In order to make the serum effective in the water supply, we had to remove the controlling element of susceptibility to temperature variations. Presto: an epidemic. An epidemic of youth! Poetic justice, for a society that's chosen to reject age and experience and celebrate novelty and youth."

"As a matter of fact," John said, with a touch of malice, "I think I remember that in my dreams you tried to say that to the Woman in the White House. She was not amused. She asked how much of the water supply you yourself had been drinking."

"By the way, how much had I been drinking?" Norman asked, suddenly realizing another possible direction for the dream.

"Quite a lot. Too much," John said. "You got it bad. I was more careful, naturally, and I escaped. "

He then described how, in the dream, Ella Shearer had come to John complaining about Norman's strange behavior. His moodiness, his unpredictability, his restless energy. How Norman visibly regressed to his young manhood when John first knew him, girl-crazy, always rushing off to see the latest pornographic show. How Donna also complained in due course about her father's constant teasing and rough play and lack of consideration – just as if she were talking about a younger brother. How with alarming rapidity the process continued until Norman began to lose his adolescent male characteristics, stopped shaving, lost direction in his sexual energies, dwindled physically into a pre-puberty child. There were still times of adult awareness and consciousness, which they attempted to capitalize on.

"In the interests of science," Norman interjected sarcastically. He was not particularly enjoying the part he had been assigned in John's dream.

"In the interests of science," John agreed, determined to tell the story out to its end.

They decided that as Norman daily became more child-like that they must get him to record in whatever way possible his psychological reactions. He was given a recorder among his other toys to play with, and he often chattered into it.

Gradually, however, he was losing his manual dexterity, and his spoken language sounded more and more like baby talk. He succumbed to fits of anger and destructiveness, obviously deeply frustrated at not being able to articulate or accomplish with his tongue and body what his mind wanted. All too soon he was returning to the toddler stage. .

I WANT A CHOCOLATE MILK AND A BICKY.

"Bicky!" Norman protested, breaking into John's account. "I never in my life talked like that. Baby talk! I spoke in coherent sentences from the age of three."

"I didn't know you then," John said calmly. "And it was my dream."

For longer periods of time the communication from baby Norman was pure nonsense. What kept the observers watching and recording were the occasional intervals of meaning. And the pathetic sense that somewhere within that helpless, bawling infant was a rational adult mind, craving its weakening link with its peers.

I WANT A DRINK
I WANT TO GO WEE WEE I GO
I WANT MY MOMMY I WANT MY MOMMY
DADDY
I WANT I WANT
WANT
I WANT MY DADDY

"That's horrible, no more!" Norman broke in, his face grimacing in disgust. "That's a horrible dream."

"Yes," John answered, refusing to be shifted from his calm, level tones. "I thought it was. I woke up in a cold sweat with the image of me holding a baby in diapers in my arms. Bawling its heart out, and I didn't know what to do. A baby with your face. It should have been funny, I suppose, but I was pretty shaken. Horrible, yes, that's a fair evaluation."

As if drained by their dreams, the two friends sat looking at each other beside the big telescope that was pointing aimlessly at the ground in front of its stand, no longer sweeping over the wide vistas of Notlimah. Neither of them had anything more to say. It was clear just how deeply the events of the past few days had stirred them. Both felt tired, too exhausted to think seriously about the future. Maybe now afraid even to dream.

Before they were obliged to continue, or bring to an end their unsettling conversation, an outburst of activity in the crowd around the edge of the lake made them aware that it was time for them to walk back. To witness the success of the divers. Not that they doubted what the outcome would be.

They waited there until their first expectation was confirmed. Chadwick Hamilton, and only Chadwick Hamilton, had been in the Lake Room, at the time of the collapse of the structure. And the long shape wrapped in blankets was his body, recovered from the depths and taken to the waiting ambulance. Then they left for their homes.

It is a fact of life that every scientific advancement has its setbacks to overcome. A year later Dr. Norman Shearer and Dr. John Hornby were well on their way to producing a new, more refined, hopefully more effective and less hazardous strain of their cancer serum. Meanwhile Donna, living most of the time on the Farm, had given birth to a healthy, normal son, and Ella was very happily absorbed in raising her own lively thriving child.

The local responsibilities of both Garth Hamilton and Alice Devers had been handed over to others who seemed to be carrying them on to everyone's satisfaction, while they themselves, as designated by Chadwick Hamilton's will, exercised their talents on a larger scale around the globe. Neither of them ever spent much time in Notlimah.

Arriving at the laboratory for a conference on the morning of his fortieth birthday, Norman Shearer found his friend and colleague John Hornby typically absorbed in his work. From his vantage point on the table looking down at him, Norman was able to detect something he had never observed before: a balding spot on the top of John Hornby's fair head.

The sight made him simultaneously sad and happy -- to be caught up in the natural, inevitable flow of time. So they were past forty, both of them, and they hadn't yet changed the course of history. But they were still alive, and still trying. Now, though their youth was clearly behind them, that was almost enough in itself. And who knows, they might still achieve something in their ventures into the unknown that the world would remember.

About the Author

F.W. Watt studied at the University of British Columbia, Oxford (as a Rhodes Scholar), and at the U. of Toronto, where he stayed as a professor in the English Department for 33 years. In the later stages of his career he dived into town and country life north of Toronto and became a commuter. Here were people in many ways different from those he knew in the ivory tower. He could see into their complicated and varied lives from close up as never before. And he was challenged to look more deeply into the ocean of his own intimate experiences, and those of many others he encountered daily. He felt driven to try to see below the surfaces. It became a compulsion to explore his visions in words and stories. He was not writing for others, but to satisfy his own need to be able to go back and relive moments of life which made him laugh and cry, and to try to understand them. Some of his visions he captured and published in poetry, others in short stories. The remaining mass of fiction, stories and novels, sat waiting during the quarter century of his retirement. Now, at 87 years, beyond the hopes and fears of young writers, but still wanting the fruits of sharing, he takes the ultimate test, the encounter with the minds and hearts of other readers. Go, little book. Six of 8.

Printed in Canada